CARIBBEAN RAIN

Rick Murcer

Murcer Press,LLC

ISBN-13: 9780615696348
ISBN-10: 1477123456

Cover design by: Art Painter
Library of Congress Control Number: 2018675309
Printed in the United States of America

CHAPTER-1

"I bet you never thought you'd get bopped in a rainforest, did you?" rasped a perspiring Amanda Griggs as she rolled off of her new husband, Dan, trying to recapture air that love and lust had momentarily stolen from her.

The air mattress gave way as her naked, glowing frame plopped down beside him, jostling the small electric lamp at the foot of the bed.

"No, I . . . didn't," he gasped, "but if I'd known how this worked . . ." He took a deep breath, turned on his side, and focused his large, brown eyes on her face. "But I'm glad you, we, whatever, did. That surpasses incredible, even better than last night in that fancy-ass hotel with the big bed."

"Really? Do you think so?" She gently grasped his hand and kissed it several times. "I was a little worried that you wouldn't like the whole communing-with-nature bit."

He drew her hand to him and returned her affection. "I won't lie. I wasn't thrilled about the idea, but getting this tent and camping gear from my buddy as a wedding gift made it easier to say yes. Besides, you can't do this in Michigan in January. Talk about frostbite on your ass."

Amanda grinned. "Literally."

Dan gathered her close, and she nuzzled his neck. Outside of the domed tent, the tiny Coqui frogs crooned their distinguished song, as if made just for the newly-weds. She didn't think there would ever be a better moment in her life. She pulled him even closer. For one of the first times in her life, she felt wanted, loved, even needed.

They'd both overcome a rough start to life. Dan's mom had divorced four times, and their family had moved eleven times in nine years. Their last move, just Dan and his mother, was to Tampa, Florida, from Ithaca, Michigan, and it was there they had settled.

Amanda's mom had been killed in a head-on collision when she was ten, so she and her dad, if you could call him a dad, "toughed" it out for about three months until poor, grieving daddy decided he had to marry again. Three years later, number two died in a mysterious boating accident. The next time, he'd waited a whole four months before wife number three stepped into her life. The woman was a bitch of the highest rating, and near the end, Amanda saw her only once a month or so—another advantage to living in a ten-thousand-square-foot mansion.

She was secretly glad when number three came up missing four years after. She was found in a parking lot in Vegas, full of heroin and void of life.

Her father had exercised amazing control by waiting two whole years before drawing in number four, who was just four years older than Amanda herself. Talk about old shit hitting the new fan.

After that wedding, Amanda had considered everything from suicide to stealing money from daddy's obscenely huge bank account and hitting the road, becoming an unknown. That all changed, of course, when she laid eyes on Daniel Griggs the first day of school, senior year. He was so handsome with a quiet but strong demeanor. It took all of about three seconds to fall head over heels, and eventually, to start thinking that maybe life wasn't such a shithole after all.

"Penny for your thoughts?" Dan asked, putting his hand on her hip.

"Oh, I was just thinking about how we met."

Rubbing her buttocks, he smiled. "I still can't believe the most beautiful woman I've ever known fell for me. Those green eyes and blond hair put me under such a spell; I would have done anything for you."

"Would have?" she cooed.

"Okay, I *still* would do anything for you."

"Good to know," she grinned. "Well, after I stand you up straight again, I'm going to want to see the rainforest in the moonlight, and I'll need some big, strong man to go with me in case an iguana, or some horny boa snake, tries to take advantage of me."

Dan reached behind his head and pulled his backpack to him. He withdrew an eight-inch hunting knife. "That's why I bought this yesterday."

"Dan, you know I hate knives like that . . . but I'm sort of glad you did."

Thinking about what good old dad did for a living, she was even more glad.

Nodding, he slid the knife back into the pack and cupped her breast then kissed her gently. "That's why you're the perfect woman for me."

The rain began to prattle against the leaves and the aroma of lush vegetation served to heighten the romantic ambience. It captured Amanda's senses, and for the next hour, she was lost in it, and him.

After they'd shaken the tent a second time, Amanda sat up, pulled on gym shorts and a tank top, and stood as tall as the tent would allow.

"Come on, Romeo, time to pay up. Plus, I gotta pee."

"I'm there; just give the big guy a chance to settle down."

"But I have to go, now."

Dan sat up, grabbed his denim shorts, and slid them on, almost. "Okay, but if I snag him on something, it could be a boring rest of the week."

"I'll take my chances," she laughed.

Grabbing the lantern, Dan unzipped the tent, started to stoop through the opening, and stopped. A scowl highlighted his brow.

"What?"

"Do you hear that?"

Amanda cocked her ear, and then shook her head. "I don't hear anything."

"That's my point. Those frogs have been mouthing off all night, and now there's nothing."

"Maybe you scared them when you . . . ah . . . were yelling 'don't stop,'" she panned.

"Real funny. Just the same, I'll scope the area and come back to get you."

"You better hurry, Ranger Rick, or this place is going to be very wet and will smell bad too."

"I'll hustle."

Even though there was partial light from the full moon, the darkness swallowed him. A second later, the beam of the lantern swept from one side of the campsite to the other. It swung up, back to the right, and then vanished. She heard a muffled thump, then heard nothing. Amanda let out the breath she'd been hoarding. The man loved a practical joke, but she didn't think she could hold her bladder another second.

"Dan? What was that?"

She waited. Silence. Amanda moved closer to the tent's door and spoke louder. "Dan? Where are you? This isn't funny. If you're screwing around, you're not gettin' any for a month." More silence. She ran her hand over her arm. This was over the line, even for him.

"Last chance, buddy. Speak up or be lonely." Her voice carried a confidence she didn't feel. Not even close. More uneasiness reached out and stroked Amanda's shoulder.

Another minute crawled past, and she found herself becoming angry. Her shorts were about to become very wet, and he thought this was a great time to screw around? She bent over, grabbed the backup flashlight, hit the on switch, and bent through the doorway.

Panning the area, she saw Dan's footprints in the moist grass moving away from the tent then, about twenty feet further, her beam caught something shiny. She stepped closer and recognized their lantern. The lens was broken, and there was something smeared on the handle.

"Dan? Come on, baby, this is starting to scare me." Standing still, all she heard was the breeze filtering through the trees. Dan was right—not one peep out of the Coqui frogs.

Amanda stepped cautiously in the direction of the broken light and jerked her hand to her mouth. The handle of the lantern was covered in . . . blood?

In the next instant, a strong hand covered her mouth; another lifted her off the ground and carried her into the thick dwarf trees and ferns just off the path. Her scream was muffled, but it didn't stop her from struggling. She kicked and flailed her arms, dropping the flashlight in the process. The man held tight, dragging her deeper into the rainforest. She kicked again and tried to bite his hand, but he held fast with the strength of a madman. Ten steps later, he stopped and spun her around, clamping his hand over her mouth, again. She recognized her husband immediately, and in the full-moon's light, saw he was bleeding from a long cut on his forehead. But that wasn't the most startling thing she saw in her husband's face. Fear reigned in his eyes. Her heart went cold.

"What—?"

"Shhh," he whispered, his eyes darting from side to side. He gripped both of her shoulders in his hands and brought her close. "Someone hit me from behind and then tried to drag me into the trees. He slipped, I managed to push him, then I ran like hell."

"This is crazy. Who—?"

Dan shook his head vigorously, blood flying from the wound on his forehead. "Don't talk. He's still out here."

"What should we do?"she rasped, her own fear rising to a level strange to her.

"We—"

At that moment, she heard it. An obscure rustling from the brush, then the most sickening sound she'd ever heard as a glint of long metal protruded through the meaty part of her husband's shoulder. Staring at the metal, she felt her spirit leave her body. She was frozen in place.

This can't be real.

Looking at his shoulder, Dan's disbelief turned to agony. His hand fell from her mouth as she watched the sword leave with an obscene sucking sound. She wrestled her gag reflex and won as strength returned to her legs.

Dan dropped to his knees, and she bent down, trying to get him off the damp ground, but he only slumped further.

"Get up, damn you," she cried. "We've got to move."

The next instance, she heard more than saw the blade rip through the air and watched in horror as Dan's arm bounced on the ground.

Her tears clouded her vision, as she slumped down to reach for Dan's face. "No, No, No! This can't be—"

"Oh, but it can and is," answered the voice from the dark.

"Why—?"

A sticky hand gripped her left arm. She jumped up, heart raging in her chest, and tore herself from the grasp, then realized it had been Dan's hand.

"Ru—run, Amanda. Run."

She hesitated, not sure whether to leave Dan or listen to his plea. Then she heard a *swoosh*, and her husband's handsome head rose into the air and flipped twice, landing at her feet. She screamed, then screamed again, unable to do what her husband had commanded.

"Scream all you'd like, Amanda Griggs. The only people within two miles of you are, well, unable to help."

Then the killer laughed.

Sometimes fear is a paralyzing agent that works for the predator and makes an easy meal; sometimes it prompts the fight or flight response that can save one's life. Amanda wanted to live.

Her indecision now gone, Amanda turned and sprinted away from the insane man armed with the blade, realizing somewhere in her muddled thoughts, that, if she didn't, she would join her husband.

The moonlight allowed her to see past the scattered trees to a bit of the trail that looped behind their campsite. She raced in that direction, and then promptly hit a low-hanging branch that knocked her off her feet. Dazed, she propped herself up on her elbows, shaking her head, and trying to chase away the mote of stars and colorful lines dancing in front of her face. She blinked, noticing the light glowing from inside her tent some forty yards away. She struggled to her knees, looking around for Dan's killer.

There he was. Standing ten feet away, twirling a sword, grinning.

"Come on, Amanda, you can do this," she whispered, struggling to rise.

The sound of heavy footsteps echoing from behind forced her all the way up. She staggered toward the tent, got her feet underneath her, then picked up speed, as did the maniac behind her.

Adrenaline and the will to survive rushed her body. Fifteen yards and she'd be inside the tent, and maybe with Dan's knife, she'd have a fighting chance.

The footfalls behind her made squishing sounds as they rapidly hit the moist grass and mud. He was gaining on her. She could hear his labored breathing.

Ten yards. She stumbled over a root, wobbled, then regained her balance.

Five yards. Her pursuer was closer than ever.

A millisecond later, she felt his hand clutch the

back of her hair, yanking out a few strands, but unable to get the grip he needed. But then he did, jerking her head backwards with a strong hand. She pulled hard and felt her hair give way. It hurt like hell, but she was free. Just in time to hear the sword tear through the humid Caribbean air and nick her bare back. She moaned, but ran faster.

The tent. She dove through the opening, reaching for Dan's backpack at the same time she hit the air mattress. Her hand probed the bag with frantic desperation —and couldn't find the knife.

"Oh God, please. Where is it?"

"Looking for this?"

She flipped to her back, and stared at the man leaning inside the tent. He was holding Dan's knife in his left hand.

Amanda threw the canvas bag at Dan's killer and crawled on all fours to the rear entrance, grasped the zipper, yanked it down, and almost made it through. Almost.

A searing pain shot up her ankle, pounding her brain with unimaginable force. A second later, there was another, and she lost control of both legs.

Rough hands flipped her on her back, and she gazed into the eyes of the man that had chased her down. She expected to see a crazy, wild expression born of Satan himself, but instead she saw a calm, quiet, but determined face, one that she vaguely recognized.

"Please, don't . . ." she sobbed.

"I've learned, young Amanda, that begging is for the weak."

The flash of steel was the last sight Amanda Griggs saw.

CHAPTER-2

Alex reached for Sophie's test results sheet from across the wide table at Kewpee's restaurant. "You passed the psych exam? No shit? I got to see this."

She snatched it off the table and pulled it to her chest. "Just keep your hands to yourself, Dough Boy."

"Come on," he grinned. "I'll show you mine if you show me yours."

"Oh man. I can't believe you went there," said Manny, who'd been watching the familiar tug-o'-war with amusement.

"Yeah, me either, and that ain't ever gonna happen," she scowled. "The score was high enough, and that's all you need to know. In fact, you don't need to know that."

"I guess you're right." Alex grinned. "I've worked with you for years without a psych evaluation like this one, even though you needed it . . . but it's all good."

Nibbling at the warm bacon on his plate, Manny shook his head. "You're *both* crazy for following me to the Bureau, no matter what the psych evaluations say for either one of you. It's nice and snug right here in Lansing, and you could live the life of leisure."

Alex widened his eyes and lifted his eyebrows in an exaggerated surprise, "*We're* crazy? You're the one who joined the Behavioral Analysis Unit of the FBI—a beacon for every deranged psychopath in the US— exposing yourself to people who only appear human, never mind what the crime scenes might look like. Yep, that sounds normal to my large ass."

"Then why are you two coming along?"

"Hey. Somebody's got to look out for you. Besides, Josh Corner is still the hottest special agent in Quantico." Sophie winked.

"I rest my case; neither one of you are right," said Manny.

Alex drained his cup and popped it down on the table. "Yeah, but you love us anyway."

"He's not going to admit it, but we know," said Sophie.

"You're right; I'm not going to admit it. Now, both of you need to get your asses to the shooting range and finish your last two certifications. Josh will be coming into town later this afternoon to finish the paperwork that makes you official FBI special agents."

Sophie jumped up, threw on her zebra-striped winter coat, and motioned to Alex. "Come on, Dough Boy, I bet I out-shoot you so bad you'll cry for your mama."

"You're on. And stop calling me Dough Boy." He grabbed his black trench coat from the rack and hurried after Sophie. "And you ain't driving."

"Don't shoot each other," Manny called out.

Shaking his head and grinning, he waved to the waitress to bring more coffee.

A lot had transpired since he'd returned from Ireland. Especially involving his good friends.

Alex Downs was the best CSI on the planet, even though his outward appearance would tag him as more of an accountant. He was paunchy with thinning hair and black-rimmed glasses reminiscent of the '70s, but his appearance belied a brilliant mind, and even more than that, a loyal friend.

Sophie Lee. There just weren't enough words to describe his Chinese-American, longtime partner and friend. Smartass, sarcastic, and crazy covered much of it, but bright, energetic, and fearless weren't far behind. The two of them were as much family to Manny as anyone. That made him smile. And now they were both joining him in the BAU. They'd been through some intense training over the last two months and had a few more hoops to jump through, but having Alex and Sophie covering his backside like old times was, well, nothing could've suited him more.

The short, slender waitress filled his cup and moved to the next table.

Sipping his coffee, his thinking shifted to his daughter Jen. She was halfway through her senior year, embracing everything her final year in high school should be, and growing up faster and smarter every day, it seemed, in the course of time. That fact led him to remember how much Jen resembled her deceased mom Louise. Her speech, her mannerisms, even the way she spoke to Manny.

He'd be a liar if he'd said it didn't hurt, every once in a while at least, to watch her evolution from teenager to young woman. There was no question that she was going to mature into her mother's daughter. He sighed. There would always be a special place in his heart for Louise, maybe more than special, and it had been beyond difficult to move on after her death, but that's where Chloe Franson came in.

Thinking of Chloe always made his insides quiver.

Her emerald eyes and flowing red hair were only the beginning of who she was. Beautiful? Yes. Smart? Yes. But there was nothing that compared to her heart—and especially her heart for him. There had been electricity between them from the first time they'd shaken hands, but now that they'd made a vow to each other, it was more like an eternal storm. He ran his hand through his hair. That storm made *waiting* all the more difficult.

When he'd gone to Ireland to tell her how he felt, and that he wanted to be with her, he'd given her a Claddagh ring that symbolized his commitment to her. They cried, they kissed, and that fire they'd both felt had grown into a raging inferno. He wasn't sure he'd ever wanted Louise this much. But his "Boy Scout" convictions had won out. No sex until they said "I do." He knew how most of the world looked at that, but he didn't care. Some things were more important. He'd made that pledge to God, and himself, and would stick to it. He wanted to be an example to Jen. It would be hard to preach one thing, like abstinence, if he were breaking the rules himself.

Chloe had told him a hundred times since then that she understood, but it was getting tougher, for both of them. The way she touched him, her walk, her scent, her pure, unadulterated love for him confused things even more. She'd even suggested that they take cold showers . . . together. He smiled. The woman was just no help.

His Irish love had also made Jen feel comfortable. They'd talked, even laughed a time or two, but the thought of someone, even Chloe, taking her mother's place at his side was still something Jen was working through. He exhaled. Hell, they were all working through that, but Jen was a special young lady. Then there was that dream—

The sound of loud voices interrupted Manny's world, and he glanced at the front door just as two men wearing long, black coats and ski masks entered the restaurant. The first man was shorter than the other, and much thicker, but both were carrying large handguns, Berettas maybe. The taller man held one of the waitresses around the neck, moving his gun to the side of her head.

"Everyone stay where you are and you get to leave on your feet," he yelled, his voice deep and tinted with a Latino accent.

The short man scanned the breakfast crowd and honed in on Manny. He then strode toward him, raising his weapon.

"Ah. Detective Williams. Are you ready to meet your maker?"

CHAPTER-3

He stood, leaning against the antique, mahogany armoire, looking at his calloused hands. He turned them over and over, reflecting on what they were capable of and what they had already efficiently completed. Never had it entered his thoughts that they, or he, would be so important to "the work." He'd traveled a path like so many others who thought education was the trail to illumination. But in the end, he'd been wrong. His supposedly enlightened professors and colleagues understood nothing concerning what it took to accomplish a gallant endeavor; they lived and died with theory. And his mission, his purpose, was nothing, if not gallant.

When he'd set his sights on a college education, despite his humble beginnings in Chicago, he'd thought of nothing else. Each day, he consumed what his teachers were serving. Each night, he read until his mother ambled into his room to his warped, two-drawer dresser to shut off the cracked tiffany lamp that glowed bright then dim from the short in the wiring. But it was enough.

She'd kiss him and tell him to go to sleep. But there were nights when he wasn't ready. Nights where the book he had been reading had taken his mind, his emotion, his imagination to an exciting new destination, and he simply had to finish. On those nights, he'd pull out the old, yellow flashlight from under his mattress, cover his head with the tattered quilt, and continue reading until he'd finished, or had fallen asleep trying. Several times, the sun was peeking through his window when he closed his eyes. He knew his mother knew, but she wanted him to read, to learn. He loved her for it. They didn't have much, but they had that.

Then it all ended so abruptly, he'd barely had time to understand. His mom had stabbed a man at the bar where she worked when he tried to steal her purse that held the month's rent. The man died, and his mom went away for twenty years; and in essence, so did he, becoming a victim of Chicago's foster care system. He rarely stayed more than six months in any one home. Some of the families were kind; some were not. But he hung in there and finally hooked up in one place long enough to finish high school.

But he'd more than finished, hadn't he? He carried a perfect 4.0 through some thirteen schools, and it had earned him an Ivy League scholarship.

A few months later, he was on his way to the East Coast and brave new worlds.

After his first year of college, he'd spent a summer in Puerto Rico, doing volunteer work at El Yunque National Rainforest. The first time he laid eyes on her, he knew what he wanted to do. It had become as apparent as those almost-mystical revelations could be. He was going to take care of El Yunque. Educate people regarding her. It was the reason he had been born, and more importantly, he knew it.

Finishing his undergraduate degree, flawlessly and in less than three years, had set up his graduate career, and by the time he reached his twenty-fourth birthday, he was a full-fledged doctor of environmental science. His research papers and subsequent dissertation regarding rainforest habitat destruction and utility had met with international acclaim. So much so that he'd been the keynote speaker at the International Conference on Science and Technology two years in a row, an accomplishment that had never been achieved before. One of his speeches included a session on how human interaction in El Yunque could cause irreparable damage if camping and tourist interactions weren't regulated more stringently. One reporter covering the event said he was a man among children in his field, but acknowledged that tourism, and rum production, was what made Puerto Rico roll and it would take an act of God to accomplish what his lecture had suggested.

If they only knew.

During that time, he'd became obsessed with reconnecting with his mother and finally found her in one of the southern suburbs of Chicago. He remembered knocking on the door of the tiny apartment and how special their reunion had been. They'd spent the night talking about everything, especially where his life had taken him. She was so proud. The look in her eyes said so. How could he ever forget that? The love, the satisfaction. Nothing matches the approval radiating from the eyes of a parent. Nothing. But he'd never see it again, thanks to *them*.

Over the next few years, he'd visited his mother as much as he could and constantly asked her to join him, but she refused. Chicago was her home, and she wanted to stay there.

He walked away from the armoire, stood next to

the window facing the east, and watched the sun rise over his precious El Yunque. He considered moving back to be with her, but that would have taken him far away from his rainforest, and *this* was *his* home. A move back to Chicago wouldn't work for him on many levels, including his guest-teaching position at two of the local universities. The phone sitting on the lampstand suddenly drew his attention. It was nearly eight a.m. and that's when they would talk practically every morning since they'd reconnected those seven years ago. She'd tell him about the snow and wind of Chicago, and he'd tell her it was eighty-five degrees and not a cloud in the sky. She'd laugh like mothers do, and it helped to begin his day on the upbeat side of this life. But the phone hadn't rung for three months to the day. It never would again unless she, somehow, figured out how to call from beyond the grave.

Reaching for the sixteenth-century German rapier hanging from his belt, he gripped the hilt, drew it from the sheath, and hugged it tightly.

He'd begged her, again, to move to San Juan with him. He'd buy her a nice condo overlooking the ocean, and it would be like old times—before they'd taken her away from him. She always said she was thinking about it, but he knew it would never happen. Then finally, in October, she had agreed to fly down to see him for two weeks. They'd shopped, ate at great restaurants, and he'd taken her to beautiful El Yunque. In some ways, it was like introducing your girlfriend to your mother. He wanted her to approve, and she had—until they'd encountered those out-of-control campers. Gripping the sword tighter now at the memory, his hand dug into the ornate crosspiece, but he didn't really feel it. He bit his lip and closed his eyes on the vivid picture of three young men, toting full camping backpacks, hurrying down the steep steps to the La Mina waterfalls. The weather had been perfect. He could still recall the singing birds and the smell of fresh rain. She'd even commented on the difference of the air compared to the city.

They'd stopped at the bamboo-covered rest area, which was just before the last, severely abrupt set of stairs that descended to the bottom of the falls and the churning, emerald pool waiting there. They'd listened closely and heard the water rushing over the thirty-five-foot ledge. She'd grinned in anticipation.

Just then, the first camper of the three nearly ran into them both in his haste to reach the falls at the bottom of the trail, managing to avoid them at the last second. He'd turned to tell the camper to slow down and be more careful when he'd heard it. The second young man had lost his balance, and plowed directly into his mother. The third, unable to correct his path, crashed into both his mother and the second camper. In slow motion, he watched his mother tumble down the steps, entangled in a swirling mass of arms and legs. A split-second later, the sickening crack of bone on concrete echoed through the trees as the three of them churned over the steps.

By the time they'd fallen to the landing below, it was over. The two men were able to get back on their feet, but not his mother. She lay on the small deck, her head turned at an impossible angle, fractured bone sticking through the collar of her new pink blouse, her eyes staring unseeingly into a deep-blue sky. Something forever had died in him that minute.

In a swell of anger, he whirled, swinging the double-edged sword expertly at the teakwood lamp resting on the nightstand. It was slashed so cleanly and with such incredible precision that it took a few seconds for the top half to separate from the bottom. It tilted lazily, finally crashing to the carpet. He stared, trying to sort out the emotions that battered him like a hurricane.

The horror of her funeral had been the final straw, and his soul and mind grew more hollow by the second as he purged every emotion but one.

Walking away from the gravesite with the Illinois wind howling through the barren trees, he'd made a promise to his mother, himself, and to his beloved rainforest: the three most important things in his life.

He smiled, turning the rapier over in his hand.

If the government wouldn't fix the problems in El Yunque, he would.

CHAPTER-4

The shorter thug reached Manny's table, his gun never wavering as it seemed to stare intently into Manny's face, its cold, dark, lifeless eye sizing him up.

Manny glanced up to his would-be executioner and said nothing.

"Did you hear me, white boy? Are you ready?" the man demanded.

But Manny detected the nervousness in his voice. Not exactly a pro, but the steady hand told him his assailant knew what he was doing with a gun in his hand, and he was pissed. Nervous, pissed, and good with firearms wasn't usually a good combination, any time.

"I'm not," he answered quietly.

The man's voice rose higher and his accent got heavier. "Well, tough shit, man. I've waited a long time for this, and now it's your turn to pay."

"Pay for what?" Manny's voice grew even softer.

"For screwing up my life. You sons-a-bitchin' cops think you got all the answers, but truth is, you don't know shit from peanut butter."

His stout assailant stepped closer and whispered into Manny's face. "And you ain't even gonna know who I am."

Manny raised his eyebrows. "Actually, I do know who you are and why you're here. Hello, Pete Contreras."

The short man took a step back, which was all that Manny needed. Grabbing Pete's arm, Manny stood up and twisted it and, with his other hand, snatched the Smith and Wesson .38. He then wrapped his arm under Pete's neck and pressed the gun to his head. The taller gunman, seeing what had happened to his partner, shuffled his feet, twisted his head to scope the room, then turned and ran through the door at breakneck speed.

He ripped the ski mask from Pete's face. "Unless I miss my guess," said Manny, squeezing Pete's throat for emphasis, "I think your brave-as-ever compadre was Slim Zimmerman. Right?"

"I'm not telling you a freaking thing, and I don't give a shit what you think. Prick," Pete growled.

"That wasn't very nice. And you don't smell so good either. Put those together with threatening to shoot an FBI special agent doesn't bode well for you, asshole. But I'm going to tell you what I think anyway. I'm thinking you're still as dumb as the first time I busted you for armed robbery."

"Get bent."

"And pistol whipping that old lady was a real nice touch, you piece of shit."

"That'll teach the old bitch for getting in the way."

Manny pressed the gun to Pete's head and heard him yelp. "So, by your logic, I should, at the very least, beat you with this gun, then maybe shoot your ugly ass, just because you screwed up my breakfast. Is that right?"

"You ain't gonna do shit, man. You're too much of a pansy-ass do-gooder. You're just full of bullshit." Pete then jerked his head backward, trying to connect with

Manny's face, but he wasn't fast enough. Manny shifted his head to the right, barely avoiding the blow.

Lifting Pete off the floor, Manny slammed him face down on the tile, shattering his nose. The crunch was more than gratifying.

"You broke my nose," Pete screamed. "You broke my damned nose."

"Just your nose? Maybe I should try it again and see how many scars I can leave for your next twenty years in prison, just like the scars you gave that old lady." Manny took out his cuffs and slapped them on Pete's thick wrists.

"I'm going to sue for police brutality," sobbed Pete. "I'll have your damned badge."

"Can't wait to hear from your lawyer."

Just then, two LPD blues barged into the restaurant, guns pulled, followed by Gavin Crosby, Lansing's police chief, and his son Mike, the LPD's new sergeant detective.

Manny stood. "Looks like your ride's here. Have a nice trip."

"I'm gonna kill you, Williams, someday, your blonde ass will be mine," threatened Pete, his voice growing more nasal with each word.

"Maybe, but you'll have to get smarter and faster, dipshit. And where you're going, I wouldn't bend over in the shower to pick up any soap."

The two blues lifted Pete from the floor, blood soaking the front of his coat, and hurried him out the door.

Manny moved next to Gavin and Mike. "Who called?"

"The cook," answered Gavin. "These two are as

smart as ever. We were on our way over to get something to eat, so—"

"Did you get Zimmerman?"

"Yep, about a block away. The dumbass was still wearing the mask and had the gun in his hand," said Gavin.

"I'm guessing those two won't be taking over the world anytime soon," grinned Manny. "Oh, and sorry about his nose. I'll write it up and send you the report."

"No problem. But you do know how those reports can get lost . . ."

"Yeah, I do. But we have witnesses, and I got a little rough."

Mike Crosby shook his head. "According to those witnesses, he tried to kill an officer, a damned Fed no less. We're good to go."

The waitress, Tammy, who had served Manny's last cup of coffee, walked up and touched his hand. "We didn't see nothin' bad. He tried to mess up that pretty face. Hell, he should be put away for life just for that. End of story."

He bent down and kissed Tammy on the forehead. "Thank you, sweetheart. I'll leave a big tip."

Her face turned red, and she looked at the floor. "I've been waiting for that for years. Best tip ever." Then she hurried off to the kitchen.

Gavin rolled his eyes. 'Come on, lover boy, we got some paperwork to do so we can get half of my damned department turned over to the Feds."

Manny looked at his old partner Gavin and then at Mike, and couldn't help thinking, again, how they all belonged to the same fraternity; they'd all lost their wives. Mike's wife Lexy died at the hands of the deranged serial killer, Dr. Fredrick Argyle, on a cruise ship two years ago, and Gavin's wife Stella was shot by a wacked-out LPD employee, who was also responsible for killing his Louise. He felt their pain.

There was an eternal kinship between them. The sleepless nights. The quick, curious glances from family and friends wanting to help but not sure how. A few too many drinks that chased the pain to some dark recess of the mind, only to creep back stronger than before. And of course, they also shared a hope—the hope that someone would take your hand and walk you from dark to light. There are few desperations like that one.

Chloe had satisfied that hope in Manny, and rumor had it that Mike had met someone new. Gavin hadn't and probably wouldn't. He said any woman getting a foothold in his life would have to be a reincarnation of his Stella, the pre-crazy one.

Gavin frowned. "What the hell are you staring at?"

"Nothing. Just thinking how ugly you two are and how I'm going to miss you anyway."

"Well, you ain't as pretty as that little waitress thinks you are, and only God knows what the perky little Irish girl sees in ya, but there's no accounting for taste," said Gavin, his patented twinkle pulsing from brown eyes.

"Maybe she's blind," grinned Mike.

"Okay. I give," said Manny throwing up his arms. "Let's go to your office. Sophie and Alex should be back in an hour or two, then we can wrap up this thing."

The three turned to leave just as Manny's cell rang. It was Chloe.

"Hey. How far out are you and Josh?"

"Manny. I'm scared."

He stopped and switched the phone to his right hand. He'd not heard her in sheer panic mode before. Not even when her Mom had been captured by Argyle. His pulse quickened.

"Scared of what, Chloe?"

"The weather was okay when we left DC and got bad over Pennsylvania. We can't find a place to land, and we're dropping fast. Manny, I don't want to die this wa—

There was a hideous crack, and the phone grew silent.

CHAPTER-5

Randall Fogerty didn't take well to people who were late, for any reason. Promptness was how things were done. By God, he was living, undeniable proof. He'd made a practice—hell, more like a religion—of being early for every meeting, every commitment, whether by phone, telemeeting, or the classic face-to-face. It didn't matter the medium . . . he was always on time and prepared for every eventuality, and he expected the same out of his associates, and particularly his family and loved ones. Yes, contrary to what some may think, he did love, perhaps jealously, when the occasion presented itself. Timeliness was how he stayed on top of things, how he'd built this empire that afforded him, his daughter, and his current wife the best things money could buy. And make no mistake, money makes the world turn, not some misguided philosophy exalting the virtues of an invisible God, or some stupid-shit process that allowed people to come back as cows, or whatever the hell they deserved when they'd completed their "first" life. Cold, hard cash changed lives, made living better. When it came right down to it, nothing else mattered.

Take the sickly kids on this island. All of them would live a hell of a lot longer with the best medical attention money could buy, not from some voodoo spell. He proved that over and over with his generous donations. Of course, the funding was also good for his image.

Randall rose from his seat on the oceanfront deck, stretched to his lean, six-foot height, and stared out to the teal ocean that ran endlessly along the white shores of Barbados' Saint Lawrence Gap. He squeezed the smartphone a little harder. His daughter was supposed to call every morning at the same time—eight thirty sharp—for the two-week duration of her stupid-ass honeymoon that she'd insisted on taking with that harebrained shithead she'd decided to fall in love with, and for God's sake, marry.

He appreciated lust as much as most. He even understood that little touchy-feely shiver that could run through one's body after a hot twirl in the sack. That feeling had been the reason he'd been married four times, more or less. Big tits and long legs hadn't hurt the "thinking" progression either.

But to have his daughter completely go against his wishes and marry a nobody was beyond his comprehension. They didn't have that bullshit, make-believe, lovey, kissy-face relationship that dads and daughters had on those ridiculous TV shows. But he had always given her everything she'd ever wanted, and she was always well protected.

Damn. Isn't that enough?

The kid she hitched her wagon to had checked out as far as any criminal past, but he didn't have a pot to piss in or a window to throw it out, until now. Marrying into the Fogerty family was undoubtedly the best thing that had ever happened to him.

He glanced at his reflection on the patio door and

couldn't help but smile.

No matter how long the little bastard lived.

The phone unexpectedly came to life, vibrating in his clenched hand. He drew it close to his face, fully expecting to see his daughter's number printed across the screen. It wasn't, and he had no desire to talk to the low life that now wanted his attention. In fact, the call pissed him off. He made a mental note to ensure that this greaser, who had the balls to interrupt his morning, never had the opportunity to disrupt him again. Ever.

He hit the redial for his daughter and waited, his patience growing ever shorter. Her voice mail kicked on, again.

"I'm tired of this. You need to call me, now. You know the damned rules, and you're breaking every one of them. You also know that will only piss me off. Is that why you're ignoring me? I'm your father and—"

His daughter's voice mail response abruptly cut him off with a mechanical rejection that was close to a slap in the face, in his eyes.

Staring at the phone, he closed his large hand around it and hurled it against the pastel, stucco wall. It sounded like a gunshot as the impact shattered the phone.

In a flash, two muscular men sprinted around the corner, guns drawn and looking for all the world like they'd shoot anything that moved and ask questions later. Just the way Randall wanted it.

"Boss? Are ya okay, mon?" asked one of the men, bloodshot eyes accenting the concern on his ebony face. He was larger than his companion, by six inches and thirty pounds, but quicker and far more dangerous. It made him a perfect fit for his number one bodyguard.

Randall cocked his head "No, Braxton, I'm not okay. My daughter seems to think ignoring me is some sort of silly-ass game, and it's pissing me off. Royally."

"Yah, sir. Dos kids can be hard ta know."

"That they can, my friend. But given the nature of my . . . profession, I don't have room for games."

The big man put his weapon back in his holster and motioned for the other man to leave. "So do we get da plane ready ta go?"

"I can't afford not to. Make sure all of my meetings are rescheduled and be ready to go within the hour."

"All of dem, Mr. Fogerty?"

"Yes, Braxton, all. Our folks from Miami will have to wait a day. I'm going to Puerto Rico. And when I find Amanda, she and that poor excuse for a husband will wish I'd stayed in Barbados."

"Ye'sir."

Braxton moved away, and Fogerty glanced at the ocean again. He hated this feeling. He wasn't used to not having his way.

Walking to the front of the house, he realized that he'd have to teach his daughter and her husband the lesson of a lifetime. It would be best for Amanda, not so good for shithead, but life was full of choices, and he'd made this one—for all of them.

CHAPTER-6

It was approaching noon and over eighty-five degrees when he pulled his rented hybrid SUV in front of the visitor's center. His hand felt moist from gripping the gear shift. He removed his sunglasses and, through the sun roof, absorbed the magical blue sky of Puerto Rico as perspiration tumbled down his neck.

He'd chosen not to turn the air conditioning on for several reasons, but mostly because he enjoyed the raw heat that his island provided. He especially took pleasure in the humidity because it made him feel more in touch with how nature should be, how it had evolved, not how mankind was altering it. Nature had its marvelous methods, and he more than embraced them.

Certainly there was survival of the fittest. Plants would go extinct only to be replaced by others that were stronger, more proficient at adapting to the local and global environments. The same was echoed with every species of fauna he'd ever studied. They'd make it, or not. It was the only true way of life and death, and he loved the simplicity of it. It was his mantra, his passion, his reason for living, especially now.

The quiet, but energetic sounds of the water prancing over the dark rocks left a momentary, contented mark on his brain. He could live in a world void of the ambient cacophony of the human race, but not one devoid of the sounds in El Yunque.

Closing his eyes, he focused on the rhythm of the water. But as usual, the sound of people brought him back to the realization that his rainforest, his island, was no longer perfect. Instead, it was as tainted and broken as everything else man tried to "improve." It always seemed to turn to shit.

His anger rose, and his mood turned dark as quickly as the sun became obstructed by a renegade cloud. He watched the khaki-clad rangers—one young woman and an overweight, older man—emerging from the visitors center. He clenched his jaw so tightly that his teeth began to hurt.

Enter the screwed-up human race as the most destructive x-factor of all.

He clamped his hands to the steering wheel, hoping to control the uncontrollable. A moment later, the two rangers stood in front of the cream-colored center, a pimple on the rainforest's ass, gesturing to a dozen or so tourists waiting to be educated on the finer points of his beloved El Yunque.

Educated? Like hell.

They'd paid their money to hear what these imposters had to say, but they were only programmed voices with memorized fact sheets and shit for brains. In contrast, no one wanted to listen to what he had to say, did they? No one wanted to hear the real facts about government misuse and habitat destruction. They'd listen soon enough. They'd have no choice.

The sun escaped the cloud and flashed its brilliance again, caressing his face with a new rush of glorious Caribbean heat.

His heart surged with excitement. If he'd believed

in such nonsense, he would have sworn it was an omen, a divine instruct, because he immediately knew what he needed to do next.

Backing out of his parking spot, he turned right on Highway 191 for a mile, then took a quick right on Road 930. The only vehicle in the lot was a blue compact car parked near the foot of the trail that led to Mount Britton Tower. He swung in beside it.

The tower had been one of the first atrocities to be constructed in his verdant refuge some eighty years prior. He'd always hated the idea of it, but today it would serve him and his purpose. He smiled. It would serve him well.

Exiting the vehicle, he scoped the parking lot, then back to the entrance of the tiny road. It was just him and whoever else had walked the winding trail to the monument. He moved to the rear of the truck, pushed back the seat, and pulled out an object that gleamed like chrome in the sun. He guided it down the inside leg of his white slacks, catching on his belt. Then he adjusted his white panama hat, felt for the object underneath his slacks one last time, took a long deep breath, inhaling the fresh mountain fragrance, and started his forty-minute jaunt, like he had a thousand times before.

The incline to the tower was over five hundred feet up and about a mile along the winding, canopied trail, but when he finally arrived at the arched stone entrance of the tower, his heart rate had barely risen—until he heard the voices at the top of the tower, laughing and carrying on like the damn fools they were.

Fools and their lives are quickly separated.

This fresh, inexplicable excitement of his was now enhanced by a new rush of adrenaline that seemed to lift him off his feet and carry him up the forty steps that wound around and eventually reached the top of the tower.

A few feet from the top, he saw the source of his excitement: a plump, middle-aged couple, glued to the wall.

The grey-haired woman was facing the wall, her skorts around one ankle, hands braced against the stones, and wide backside exposed. Her bald lover thrust with the energy of a college boy as sweat stuck to his shirt. It wasn't clear who was moaning and who was grunting, but the couple was totally oblivious to their audience.

They, and what they were doing, were poster children for everything he'd hated since the desecration of El Yunque had begun.

He took the blade from his slacks, moved to within three feet of the man. "Are you having fun?"

The woman screamed at the sound of his voice, as the man backed away from her, grabbing desperately for his khaki shorts. The man hadn't turned to face him, but yelled, "What the hell are you doing, you pervert. Can't we even have a little privacy?"

The balding man finally got his shorts partially up around his thighs and turned toward him, woody still throbbing.

"You can have all you want, forever."

Swinging effortlessly, he severed the man's right hand. His victim looked at the stub in disbelief, then screamed. He pivoted, then reversed his position, swung again, hacking off the lover's manhood. The tourist screamed again as he drove the blade through his heart. He pulled it out, and watched him tumble to the floor. With a kick of his foot, he sent the man down two steps, and then watched as he dropped to the bottom, some thirty-five feet below. He turned back to the fat woman, grinning.

Her mouth moved, but nothing came out. She looked at the blade, then to the blood dripping to the floor. Her wide, hazel eyes captured his with a pathetic, unspoken plea. He never gave the look, or her unspoken request, a second thought, as he raised the blade over his head. He plunged it through the base of her neck, twisted, and did it again. She covered her throat with her pudgy hand and fell to the stone floor, making gurgling sounds he'd not heard before, not even from the others. His heart raced even faster at the sound. It was . . . erotic.

Finally, after she'd grown silent, he started down the steps. Then he was struck with another thought and hurried back to her. He raised the rapier and swung it four more times.

Moving quickly, he exited the tower, knowing he'd evolved to the next level and relishing the transformation. And more importantly, he had won another battle.

There would be more.

CHAPTER-7

Chloe Franson glanced over at Josh Corner just as the Gulfstream GV5 pitched left; causing her to lose control of the cell phone. It shattered as it hit the wall that was at a forty-five degree angle lower than where it had been a few seconds prior. She heard a quick, sharp scream, and then realized it had come from her.

"Hey. You afraid of a little turbulence?" grimaced Josh.

"Ya bet yer arse," she managed. Her Irish cadence became more prevalent when she was emotional.

"Me too."

She smiled, even though she felt like her insides were somewhere on the outside. It was just like Special Agent Corner to try to help ease her fear. The world needed more men like him.

The jet righted itself, and the ride continued, resembling more of an 1800s-wagon-trail jaunt than a modern-day jet flight. She let out the breath she'd been jealously protecting.

Josh touched her arm. "You're going to have to pay for that phone when we get back to the office. Those are expensive. Something else I can blame on Williams too."

"You get my arse back to the home office in one piece, and I'll buy ya two of 'em."

"Deal. And remind me to shoot the weatherman

too."

The plane dropped again, pitching to the right this time. Chloe gripped the armrest and felt her fingers dig deep. She leaned back against the seat with closed eyes, perspiration forming on her lip. The plane leveled out again and was abruptly very steady.

She looked at Josh from her peripheral. "You're gonna have to beat me to shooting that loser."

"Okay. We'll shoot him twice."

The weather report was a little sketchy for later in the day, but the trip to Lansing took less than two hours from DC, and there had been no reason to believe they were going to have trouble. Except that Mother Nature had different plans. The storm system that was to bring high winds and snow had accelerated quickly due to an unexpected change in the unsteady jet stream, unleashing the storm that had been holding Minneapolis hostage. The vicious weather had greeted them just over Youngstown, Ohio. It figured. Chloe hated wind and snow, but worse, *flying* in wind and snow.

The pilot said he'd never seen a weather change as quick as this one, and it was going to be difficult to avoid downdrafts as they flew lower to the ground. These kinds of conditions, he warned, led to an extremely dangerous type of wind shear that was difficult to detect. His equipment would help, but it wasn't always one hundred percent. Their chances were about thirty-seventy against them avoiding an incident. To Chloe, that meant avoiding a crash.

Josh had sarcastically commended the pilot for his uplifting take on their precarious situation and for scaring the hell out of both of them. The pilot had shrugged and returned to his seat without answering.

That's when her stomach really began the upside-down journey.

The jet remained fairly steady, and she felt herself relax.

"You know," Josh reflected, "I kind of thought I would go out getting shot or some other weird-ass way. Like a cut that got infected and eventually went to my brain, popped the blood vessels, and that's it. But a plane —"

"Don't say it, man. We're still floating, and the pilot may lack a few people skills, but he's good."

In response to Chloe's words, the jet dropped quicker and farther than at any time before. It almost took the wind from her lungs and was the same feeling, times a hundred, that accompanied a rabid jaunt down a steep rollercoaster. She didn't know how much longer she was going to be able to hold on to her breakfast.

The jet leveled for a moment, then dropped once more. Chloe heard herself cry out again, this time Josh joined her. It was the only sound she could muster, and she was pretty sure Josh had nothing else to say either.

The pilot's voice came over the cabin speakers.

"Okay, guys. This is it. We're down to about twelve thousand feet, and Cleveland has a spot for us. I'll do my best to get us down in one piece. It won't hurt to pray a little."

Managing one last glance in Josh's direction, she saw the grin on his face, but his eyes told a different story. He had to be thinking about his boys, his wife, and maybe more than all of that, what came next, if they didn't make it. Chloe was thinking the same way. She wanted that life with Manny, that fairytale dream of every girl thought about. Meeting Jesus sounded wonderful, but she wanted a good long drink from this life first. She prayed harder.

Fingering the crucifix draped around her neck, she contemplated the worst. She knew about the afterlife. Most good Catholic girls did, but putting her faith on the line at a time like this was harder than she ever imagined it would be. But she'd try; she had no choice.

Slipping her hand into Josh's, they waited together. She squeezed harder as the ride down got crazier. It felt like the jet was coming apart at the seams. Josh squeezed back. Then he asked her a question.

"So, did you ever get Williams into bed?" His voice shook in rhythm to the vibrating plane.

She spit out laughter and managed, "No, and if I go like this, I'm coming back one time to nail him."

"Good girl."

The vibrations grew even more intense in conjuncture with the rolling, rocking jet. The next second, they hit something with an impact she didn't think possible. Before she could scream, it happened again. She felt the left wing bend, then watched it dislodge, taking part of the fuselage with it. Instantly, Josh and she were engulfed in an incredible cold. Making matters worse was the fast-moving snow that stung her face mercilessly like so many angry bees. She bent her head close to her knees and hoped that God held Josh, the two pilots, and her in the palm of His hand. The plane hit the tarmac again, spun right, did a three-sixty in what seemed like slow motion, then suddenly reversed direction. Chloe felt her body tremble and shudder. The torque made it feel like she was coming apart.

Out of nowhere sailed a white splinter of metal. It hammered the side of her head, and then Chloe Franson felt nothing at all.

CHAPTER-8

His Cessna X darted some fourteen thousand feet above the Caribbean Ocean, and Randall Fogerty watched the sun reflect off the water's surface. There were over three hundred thirty-five days of sunshine per year in the Caribbean, and today was one of the more spectacular days. But those circumstances did little to improve his mood. He fingered the new phone. With each attempt to reach Amanda, his temper, the real pissy one, rose a notch.

She's ignoring me, and no one ignores Randall Fogerty, not even my daughter.

He swirled the glass of Caribbean rum in his left hand. This particular bottle cost more than most indigenous residents of the islands made in a year, but wasn't even a tiny blip on his daily spending radar. The "distribution" business had been good to him—and to Amanda.

The business hadn't come without risks. Risks that a poor white boy from the south side of Detroit hadn't minded taking, especially after the life, or so called "life" his screwed up parents had pawned off as an acceptable existence. By the time he'd reached eleven, he'd robbed several rich-bitch types, at gunpoint no less. He would have robbed neighborhood stores, but there was an unwritten law to leave them be. He honored that for a while, until he decided he didn't give a rat's ass about unwritten laws.

At age thirteen, he knocked off Teachout's Convenience Store, and to blow a lid off it, old man Teachout had recognized him. He had no choice. Never batting a proverbial eye, Randall Fogerty made his first kill by pumping three bullets in the tall man's chest, then grabbed the fifty-eight dollars off the counter. Ten minutes later, he sat in a fast-food dive, ordering and eating whatever he desired.

Everything he'd been taught said he should have felt guilt, remorse, even condemned for sending the old man to his grave, but he hadn't. Not an ounce of culpability had touched his thought process, or more importantly, some would say, his heart process. Instead, he had found himself embracing the power, the control of taking whatever he wanted. He drained the rum and handed the glass to Braxton for a refill.

The most striking memory of that evening had taken place when he laid down the money to pay for his meal. He realized he'd never have to go hungry again. Never feel his stomach grind and twirl because of mealless days. Never wear dirty clothes again or shoes that looked more like rags than something to strap on his feet.

"Thoughts, sir?" asked Braxton, that deep, Barry White voice bringing him to the present.

"Nothing too serious. A little reminiscing about the good old days."

Braxton nodded. "We all do dat, from time ta time. Keeps ya grounded, my momma use ta say."

He smiled. "Your momma knew a thing or two."

"Yes, sir, dat she did."

His right-hand man reached into his pocket and brought out the leather-bound notebook, already anticipating his boss's next thought. Fogerty asked anyway.

"Are all of the shipments on time?"

"Dey are, sir. No su'prizes. No heroes and none a dos new entrepreneur types yet, today."

"Good. We don't want our South American friends to get nervous because I take a day off to hunt down my disobedient daughter."

Dialing the phone again, and getting the same no-answer result, he slipped the phone into his shirt pocket, removed his shades, and bent closer to Braxton. "We'll not be going through this shit again. The risk of her being away from my umbrella leaves too many opportunities for my enemies. She's chosen this route by not staying in contact with me. I'm already tired of her married life. Understand?"

Braxton's wide jaw broke into a tooth-filled grin, and he pulled the gleaming, nine-inch dagger from his belt. "As perfectly as one a dem fine tailored suits fittin' dat frame o' yours."

Fogerty laughed. "That's what I like about you, Braxton, you get it."

"I do, sir, I do. No worries 'bout dat."

The plane began its descent to San Juan International, and Fogerty's smile slowly turned to a different expression—the one that wasn't good for anyone who got in his way.

CHAPTER-9

Staring at his cell phone screen, Manny felt the most God-awful déjà vu. The screen bellowed, *call disconnected.* He wasn't sure if the message was intended for his eyes or his heart, until the latter threatened to explode into so many indefinable pieces.

No God, not again.

He redialed Chloe's number, glancing at Mike and Gavin who'd stopped walking. He had a Crosby at each side, both peering intently at him. Chloe's voice mail kicked in after one ring. He dialed again, voice mail again.

"What the hell's going on?" asked Gavin. "You look like you're going to pop a blood vessel."

"Chloe just called and said the plane carrying her and Josh was in trouble and couldn't find a place to land. Then the signal went dead, and I can't reach her."

"My God! You've got to be kidding," said Mike.

Manny shook his head, pacing to the front door of the restaurant and back. "She sounded terrified, and I don't know what that freaking noise was just before her phone went dead."

"Don't panic. Let's try Corner's phone," urged Gavin.

"You're right." Manny dialed his good friend's number. More voice mail.

He shifted his feet, closed his eyes, breathed a prayer, and tried again. This time, the phone rang longer, and then he thought he heard a voice. But his imagination had played a cruel trick on him: Josh's message system sprang to life, again.

"I have Corner's number. I'll keep trying him, and you keep on with Chloe's," said Gavin. He turned to Mike. "Call the airport, ask for Hannah Prisby, and tell her I need any info she can find about that jet. The Feds had to file a flight plan, so she should know something."

"Will do," answered Mike.

Running his hand through his hair, Manny was struggling to speak; instead, he nodded in appreciation to his long-time friends. Emotion could be as cumbersome as any obstacle when it came to expressing oneself, but often, a glance, a wink, a touch of a hand would convey more than a thousand words—like now.

A few minutes later, he slammed his smartphone into the palm of his hand. "It's no use. I can't get a signal through to the jet, and the damn weather isn't helping."

Gavin rubbed his jowls and nodded. "You're right. What about someone in Quantico? Do you have someone else you can call?"

"Yes. Josh's boss, John Dickman."

"Do it."

Searching his contacts, Manny called Dickman. Just when he thought he was going to get another God-forsaken voice mail, Dickman answered.

"Williams? Make it fast. We've got a problem," his voice as gruff as his wrinkled exterior.

"I know, sir. I got a call from Agent Franson that their jet was in trouble, and now I can't raise her or Agent Corner on my cell."

The silence on the other end was one of those situations that sends one's mind clambering to exit the body, so it wouldn't have to hear or see what was coming next. He clutched the phone and waited, unable to exhale.

"It, the jet, went down at Youngstown-Warren Regional while they were trying to land through an unexpected, fast-moving snowstorm."

Not sure he had the strength to ask, he did it anyway. "What do you mean 'went down'?"

The assistant director of the FBI cleared his throat. "They made an attempt to land, and the plane apparently hit hard a couple of times, then lost a wing and hit a barricade at the end of the runway, moving fast."

Manny didn't think it was possible for his heart to drop as far as it did. He gathered more strength. "Shit," he said softly. "Were there . . . is everyone . . . okay?"

"We don't have all of the information, but there were at least two survivors. We don't know if there were . . . fatalities. They're still searching. Before you ask, I don't know which is which or who is missing. I'm sorry, Manny, I know you're close to Franson and Corner, but I don't have any more specifics."

The screaming in his head came from his soul, and if he didn't run away from the negative thoughts, he'd be insane in a few minutes. He did his best to shift to cop mode. It helped. Then he made a decision, because waiting just wasn't on the table.

"Thank you, sir. I'm about four hours from there, so I'm on the way," he said quietly.

"Are you sure you want to— Wait, I have another call from the Cleveland office," said Dickman.

If silence were a dagger, he would have been cut to

ribbons in the first five seconds of that horrendous wait. No matter what he tried, he couldn't keep his mind from running down the road where doubt was so willing and able to lead him. He tried focusing on his daughter Jen and that helped some, for a moment. But to lose Chloe, and Josh, especially like this, was a prescription written by insanity.

Finally, Dickman came back to him. "Williams?"

"Yes."

"They found the other two and are doing all they can, but it's touch and go. I can't discuss the details because I don't have them all, but get your ass on the road. You can meet with the Cleveland people at the hospital."

Manny was already out the door, Gavin and Mike in tow. "I'm leaving now, sir. Is there anything else you can tell me?"

Dickman's answer was strange, at best. "You're the profiler. You got a couple of hours to think about this call, so profile me. Meanwhile, do what you're told and get to Youngstown."

The line went dead. Manny stared at the phone. He briefly wondered what it took before people just ditched their emotions and opted out of the rat race. Losing Chloe would do that for him.

Dickman was right. He *was* the profiler, and if he'd read the man's voice correctly, he had little time to see Chloe or Josh alive.

CHAPTER-10

Hiking through the wilderness of El Yunque was as close to a legitimate paradise as Rainer Johns had ever imagined. He was familiar with what the concept of Heaven, but what could be better than this? The smell of the Tabonuco trees and the Sierra Palms combined with the lush, green essence of the forest caused him to stop, close his eyes, and attempt to grasp it all.

When Rainer finally opened his eyes, the view had evolved to something even more stunning. He'd heard that the vistas were ever-changing at El Toro's peak, and he had previewed the unimaginable beauty of the north and east parts of El Yunque, but this was living proof. The landscape caused his heart to skip a beat.

Shifting the position of his long legs a little wider, he could barely contain himself. Even the high-rise hotels waving in the distance proved to be little or no reminder of civilization. Braced against the clear blue sky, they looked more like paintings than anything tangible.

Taking out his new, high-end digital camera, he proceeded to take pictures of everything and from every angle. He zoomed out, zoomed in, and held the camera at arm's length to take several shots of himself against the lush backdrop. He was sure his friends in Boston would turn green with envy when he posted the photos online. Especially Shari, his girlfriend. She had to work and couldn't make this trip. He'd get his ass kicked after she saw what she'd missed, when he got home, but it would be worth it. He loved her, but getting one up was a nice benefit.

"Nice? It's just plain awesome," he said out loud.

Finally, he launched back down the trail, mud and all. It was getting late, and he only had a few hours before it would be a whole different trek as the Caribbean sun settled.

After a quarter mile of muddy going, the path dried significantly, and he practically flew down the rest of the two-mile path, only stopping to snap an occasional picture of a green lizard or a red-legged thrush.

Less than three hundred yards from his parked SUV, he did something very different for a man of his nature. He'd planned every moment of his vacation, but now he decided he should try to be, as Shari suggested, more *impetuous* from time to time. *Impromptu. Spur of the moment.* He usually steered clear of acting on those terms and phrases, but not today, not at this moment of pure randomness. *What could go wrong?*

His eyes grew wide as he motored toward the less-maintained side trail that led farther into the jungle and the backside of the Bano de Oro trail.

Why not? I'm not a child. I'm on my own time. I'm free!

After ten minutes, he slowed and enjoyed the less strenuous alternative to El Toro. The path branched into several single-file trails where people would camp or just go off to commune with a side of nature not available in the northern states, especially in the winter. Stopping, he put his hands on his waist, just as the rain began to fall. Rainer turned his face to the sky and raised his hands to the new rainbow. This was just for him; this moment of Caribbean rain was his alone, and in a sense, eternally his. No one would or could experience what El Yunque was giving only to him. He felt himself getting hard and laughed out loud.

That's a new one.

Then he heard it. He suddenly glanced in one direction of the trail, then the other. The noise hadn't been born of the breezes and the trees. It'd sounded . . . guttural. Primitive. He swallowed hard. Those were words used on TV or in the movie theater and shouldn't apply to his joyous trip to El Yunque.

Standing rigid, he waited, his angst living just short of panic.

He listened intently and heard nothing but the multiple voices of the rainforest. After thirty seconds, he let out a breath and chalked one up to imagination created from excitement. But then he heard it again, closer this time, accompanied by a slight rustling of the thick underbrush about fifteen feet to his left. He waited.

A large mongoose unexpectedly burst onto the trail, dragging something he couldn't quite make out. His heart fell to his stomach as he leaped back. He'd read that the forest service had made an attempt at reducing the rat population by introducing mongooses to the rainforest. It hadn't worked, plus these vicious little vermin had a propensity for carrying rabies. But Rainer Johns seemed to be the last thing on this critter's mind. It was pulling hard on its apparent next meal, trying to get it loose from some impediment. When the mongoose finally succeeded, the meal was not only freed, but flung into the air. Rainer's eyes followed it, growing wider with recognition. He'd never seen a human foot detached from the body. Especially one half eaten.

The last floodgate protecting him from total panic sprang open, and he ran in the opposite direction, veering off to one of the other side trails, running like Jesse Owens in the '36 Olympics.

And he didn't stop until he saw a large, camouflage tent and heard saxophone music.

Thank God. There is strength in numbers. Everyone knows that.

"Hey. I need some help. I think someone's hurt," he yelled as he hurried to the opened mouth of the tent. No response, but it didn't matter. The music meant that another living soul was inside, and that was the important thing right now.

Not caring if anyone would be upset, he bent low and rushed inside.

Amanda Griggs stared at the entrance of the tent. Not unusual, except that her head was hung from the tent's cross supports, her naked, drawn-and-quartered body scattered throughout the tent.

This campsite hadn't been Rainer's salvation. Instead, when reality crossed the border from the realm of the unreal, something in him gave. He felt it.

He scrambled out of the tent, falling face down into the dirt. That's how the park rangers found him, still screaming, some thirty minutes later.

CHAPTER-11

Passing another eighteen-wheeler like it was standing still; Manny felt the Explorer slide then straighten. He knew he should slow down, but getting to Cleveland was all that mattered.

"This must be driving you crazy," said Alex quietly.

Manny glanced at the chubby CSI, swerved around a slower-moving truck, and nodded. "That might cover it. You know, when you deal with all the shitty things life throws at you, you think maybe you're ready for a few good rolls of the dice."

"True enough, but we've all been around the block a time or two, and we know life's a crap shoot. So we've got to be ready for anything, but that's easy for me to say —at least today," answered Alex.

"I know that's true, but sometimes I'd just like to have the dice in my hand."

"Yeah, I think you're right on that," Sophie strained from the backseat. "But the way you're driving on this snow, I'd say you're getting a few lucky rolls."

"Sorry. It's making me nuts not knowing, and AD Dickman won't take my calls."

"I know," she said, "and I'm hanging. Might need some new underwear, though."

"Why?" Manny asked.

"Mine went out the window after Toledo." The

next second, Manny felt Sophie's hand on his shoulder. "But me and old Dough Boy can handle whatever it takes to get you there. Right?"

Alex flashed a grin of his own. "She's right." He turned to look over his shoulder. "Toledo, huh? Mine never got out of Michigan."

Manny smiled, despite the situation. "I'll buy you both a new pair . . . and thanks, I needed that."

They drove in silence for another twenty minutes when Alex pointed to the road sign. "That's the exit."

Cranking the wheel to the left, Manny felt the Explorer fishtail back to the right, then straighten as if an unseen hand held the SUV steady.

"Damn it, Williams. I'm driving next time," said Sophie, her voice an octave higher.

"I hope we don't ever have another next time like this."

"Good point. But the next trip is mine."

"Fair enough. You're better than me, but I couldn't just sit in the seat. *That* would've driven me nuts."

Manny swung the Explorer into Cleveland's Memorial Hospital. The tires had hardly stopped turning when he jumped out and ran through the driving snow and wind toward the emergency room's entrance.

Alex and Sophie hollered for him to wait, and he heard their staggered steps crunching the crisp snow, but waiting was out of the question. Hell, anything except a full sprint was out of the question. He'd managed to keep his composure for the three-and-one-half-hour drive, but now his bundled nerves were fully released, along with a once-controlled imagination. Dread was his new best friend. To lose a love of your life once was obscene, twice made it flat out unbearable.

The automatic doors hesitated, slid open, slid shut, then crawled to reopen. In those moments of pause, after he kicked the thick door, he thought of Chloe's face and all that contributed to the essence of who she was. He brushed at tears.

What will I do if she's gone?

His panic escalated thinking about Josh. This cop world was a bitch and when you have people like Josh to cover your ass, well, it was the difference between sane and insane. Life and death.

Rushing through the now completely opened door, Alex and Sophie at his back, he charged the nurse at the counter.

"Chloe Franson and Josh Corner, where are they?"

The nurse raised her eyebrows. "Didn't your momma teach you any manners?"

Before Manny could move, Sophie had the nurse by the lapel, her face an inch from the nurse's rotund face. "This ain't no time to think about teaching manners. If you don't want your fat ass kicked through that door out into the freeze-ass parking lot, answer the man."

The desk nurse's eyes widened, and she pointed down the hall. "IC. . . IC room two on the third floor," she stammered.

"See, that wasn't so damned hard, now was it?"

Sophie smoothed out the woman's jersey and then followed him toward the elevator.

"Not nice, you know," said Manny. "But thanks."

"Yeah, yeah. Just don't tell Santa . . . and you're welcome."

Bursting through the elevator door, his eyes searched the room numbers. Two was on the left. He hurried to it and then stopped.

Maybe I don't really want to see this.

But he knew no other way but to be bold. He said another prayer and took a step. Alex grabbed his arm.

"I got this one, boss. I'll be right back." With that, Alex strolled ahead.

Running his hand through his hair, Manny let Alex enter the hospital room first, and in doing so, felt some momentary relief. Maybe there was only so much of this heartache thing that people could handle. Maybe that was how it's supposed to be. Then we'd have to lean on others just that much more. Somehow that made perfect sense.

Alex was gone for about fifteen seconds when Manny couldn't take it any longer. He took a deep breath, inhaling that inherent hospital smell, and headed through the wide doors.

There are shocking situations in life to be sure. Manny had seen more than his share—good and bad— but but all of heaven and earth could have convulsed into some other dimension, and he wouldn't have been as surprised.

Chloe sat on the first bed, facing the door, with her legs crossed, a small bandage on her temple. Her left arm was draped across her ample chest resting in a beige sling.

In the bed sat Josh. Circling around his head was a gauze wrap. There were scrapes and cuts on his face and arms, but he looked to be relatively unhurt. It took a moment for the scene to register. Chloe and Josh were alive and kicking.

Odd where the mind ran at times like this. His first reaction was one of disbelief, and the second was to thank God that his expectation was not a reality.

"About damn time you got here, agent. We were thinking you didn't love us anymore," said a grinning Josh. "Oh, and you can close your mouth now."

Struggling to her feet, Chloe rushed Manny, who met her halfway. She was a strong woman, and even with one arm, she held tight enough to stop the air from coming, but he didn't care. He gently wrapped his arms around her.

"Is that all ya got, man?" she whispered.

"I don't want to hurt you."

"I'll let you know if ya do."

He kissed her and pulled her tight. "Better?"

"Oh, much better."

Manny had no more words, but then again, he was pretty sure he didn't need them.

After a minute that seemed like a second, he kissed her, held her at arm's length, kissed her again, helped her onto the bed, and then moved to Josh.

"You're not going to kiss me too, are you?" he smiled. "There are manly rules about that kind of thing."

"Not gonna happen, even on your best day," he said as he leaned and gave him a hug.

"Shit. I will," said Sophie.

She brushed past Manny and gave Josh a long kiss, square on his lips, then stepped back. "Damn. That was even better than the dip-and-kiss you pulled on me in Lansing."

Josh's face turned red. "Ah thanks, Sophie."

"Don't mention it. Somebody has to be willing to do what it takes in this group."

Alex shook his head. "None of you are right. This is supposed to be a Behavioral Analysis Unit, not freaking Woodstock." But Manny could see the sparkle in his eyes. He was as relieved as Manny.

Manny sat on the side of the bed. "About time? Is that what you said? You're lucky you're gimped-up. I thought we were dead three or four times with me driving here."

"Sorry about that. We couldn't call. Lots of tests and no phones. Besides, the boss wanted you here."

Chloe hobbled to his side, her hand slipping into his, leaning her head on his shoulder. The way he felt as she touched him was the substance of answered prayers.

Letting out a deep breath, he located what was left of his composure. "We'll talk about that in a minute. What happened up there?"

Josh turned his head and looked down, then his cobalt blues caught Manny straight on.

"That weather front went nuts, and the next thing we knew, we were dropping like a lead balloon. We bounced on the runway, but the plane hung in there, and for some unknown reason, Chloe and I woke up, side by side, in the snow at the end of the runway, virtually unhurt. She's got a sprained ankle and a bruised shoulder. I got my brain rattled around, and my back's sore as hell, but nothing too severe."

"The pilots did a great job of keeping Josh and I alive, but . . ." said Chloe, her voice breaking.

"They were both hurt worse than us," finished Josh.

The room grew quiet.

Manny again marveled at the mind's ability to balance several simultaneous, gut-wrenching emotions into something that drew order out of chaos. Relief.

Angst. Joy. Sadness. Frustration.

They were all grateful for Chloe's and Josh's survival, but at what price?

"They're both in the other IC unit, hanging in there, but they won't tell me anymore than that. Funny. I was on the pilot's case for telling me how it was, instead of trying to make Chloe and I feel better. A few minutes later, he and the co-pilot were saving our bacon," Josh whispered.

"He sounds like my kind of guy," said Alex softly.

"Mine too," said Manny.

"Okay. Enough of the trip down Guilty Lane. It can't change anything, and I don't know about you guys, but I've had enough of the emotional rollercoaster ride for the day. Those guys are going to make it because it's how it's supposed to go. They did their jobs, and that means they won't be checking out anytime soon."

Running his hand through his hair, Manny smiled at Sophie. "Pretty profound for someone who thinks she's not."

"Hey. I have my moments."

"And you're also right," said Josh.

"Changing gears from Agent Lee exhibiting more than a sixth-grade level of profoundness . . . Josh, you said the boss wanted Manny here, and I'm assuming us as well. So, why?" asked Alex.

Josh nodded and immediately winced. "Ouch. That's not a good idea. Anyway, the assistant director has a case for us, your very first as FBI agents. It's not exactly up our alley, but the DEA arrested three suspects in San Juan that they believe to be a part of one of the most prolific cocaine cartels in the Caribbean."

"We get a road trip to San Juan in January? I'm

already loving this gig," said Sophie, clapping her hands together.

"Down girl. Josh is right. We really don't have much experience in that world," said Manny.

Sophie raised her hand. "Ooo. Ooo. Does experimenting with crack in college count as experience?"

"I'm going to ignore that, agent," said Josh, grinning. He turned back to Manny. "What he's hoping we can do is complete an in-depth profile and then apply that to the next step of interrogation. The DEA is desperate to get anything on this cartel. They think the head of this organization was responsible for getting over three hundred tons of coke in the US last year."

Alex whistled. "Damn. That's a lot of blown-up sinuses and septums."

"Not to mention tax-free income," added Chloe.

"So when will you two be able to leave?" asked Manny, moving closer to Chloe.

"The doc said I can fly in a few days, but Chloe could be ready to go, depending on the x-rays. You might have to go without me this trip. It's you they really want anyway."

"As profilers?" asked Alex. "I can understand Manny, but Sophie and me?"

"You two are very good at what you do, and the three of you have been a team for awhile. You can kick around ideas with each other, and it'll help."

"It won't take long to profile three drug runners," said Manny.

"Yeah. They want you to leave tomorrow and probably come home in a day or two. Home, as in Quantico. You've all got a shitload of paperwork to finish and you haven't met everyone you need to meet. Then there's the swearing-in ceremony for Alex and Sophie."

"That'll be a switch. Sworn in instead of sworn at," said Sophie.

"For you," said Alex.

"Bite me."

"On your own time, you two," said Josh, not hiding his smile.

"I'm assuming you all brought your travel bags," he continued, "so go ahead and get a hotel. You'll leave tomorrow morning, early."

The phone on the nightstand rang, and Josh picked it up.

"Corner here. Yes sir, thank you. We're glad we made it, too."

As Josh listened, Manny saw his friend's expression change like a dark cloud had just blocked his sunlight.

Josh hung up the phone, then swung his bare feet to the floor. "Circumstances have changed."

"How?" asked Manny.

"The rangers in the El Yunque rainforest have just discovered four bodies. Two near a campsite and two in a tourist attraction, the Mount Britton Tower."

"And . . . ?" prompted Alex.

"They were all four hacked to death, and it looks like the killings could have been less than twelve hours apart. They want our help."

"What does hacked to death mean?" asked Manny.

"I don't know, but we're going to find out."

"So we're invited and still leaving tomorrow morning?" said Manny.

"Yes to both. Well, we're going to leave as soon as the weather clears and we can get a jet here. I'll talk to the doctors and find out their bottom line for when I can leave. I have an 'in' at the rainforest so I need to get there ASAP."

"In?" asked Manny.

"I'll tell you later." Josh paused then added, "There's another thing. We need to talk about you and Chloe getting tight when this one's over. There are regulations that address relationships at the Bureau, let alone in the same unit. Especially when it could affect judgment in a dangerous situation. Is that a problem here?"

Manny nodded. "We kind of thought this was coming, so no surprise. But no, there's no problem, so far."

"He's right, none so far," said Chloe.

"Okay. We'll talk more later on. Right now, let's get the docs to do their job so we can get the hell out of here."

"Are you going to be able to fly so soon?" asked Alex.

Raising his palms to the ceiling, Josh shrugged. "What choice do I have? I either fly or take a bus to DC and get a job serving burgers."

"I guess that's true, but that may be easier said than done," said Manny.

"It might."

Manny noticed that Josh was trying to avoid eye contact and knew immediately there was more. "What else?" he said.

"Two things," Josh quickly responded. "We will be meeting the new CSI assigned to this unit in San Juan. His name is Dean Mikus. We just hired him away from the Los Angeles PD. Very bright, but a little quirky."

"He'll fit right in," said Sophie.

"He will. And the other thing?" probed Manny.

Agent Corner glanced at the floor, then to the ceiling, finally settling on Manny. "This might be my last case in the BAU."

CHAPTER-12

"We've got six bodies, all killed the same way. I think that qualifies as freaking rampage, a serial-killer trifecta. Shit. Why us?" said Detective Julia Crouse.

Detective Carlos Ruiz started to answer his partner, but paused to look at her for a moment. She was taller than he, better-than-average-looking with huge, dark eyes and short, black hair that perfectly framed her oval face. She was damn near attractive when she let go of the seemingly eternal frown. Today wasn't going to be one of those days, however.

He stroked his mustache, shrugged, and said, "What'd you think homicide was when you signed up? A Girl Scout get-together with barbeques and piñatas? I mean we get more murders than New York."

"No, smartass, I knew we'd get the drug and gang-war crap. A few road-rage shootings, and of course, the old standby, domestic violence, leading to more funerals than reconciliations. But this? Good God, did you see those bodies?" answered Julia, hands flying a mile a minute.

He sighed. He *had* seen them. The horrific scenes would no doubt stoke the fire that fueled his perpetual migraines and the never-ending nightmares.

Ah. The joy of law enforcement in San Juan.

"Even worse was the position of the bodies. It

was . . . organized," he said.

"I saw some of that, but I'm not sure it was the case for the last two."

"I'm not sure of a lot of this, and the CSI teams are going to go nuts trying to find *anything* where these folks were found. That's why I called the cavalry."

Crouse rested her backside on her desk and crossed her arms. He smiled. She wasn't anything if not a classic, strong-willed woman. She hated not being the first to know. He thought that trait was part of what made her a good cop.

"What? Who's the cavalry?" she asked, lips tight.

Gathering his thoughts, he gazed out the second-story window and caught the beginnings of a Caribbean sunset. It was as vibrant as any in the world. He felt himself drawing strength from it, strength he needed whenever he talked about *her*.

"A couple of years ago we had a murder at one of the Condado Strip's elite hotels."

"I remember that one. Ended up being some psycho serial-killer tandem, right?"

He nodded. "It did. The FBI got involved, and this Michigan cop, Manny Williams, helped in ways that only those profiler types can. But it was too late for my partner, Christina Perez."

Crouse's expression was immediately altered by the softening of her eyes and face. He'd only witnessed this look a time or two in their partnership. "I remember that too," she said softly. "I was still in blue, but I heard the rumors about how she died." She tilted her head. "And the rest of those rumors."

He rubbed his face with both hands. "Well, they were true, mostly. She died horribly, and I should have been there. She said she could handle it, and that our caseload here was too crazy to leave, so I agreed." His hand started to shake, and he clenched it with the other. "I've not slept well since her funeral."

Crouse stepped close and took both his hands. "It wasn't your fault."

"I know, but I can't help wondering how it would have gone if I'd been there."

"You'll make yourself crazy trying to figure that one out. So stop. I kind of like my partners not spending their nights in the loony bin."

"Believe me, if I could, I would. It's just not that easy."

Squeezing his hands, she stepped back. "Did you love her?"

Ruiz gave her an even, steady gaze. "The other rumor?"

"Yep. Hey, there might be seventeen thousand cops on this island, but stuff like that gathers no moss."

"I suppose it doesn't. Let's just say we were close."

"Fair enough."

"Anyway. The FBI's BAU is the best, and I hear Detective Williams is now part of them. We have enough shit going on and could use their help on this one."

"Okay. When will they be here?"

"Hopefully within twelve hours or so. Hell, they don't even know about the other two bodies found near the La Mina Trail."

"So all bullshit aside, do you think this is drug-related? I mean half the damn killings on the 'Isle of Enchantment' are."

Ruiz opened his hands. "I don't think so. I could be wrong, but I don't see it. We've seen some gory shit between local drug lords and all of that turf war violence. I mean the throat slashing and the execution-style crap. But I've never seen anything like this from them. They almost have a code, not always, but mostly. There's no freaking code here. This killer didn't attempt to hide anything and left everything of any value at each murder scene."

"And . . . ?"

"And my gut tells me it's different, for whatever that's worth. But that's where guys like this Williams come in. He'll know, and that can only help find this warped bastard."

The cell on his desk began to chime, the ring tone set to a famous piece by cuatro player Yomo Toro. He glanced at the screen and did a double take.

"Shit," he whispered.

"Who is it?"

"The coroner." He picked up the phone. "Ruiz here."

A moment later, he dropped the phone from his ear and shook his head.

"I hate it when you look like that," Julia said.

"Yeah, well, I hate it too. They found another body, only one this time."

"In El Yunque?"

"Yes. But it's bad."

His partner's eyes grew larger. "What do you mean, bad?"

"They found the commander of the park ranger division, sliced beyond recognition."

"Shit." Her eyes widened. "Oh man. Isn't he the brother of a—"

Her words were halted by the slump in Ruiz's shoulders. He'd forgotten about the park ranger's connection with the Feds.

Picking up the land line, he slowly dialed the number he'd already memorized.

CHAPTER-13

"What the hell does that mean?" asked Manny, watching Josh's eyes closely.

Sophie was more abrupt. "Are you leaving the bureau? If so, I'll have to kick your ass right now. Then nurse you back to health the Chinese way."

"Relax," said Josh. "It just means that there might be something more on the horizon for me. And what does 'the Chinese way' mean?"

"Let's just say you won't be feeling any pain."

"That works," grinned Josh.

"A promotion? You've only one way to go, man. So that means—" Chloe began, walking gingerly to the head of the bed.

"Assistant director," Manny finished.

"Well, maybe. The assistant director over the BAU and a couple of the drug-trafficking units is retiring due to health concerns and AD Dickman wants me to throw my hat in the ring. I said yes, that's all."

"That's all? I think that's pretty significant," frowned Alex.

"Yeah, that's like calling Lake Michigan a pond," said Sophie.

"Hey. Guys. It's just a hat in the ring. There's a bunch of agents with more experience, so I'm not even in the top five, I'm sure. Okay?" Josh had a hard edge to his otherwise calm voice when he said "okay?"

"Okay it is," answered Manny, knowing Josh knew more.

Manny watched Josh's hand move to the back of his neck and the particular way he looked down and away. Not Josh Corner traits. There was more to the scenario than his friend was letting on. He was hiding something, something deep that birthed a level of anxiety he kept to himself. Josh turned Manny's way, peering intently at him.

That's more like Josh Corner.

"I should never talk about these things in front of profilers. Didn't we have a deal? No profiling the boss, right?" he said.

"I don't remember that one," said Manny. "It's just obvious you're less than comfortable with all of the attention. So we'll back off, for now. Not to mention you must have a headache the size of Texas."

"Like hell we will," said Sophie. "I sign up and you leave? Not happening. Oh, and I have an old Chinese cure for that headache, but I ain't telling, or showing."

"Come here," said Josh.

Sophie looked at Manny, then to Alex, then to Chloe. Each glance reflecting that wonderful uneasiness that was so rare to see in his partner.

"No. I'm—I'm pissed at you," she sputtered.

"Now, Agent Lee," demanded Josh.

Taking a deep breath and leaving the uneasiness in the dust, she marched to the left side of the bed, her hair bouncing in rhythm with her steps.

"What?"

"Closer."

She shuffled a step closer. "This is all you get.

What?"

He pulled her head close and whispered in her ear. When he was done, she moved back and folded her arms. "You can't play that card, especially now."

"My badge, and our friendship, says I can. Do we have a deal?"

Rolling her eyes, she bent to Josh, kissed his forehead, then moved back to Manny. "Freaking men. Yeah, we got a deal, for now. Asshole."

"You're too kind."

Josh got out of bed and stood in the middle of the room, looking directly at Manny. "No grilling her either. This one is between us."

There existed almost a pleading in his boss's eyes. He found himself, once again, wondering what the hell was going on, but nodded his agreement.

"All right," said Manny.

Chloe moved to Manny's side, looping her arm through his.

For the second time in ten minutes, he felt the elation of knowing someone you love is safe. What could match that?

"Let's get organized," Josh said. "The docs will be here in a few, so Chloe and I will harass them into a positive update on our conditions."

Chloe slipped off the sling. "What conditions?"

Josh followed suit and unwrapped the gauze from his head, revealing another semi-bloodied bandage on his forehead. "She's right. I feel better already."

"You both look good too," said Sophie.

"I'll say it again, none of you are right," said Alex. "Doctors usually know what they're talking about, but none of you are going to listen."

"Hey. We've got work to do," said Josh. "The next thing will be to check out the weather and get us to San Juan as quickly as possible. That means you'll have to be ready when the pilot says *when*."

"I hate to be a wet blanket here, but are you two sure you're ready to get back inside a plane right now?" asked Alex, again.

Josh and Chloe exchanged a look and shrugged in unison.

"My mum used to say you got to get back on the seat when you fall off, so I'm okay," said Chloe, her eyes full of determination. Another trait Manny loved about her.

"Her mom and my dad must have been from the same school," added Josh. "I'm as ready as I'll ever be. Besides, I hate buses."

"You had a traumatic experience, and it might not be that easy."

"Thanks Alex, but we're done talking about this."

The door swung open, and a team of three doctors entered. The first one was a short, lithe woman, who was probably older than she looked, with intelligent, deep-brown eyes and high cheek bones on a handsome face that demanded respect.

"Agents. My name is Doctor Mary Gilger, and I'll be ensuring you walk out of here in better condition than before the accident."

"Thank you, doctor, but I think we've made miraculous recoveries and are ready to check out," said Josh.

Grinning, Manny thought how charming Josh could be, but judging by the doctor's body language, *bullshitter* wasn't anything she embraced.

"I'll be the judge of that, Agent Corner. None of you police types ever think you're hurt, or you all have some damn Guardian-of-the-Universe attitude that makes you invincible."

"Well, that would be him, the blond, blue-eyed cop over there. I'm just a fast healer," said Josh.

"I can see that about Agent Williams."

She eyed Manny and winked. "Yes, I know who you are. We know who all of you are. Just because you're good-looking doesn't mean we don't check out who comes to visit injured FBI agents. No one got into this room unless I knew about it. Even Asian women who threaten nurses."

"Sorry," said Sophie, running her shoe back and forth on the floor. "She was being a bitch."

"That's her job."

The doctor turned back to Josh. "But you're also full of shit. You're not healed and neither is the Irish Princess."

"I assure you doc—"

"You're not assuring anything until I get a closer look, got it?" she growled.

Sophie covered her mouth and laughed. Alex didn't bother. He just laughed out loud. Manny joined him.

"Did ya hear that Williams? I'm royalty. I need to be treated that way," Chloe reminded him.

"I got it handled," said Manny.

"I've got other patients who might actually listen to what I've got to say, so let's get this in motion. Both of you, on the bed, chop, chop."

"You guys are in deep do-do," said Sophie.

Just then the phone rang, and Josh snatched it off the nightstand. "This is Corner. Yes, Detective Ruiz.

Good to hear from you, too."

The expression on Josh's face changed, and Manny felt his heart climb to his throat.

"What's the bad news, detective?" asked Josh.

A moment later, the phone slowly slipped from his hand and bounced off the tiled floor. Manny grabbed it before it could rebound a second time. He brought the phone to his ear and heard only static and line noise.

The room had taken on one of those eerie quiet reversals of ambience with which this group had grown far too familiar. Joy one moment, hell the next. By the look on Josh's face, hell had left another calling card. Manny wondered if it would ever stop.

"What is it, Josh?" he asked softly.

"Remember that 'in' I have, uh, had at the rainforest park department?"

"Yes."

"He was the head of the division. They just found his body, and he was murdered like the others."

Josh looked at Manny with a sadness he thought only possible in his own world. "His name is Caleb, Caleb Corner, my brother."

CHAPTER-14

Wiping the blood and tissue, not to mention the pesky strands of hair from his blade, he couldn't get the smile off his face. The task of cleaning his sword had been very unpleasant at first, maybe even morbid. However, after the second executions, the cleaning began to lend itself as pleasurable on some level. He had studied other areas of academia but had little desire to delve deeply into the human psyche. He still didn't, but his natural curiosity couldn't, wouldn't, be dismissed as easily as a confused student in one of his classes. Nevertheless, he had little time to research what his emotions might mean. He was far too busy, and in a real sense, enjoying himself far too much to care what any such analysis would reveal. His overall purpose was noble, enlightened, even destined, if one chose to travel down the road leading to any kind of spiritual superstition or religion. God never entered into his definition of existence, but if there was a God, He would surely approve of what he was doing. After all, sacrifice was a part of any equation that leads to advancing human knowledge. His smile grew wider.

Never mind that each lesson I deliver to the infidels in my rainforest is becoming almost as satisfying as any sexual encounter I've ever experienced . . . maybe more.

He carefully placed the rapier back in the sheath

and took it into the den, securing it in the oblong safe he had built just for his collection. He bent lower and frowned in concentration, examining the safe's contents with the gaze of a protective, proud father. Each one was perfect in its own right. Each one carefully constructed by men who shared his passion for perfection and purity, albeit centuries in the past. The type of genius required to create such objects of sheer precision was as rare then as it was today.

After touching and affectionately caressing each of the other five rectangular cases, he chose one that was a little shorter than the rest. There was no question that his attempt at impartiality was compromised by what lay hidden in the felt lining of the customized leather case. It was his favorite. He felt a tinge of guilt at that admission, but truth is always truth, no matter how much makeup one uses to disguise it.

Carefully pulling out the container, he released the combination locks at each corner and opened it. He could only stare for a moment, then was compelled to glide the fifteenth century Koto Katana sword from its resting place. The ivory handle had been restored and the gold inlaid inscriptions running down the blade were almost as bright and colorful as the day they were created.

The hilt was curved in the classic two-handed custom of that era and it felt like it *belonged* in his hands. There was a sense of oneness he could barely comprehend, but it didn't matter. Love is never predictable or understood; it just is. And make no mistake—he loved this blade like a man loved his new bride.

He tenderly fingered the inscription. He'd spent long hours researching and growing in understanding of each message and the incredible culture behind the craftsman, known as Ippo, who'd built this blade. He knew that it had all of its dimensions recorded in the inscription and how rare a six-fold carbon construction was. The legends surrounding the forging of this weapon included the adding of human blood in the molding method. All very interesting, but not as interesting as the cutting tests. The tester of this blade had accomplished a rare feat with this particular sword. It was called a two-body cut. The tester had successfully cut clean through two living human bodies, according to the inscription, in an attempt to reveal the quality of construction the Katana possessed. Closing his eyes, he could picture the test being accomplished. He felt himself swoon with emotion.

"What a seal of approval that must have been," he whispered. "If only I'd been there."

He brought the blade to his face. The aroma of old ivory and steel caused him to close his eyes in pure ecstasy. This instrument, this lover of justice and vengeance, would accompany him on the next step of his purging mission. If the defilers of his rainforest wouldn't leave El Yunque, the blood of the sacrifices would be on the hands of the bureaucrats that let them in, not on his.

Thrusting the sword in the air, turning two perfect pirouettes, he stopped in a striking pose as gracefully as any dancer. He then placed the sword back in its home, laughing out loud as he did. It was getting late in the afternoon, and as much as he wanted, perhaps needed, to visit the rainforest and teach another lesson, he'd get an early start at dawn. After all, morning surprises were always the best. They radiated a semblance of Christmas morning, and who didn't appreciate Christmas morning? Besides, he loved being the bearer of surprises. Who knew, after a few more bodies, maybe the government would shut down public access to his rainforest. He sighed. It wouldn't be for a while, he suspected, because humans are innately stupid. Of course, law enforcement would have to make its usual ridiculous attempt to figure out what was going on and to capture the immoral person responsible for the murder of innocents.

He felt his blood instantly boil, his heart rate climb. There was no justice for his mother and certainly hadn't been any for El Yunque over the years. He knew that double standards and concepts of right and wrong prevailed in this age. But they hadn't counted on someone like him. He would win. He would change perceptions. Nevertheless, he'd begun to leave them clues, a fighting chance to meet him. Something his rainforest, and his mother, no longer had.

CHAPTER-15

"Perhaps I've not made myself clear," spoke Randall Fogerty, leaning on the counter of the car rental office. "I need the limo I always rent when I come to San Juan."

The attendant stepped back, eyes widening to the sweet venom in his voice. But she repeated what she'd said a moment earlier, her Latino accent heightened by stress. "I'm sorry, sir, that vehicle is reserved, and I cannot give it to you. I hope you understand. It's our policy."

He leaned closer and spoke softer. "What's your name?"

"Evita, sir."

"Ah. That means life, yes?"

"Yes sir, it does."

Her nervousness was escalating. Good. "Well Evita, does it look like I give a lizard's ass about your policy?"

"I . . . I, no it doesn't, but—"

At that moment, a man emerged from the back office, and he immediately rushed to the counter, eyes showing more than just a concern for customer service.

"Mr. Fogerty. We weren't expecting you."

"That seems fairly obvious, muchacho. This fine young lady refuses to give me the limo; she says it's already reserved."

"Let me take a look."

A moment later, after a few hurried key strokes, he looked up smiling in relief. "It seems that reservation has been canceled. I'll have the car brought up, *señor*."

Evita looked at her manager, then back to Fogerty. "I'm sure that reservation is still—"

"Evita. Please go tell Alfredo to bring the limo up, now."

"But—"

"I said now, if you want to work your next shift," his eyes on fire.

She bowed her head and moved to the back office.

"Thank you, Benito. I appreciate the way you handled that." Fogerty shook his hand. "For that kind gesture, we'll leave the interest rate for your loan at twenty-five percent. You've been a day late on the payment twice, so we could raise it, but you did well."

"Yes sir, Mr. Fogerty. I appreciate that. My daughter is doing well from the surgery and her chances are good."

Fogerty smiled wider and leaned closer. "I hope that makes you feel better, because frankly, I don't give a shit. If you miss another payment, you'll have more trouble than she. Got that?"

Benito's voice shook. "Ye. . . yes sir. It won't happen again."

"I know it won't."

Fogerty spun on his heel and walked through the doors to the awaiting limo. Braxton instructed one of the bodyguards to take the wheel and the other to ride shotgun, while he climbed in back with his boss.

Fogerty grinned as Braxton folded into the backseat opposite him. Not a small man himself at six feet and two hundred pounds, he was nothing compared to his number one man. Watching him get into the limo and get comfortable was always a show.

Braxton returned the grin. "Dey don't make des like dey use ta."

"I'm sure you're right."

Braxton nodded, then abruptly hit the dividing glass that separated driver and passenger.

"Let's go, mon. Get dis ting up to the rainforest, now," he yelled.

Fogerty nodded his approval.

It was time to end this charade, and no one could do that better than he.

CHAPTER-16

Manny waited for Chloe and Josh outside the sterile examination room. Sitting in the padded chair, he ran his hand through his hair, contemplating Josh's revelation regarding his brother. Shock was probably too strong a word, but it seemed his world was never devoid of the type of surprises that raised his blood pressure and made slack-jaw the expression of the day.

The waiting room was empty, and for that, he was glad. He could use the quiet. Sophie and Alex had gone out to fill the SUV with gas and retrieve their baggage. Alex also wanted to call the Bureau for an updated time frame for when they could get another plane into Cleveland. The cell phone reception in the hospital was terrible, maybe by design, so he tagged along with Sophie. He said they'd be back in thirty minutes. Manny smiled to himself. Sophie was driving, and she had said twenty.

After announcing his brother Caleb had been murdered, Josh had explained what he meant by brother. Caleb was actually his half-brother and had come to the Corner family at age thirteen. Josh's father had had a bit of a wild side growing up and had gotten a young woman pregnant. She wanted nothing to do with him, married another man, and moved to the West Coast. The family apparently had trouble to staying together. Then Josh's family had gotten the call, out of nowhere, and he had a brother.

Josh said Caleb had come from an extremely troubled home, where beating the children for no apparent reason and smoking crack cocaine had been routine for Caleb's parents, especially for his stepdad.

The four-year difference in age, with Josh being older, prevented them from being close, but they talked a few times a year and up until Josh's mom passed away two years ago, saw each other for Christmas and her birthday.

Watching his friend's face and body language as he told the story, Manny could tell that Josh was creeping close to the level of stress and anxiety that could be a little more than any man might be able to handle. As surprised as Josh was at the news of his brother's death, and the way he'd died, Manny was sure there was still something else going on. The reaction he'd seen just before the doctor had entered told Manny he was right. But then, like he'd seen him do so many times over the last two years, Special Agent Josh Corner set his face and eyes in that familiar *I got this* mode and became all business. If ghosts were enjoying the haunt in Josh's head, he wasn't telling anyone about them. Josh could shift gears almost as well as Manny—and Manny knew that dance.

He stood, stretching his back and legs. Soon enough. Josh would tell him soon enough. However, timing was the spice of life, and in this job, good timing was a constant guessing game. He hoped he didn't have to wait too long for Josh to unload.

The heavy steel door swung open, and Chloe walked out. There was a small bandage on her head, and the sling was gone. That made him feel even better.

His insides did that old "jumping in the chest" routine as she sauntered close to him. He'd never get tired of the way she walked. The shape of her body, the sway of her breasts, and the blatant beauty that always turned his heart, if not his head. She stopped a foot away and smiled with those eyes. It was brilliant. He felt his temperature rise.

"I could file sexual harassment charges against ya for the way you're looking at me, man."

"File away. But I doubt I'd be the only defendant."

She wrapped her arms around his neck, delivering a kiss that would thaw an iceberg.

"You're the only defendant that matters, though," she breathed, her voice husky and provocative. "Manny Williams. How long are you going to make me wait? Sometimes I think I might explode."

For a brief moment, he thought she'd only have to wait another ten or eleven seconds. His whole body ached with the anticipation of sleeping with her—all night.

"Why, Agent Franson, whatever do you mean?"

She tightened her grip, moving her body closer. "Oh, I can tell you know what I mean, or is that your gun in your pocket?"

"Got me there," he grinned.

He reached for her hand and felt the Claddagh ring he'd given her in Ireland. "I made a promise and you said yes, so let's—"

Just then, Josh burst through the door, Doctor Gilger on his heels, white coat flapping and her notebook held high.

"Don't twist my words, young man. You *might* be okay to fly, I said. I need to run a few more tests."

"I heard you, but I'm leaving on the next flight to San Juan, with or without your approval," he said firmly, his face draped with determination.

"Like hell you are. I got sons your age, and they still listen to their mother when I speak to them. Never mind that I'm your doctor."

He stopped and turned to face her. The look changed to a softer, but even more determined, demeanor Manny hadn't quite seen before. "I respect that, doc, but this killing bastard just made it personal. Give me some pills that will help, if you'd like, but I'm going to be in Puerto Rico in a few hours."

She stared at him, then slowly reached for his hand, patting it like mothers and grandmothers do when they're proud and pissed at the same time. Manny felt the attack of déjà vu. That gesture had been one of Louise's favorite. He pushed it way. The last thing he needed right now was more emotion kicking the shit out of him.

"I'll get you some non-aspirin pain medication and hope you don't develop a subdural hematoma and die drinking your coffee."

"Deal. And if I do, you can say you told me so." He winked at her. "Thanks, Doc."

"That charm stuff doesn't work with old ladies like me, but you're welcome." Then she left.

"You still have a way with the women," said Manny.

Josh gave him a tired grin. "You gotta use it when you have it."

Sophie pranced through the outside door with Alex a few feet behind her, his face pale as the drifting snow.

"Never again. I keep saying that, I know. Then she

sucks me in with promises to drive like someone from this planet. She thinks she's driving the freaking Starship *Enterprise*.

"Stop whining, Dough Boy, we got back seven minutes sooner than you said we would."

"Yeah, but my guts will never be the same. And don't call me Dough Boy."

"Never mind your guts, tell them what we found out."

"That'd be good," said Manny.

After letting out a breath, Alex straightened up. "The weather is breaking, and it looks like we'll be able to leave in a couple of hours."

"That's good. We need to get down there," said Josh.

"What else?" asked Manny.

"The detective that called you, according to AD Dickman, didn't tell Josh everything."

Tension sang in the room as all eyes focused on Alex. "There have been seven murders, not five, all in the last fifteen hours."

Manny ran his hand through his hair. "Shit. That means the killer is on a spree."

"And is very pissed about something." added Sophie.

He nodded. "I keep thinking I'll get used to crap like this. What else, Alex?"

The CSI looked down to the floor then back to Manny. "Yeah, that's not all. Apparently we have three more missing persons."

CHAPTER-17

Dean Mikus stroked his long, uneven beard and wondered what it took to get a taxi in San Juan. In Los Angeles, they'd be on him like flies in a landfill, and in several different languages. But he wasn't in LA anymore, was he? The FBI had made an offer, and he only had to think about it for a few seconds.

Hell yes, I want to be an FBI agent.

This job gave him the opportunity to specialize in forensics, instead of the *jack of all trades* gig he had in LA. The pay was better, the cost of living in the DC area was less expensive, and goodbye morning smog. That might have been the best reason to leave the LAPD. He wanted no part of emphysema or any other situation that would turn his lungs assorted dark colors. Sure he'd miss the beach, and of course the bikinis, but at thirty-eight, he was feeling more and more out of place going down to the ocean and sitting under an umbrella to watch the waves and the chicks. Even the "older women" pushing thirty were starting to look like his kid sister. He smiled. Not quite, but almost.

Reaching his hand high in the air, he hailed another taxi; it zoomed past with defined purpose and a backseat full of tourists. The driver waved; Dean fingered him.

My first California Salute out of the state. Got to like

it.

Stepping out a little further into the street, he started to hail the next yellow vehicle that caught his attention, when he heard the horn. He glanced to his left just in time to see the white Hummer limo bearing down on him, looking more like a rhino than a vehicle. He jumped back, falling over his bag and hitting the sidewalk with both cheeks. Never missing a beat, he jumped up quickly and yelled obscenities toward the limo that was, by now, far down the street and out of ear shot.

Brushing off the dust, he mumbled under his breath, "Paybacks are a bitch that will not be ignored, and she's a friend of mine."

He reached down and picked up his sunglasses, minus one lens, shook his head, and put them on anyway. Might as well add to his reputation of being a little different, whatever the hell that meant. Just because he liked things a certain way didn't mean he was weird. For instance, didn't everyone prefer a certain kind of hairdo or type of clothes? His style preference was to ignore the barber shop for three years. The same time frame applied to his beard. He liked it that way, and it was his choice. And what was wrong with argyle socks and shorts? They were always color-coordinated and clean. Besides, they were practical. The socks kept his legs warm, but the shorts reminded him that he lived in California and that the sun shone every day, almost. His dress was the best of both worlds: warm, but not too warm; cool, but not too cool.

And what about personal preference when it came to the opposite sex? Women loved big guys, little guys, good-looking men, long hair, short hair, beards, hairless, all shapes and sizes. Women were better at tapping much deeper, at least initially, into relationships. But men would come around, given the right woman.

Men, himself included, all had the perfect woman pictured in some mysterious part of themselves, not driven totally by the small head. The color of her hair, the size of her breasts, the shape of her hips, the curve of her legs were all important. Was she quiet or boisterous? Pale or dark? Some people called it compulsion; he called it simply a matter of taste.

His friends all thought him a little odd when it came to *his* perfect woman, claiming he was far too picky given the list of requirements he desired to fall head over heels. He'd shrug and tell them he wasn't in a hurry, and she was out there, somewhere. Dean had no idea where his preference for that flawless mate had come from, but he couldn't help it if he liked Asian women with big hooters and a thinking practice that didn't revolve around shopping and painted fingernails. He looked to the late afternoon sky and stroked his beard again. And what was wrong with restoring old lawn mowers? Didn't everyone have a hobby?

You bet your ass they do.

Feeling more of the Caribbean heat than he was ready for, he renewed his search for another taxi. Looking left, then right, he noticed a couple avert their eyes from him and glance to the cement as they hurried past. He looked down, admiring his red argyle socks and the blue-and-red-paisley Bermuda shorts, set off by his brand new, green island shirt, and his royal-blue LA Dodger hat. He shook his head again. Some people just had no appreciation for a true sense of style.

Finally, a blue-and-white taxi rolled up. The female driver jumped out almost before the vehicle had stopped. She sprinted around the front of the car, stopping in her tracks, covering her mouth with her hand, ever so briefly—but Dean noticed the twinkle never left her eyes.

"I take you to where you want to go, senõr." The plump driver tossed his bag in the trunk. He scooped up his laptop case before she could reach it. She opened the door, then cocked her head in one of those inquisitive looks people throw out when the question they want to ask is much more powerful than any sort of personal restraint.

"You dress very . . . colorful. Is there somewhere special you wish to go?" She drew out the go in a classic Puerto Rican accent.

"Well, thank you, but no. Just to my hotel, the Condado Hotel on the Condado Strip please. I'm meeting my new team there."

She nodded her head with enthusiasm. "They will be impressed."

Stepping toward the door, he noticed the Hummer limo coming back in his direction, heading out of the airport. The back windows were tinted, but he got a good look at the driver because the window was down.

He yelled. "Watch where you're going; you almost hit me."

The driver threw back his head and laughed, speeding up without responding further.

The cab driver's face grew somber. "You shouldn't talk to that one like that. He's trouble, senõr."

"That's okay, I'm with the FBI, and I can be trouble too."

She nodded and got into the car.

Dean Mikus frowned and filed away the taxi driver's reaction to the driver of the Hummer. Could be nothing, but in his line of work, it didn't pay to ignore fear, no matter the source.

The cab moved away from the terminal, and he remembered he hadn't checked his email or messages. He pulled out his new smartphone and hit the email button. Two messages from friends, one dating service, one that wondered if his woman wanted his manhood to be three inches longer by the weekend, and one from Agent Josh Corner, his new boss. He thumbed the screen and the message popped open.

Hi Dean,

We'll be in San Juan by the early morning, so enjoy your first night because tomorrow will be a big day.

P.S. Attached are some preliminary reports and photos from the SJPD of the first two victims. For your review, in case you're bored.

Agent Corner

He smiled. Corner knew guys like him couldn't resist a good crime scene report, pictures and all.

Tapping the file with the photos, the first one came up. He felt his stomach turn inside out. The man's severed head hung from a branch, glasses still on his face and blood splattered on the left lens. The second showed the rest of the parts of the drawn-and-quartered body, laid out in approximate order, with six-inch gaps separating the limbs and the trunk of the camper's body.

After three more photos, he shut down the attachment, his mind settling on the beautiful San Juan weather. Almost.

"Shit. I thought LA had sick bitches," he whispered to himself, his mind churning.

He was struck with another idea.

Maybe LA wasn't such a bad place after all.

CHAPTER-18

"Good God, I hate this," said Sophie as the Gulf-stream V sprinted down the runway and lifted effort-lessly into the still Ohio night air.

"I know what you mean," answered Chloe. Manny noticed her face was a shade paler than it had been a moment before.

Sophie sat to his left, Chloe to his right; each one had a vice-like grip on one of his hands. "I'm going to need surgery on my phalanges if you two don't let go."

"You've been reading again, haven't you? Pulling out those new words for fingers isn't going to save your ass this time, or your hands. I'm not letting go until we get to San Juan, or I have to pee, whatever comes first."

"I got to agree with Sophie on this one. And if *you* have to go to the rest room, we're going with you," agreed Chloe, still sounding a little shaky.

"Okay. I guess I can sit here for a while with two beautiful women, but no one goes into the john with me, got it?"

Leaning forward, Sophie narrowed her eyes, scop-ing Chloe's face. "Have you told him?"

"About what?" Chloe frowned.

"The Mile-High Club. I mean, how many more chances do you two think you're going to get? I'll even stand guard outside the door so no one interrupts."

"Uh, well. Thanks for the offer, but . . ." answered Chloe, more color returning to her face than Manny thought he'd seen for a few hours.

"It's good to see you're as sick as ever," said Manny.

"Yep, I'm starting to feel like myself."

"If we ever join that club, you won't be around to know it," said Manny.

"That hurts."

Manny leaned forward, trying to shake at least one of the women's hands loose. They only hung on tighter. He turned to Sophie.

"I thought you were feeling like your old self."

"I am, just being a little cautious."

"So how will you be feeling when we start that landing process?" teased Manny.

Alex, sitting across the aisle, began to laugh. "Oh, I can answer that one. She's the reason they supplied more puke bags on the Gulfstream's. She'll toss her cookies faster than an old man on a merry-go-around."

"You should try that, Dough Boy; at least you'd get rid of a couple pounds. And another thing—"

Just then, Josh emerged from the cockpit area, carrying a stack of papers and folders in one hand, a briefcase in the other. He sat down beside Alex, plopping the files down on the table. He sat the briefcase on the floor, sliding it behind his leg as if he were trying to hide it. Manny wasn't even sure Josh was aware that he'd done it. But who could blame him for being distracted? He'd found out about his half-brother's grisly death hours just after he'd almost died in a plane wreck that would have most people walking, or taking a bus, to San Juan.

Talk about a recipe for drinking early—and often.

Manny felt Josh's stare and greeted it with his own. "You don't miss anything, do you?"

Smiling, Manny answered. "I miss more than I catch, but some things just jump out and grab me by the shirt, then shake me. Like sliding that briefcase behind your leg, why'd you do it?"

"Good question. I'm not sure why, but I'll tell you what's going on with it later."

"Damn. I didn't see that," said Sophie, a scowl across her pretty face.

"That's because you're focused on cutting off all of the circulation in my left hand. If you two don't let go, I'll need bionic fingers."

"Fine. But if it gets bouncy, I'll be on you faster than a hundred-dollar-a-minute lap dancer," said Sophie.

"You'll have to beat me to him," grimaced Chloe.

"No problem," said Manny.

The two women released their grip, and Manny shook his hands, feeling the tingling sensation as blood again flowed freely to his fingertips.

"Hey, I'd pay to see that," said Alex.

"That's what I heard; you like to watch," said Sophie.

"I'm not going to justify that with a response."

"Oh, that one must have hit a nerve. Didn't it?"

"Okay, you two can finish your conversation on your own time. Let's get to work," interrupted Josh. Manny noted the stress in his voice. Again, understandable, but . . . "Listen, before we dive into these murders, I want you three to know that I'm scared shitless to be in this plane. Chloe and I both are, but we talked to the doc, who's also a shrink, and she agreed that we should jump back into the air as soon as we were ready. And given our job situation, there was no time like the present. That jumping into Manny's lap thing goes for me too. Hell, I'd even jump into Alex's."

"Glad to help," grinned Alex.

"Just know we'll be ready. It seems Chloe and I have many of the same personality traits, and the doc thought we could handle the flight to San Juan, mentally."

"What about the physical?" asked Manny.

"I think we'll be fine. It was ultimately my call. We'll both be sore for a day or two, but we'll be fine. Providing my concussion doesn't cause my brain to pop a few thousand blood vessels."

"You okay now?" asked Manny.

"Yep. A little nauseous, but good to go."

Josh looked around the table. "There'll be a time to talk about my brother, but this isn't it. Doctor Gilger gave me a couple of pointers on how to handle his death, but the biggest thing for me is to find his killer. I'm going to focus on that. I want you all to do the same. That's why we're going."

Sliding the first set of files to Manny then handing out the rest, he motioned with his hand toward the briefcase. "My brother's preliminary file is in that briefcase, what there is of it, and Manny's the only one who gets to see it before we land."

"Why?" asked Chloe.

"Lots of reasons, some personal, but the main reason is that the initial report says there are some different characteristics about the scene and what the killer did to . . . to Caleb."

He fought to control his emotion after he said his brother's name and won the battle—this time. But

Manny knew, from experience, that it was a matter of time before Josh wouldn't be able to control it.

Josh continued. "Anyway, I want Manny's first impressions. Nothing personal to the rest of you, but that's why he's making the big bucks."

"You thinking trance?" asked Sophie.

Looking around the table, a small smile tugged at the corners of Josh's mouth. "Trance would be good."

The five agents grew silent, all feeling the same thing, Manny guessed. Josh had expressed a dozen ideas in those four words. Not the least was a silent thank you to his crew, his friends.

Josh cleared his throat and did what he did best: he took control. "The crime scene files you have, except for Caleb's, are a little sketchy, but the crime scene photos are as graphic as anything I've ever seen, including the work of Fredrick Argyle."

"Freaking great," whispered Sophie.

Opening the file, Manny felt his eyes grow wide, and his stomach turn south. The first picture of victim number one was beyond sick. The head of the fortyish man was hanging from what looked to be a clothesline. His face was partially eaten by whatever scavenger decided that human face was on the menu. The next showed the precise display of the body's four limbs, a six-inch gap between each one, spread like he was preparing to make a snow angel. Each cut seemed smooth and clean, not jagged or torn.

What the hell could have done that?

The man was void of clothing, but oddly, his belongings were stacked near his right hand in a neat, orderly manner. The next two photos were close-ups, showing two of the numbered yellow tabs that indicated possible evidence areas near the victim's right foot. Squinting, he was pretty sure both areas displayed small pieces of leather. The next few photos showed the body from different angles, and he saw nothing that jumped out at him until he turned to the last page. There was a long, creased gouge on one of the Yagrumo trees that he wanted to see for himself.

He fingered through the other three files, all telling the same story in a different setting. The two victims in the Mount Britton Tower seemed to have been more hastily displayed, like the killer was in a hurry.

Looking at the next file, he closed his eyes and ran his hand through his hair when he reached the photos of the young lady whose body had been found in her tent—the images were far past sickening. She'd been a beautiful woman enjoying her honeymoon before this deranged son of a bitch had hacked her up like an animal in a slaughterhouse. His gut tightened even more. She'd had a future, a husband, a new life to create and enjoy. It struck home even more when he saw Amanda Griggs's birthday on her bio. She was only five years older than his daughter Jen.

He looked up just as Chloe slammed the last file shut, her color once again gone from her face.

"You okay?"

"Hell no, I'm not okay. Are we looking at the same files? Just when I think I've seen the worst . . ." she answered, biting her lip.

"She's got a point, Manny," said Sophie quietly. "This is way out there. Talk about a snake in the garden."

"I agree, but we've got to do the drill in order to take the next step."

"You're right, of course, but this stuff is disconcerting as hell. I thought looking at Liz's body in the morgue on the cruise ship was bad," said Alex.

Josh cut in. "I know these pictures and reports are over the top—like you all have mentioned, beyond horrible. But I need your ideas now." Four sets of eyes turned to Manny.

Letting out a breath, he began. "All right. This person, like Sophie said before, is pissed. The unsub's rage has probably been brewing since he or she was a child. This kind of violence and spree-killing escalation indicates the unsub has recently gone through some event that triggered the latent anger."

"So that makes him more of a spree killer than a true serial killer," said Chloe.

"I think you're right. My guess, based on the first pass, is that the killings are a result of revenge or some type of goal."

Manny leaned forward to get his bottle of water just as the plane hit a small pocket of turbulence. Josh's lips and face were equal shades of white as he grabbed the arms of his leather seat. Chloe slid her hand under Manny's.

"It's okay, guys, just a bump," soothed Alex.

"Yeah, well, a bump to you, hell to us," said Josh. He waved to Manny. "Keep going."

Manny nodded. "Then, if my first assumption is true, this has Mission Serial Killer tendencies painted all over it. The killer wants to rid the world of some segment of population."

"So we have some asshole hybrid spree- and serial-killer?" asked Sophie.

"I think so, and that's not all. There are too many

prepared details to think this one is unorganized. That fact, except maybe for the tower killings, where I think the killer was hurried, means the unsub is extremely intelligent; not to mention, the killer took time to finish what he or she started. I think that means they know the area. Sprinkle in the desire to display the bodies, either to show us that he or she has all of the power, or that all things must have an order. And this murderer is just the one to do it. Put that all together, and we've got a serial killer that is more deadly than any we've encountered. The fact that there isn't any apparent social or physical link with the victims, at least yet, makes these murders more pointed."

Releasing his grip on the seat, Josh exhaled. "In my book, this reeks of unpredictability."

"It does," Chloe agreed, adding, "Not exactly a formula for a fun trip."

"The thing about someone like this is that they are fearless, but cautious at the same time. They won't make any mistakes," said Manny.

"Alex, what about the forensic reports?" asked Josh, sounding more and more like his old self.

The CSI shrugged. "I need more info, and I need to get to the scenes. I think the big question, and it might be a key, is what is the method, the weapon or weapons? There are no gunshots, doesn't look like any chloroform indicators on the faces, yet he was close enough to dismember them, and at least some of it looks like antemortem."

"A guess?" said Josh.

Alex searched his hands, scowling. "I saw some cuts similar to this made with a meat cleaver, but they were always a little jagged, based on the power used to make the swing. Hell, I don't know. A sharp machete?"

"How about a sword?" asked Sophie, her eyes coming alive. "When I was a kid, we used to go to these shows where experts with swords did some pretty amazing stuff. One time, the two men got too close to each other, and one of them lost part of a hand. It happened so fast that at first, I thought it was part of the hocus pocus, but when the blood started spurting, I realized what had happened."

Raising his eyebrows, Alex grinned. "That could be it. Not bad for an Asian with a boob job."

"Why, thank you, Dough Boy."

"Shit. Damn it!" swore Chloe. "I think I know this woman. I've seen her before."

Manny turned to her and watched as she traced Amanda Griggs's bloodied face with her finger.

"Are you sure? Where?"

"Just a minute."

Chloe dug for Amanda's bio on the next page. After reading it, she pointed to Josh.

"We've got big trouble."

CHAPTER-19

"What the hell do you mean we're not headed for the rainforest? That's where she and shit-for-brains were going to stay for two weeks."

"Da signal says ta go west, not to da east," said Braxton.

Leaning forward, his large hands clasped together, Fogerty fought to control his monstrous temper. If the tracker was broken, it wasn't Braxton's fault, but he needed to blame someone. He'd never told Amanda about the GPS chip he'd had imbedded under the birthmark on the back of her left arm. No reason to. He may have, as she grew older, and if she hadn't developed such a blatant disregard for his warnings of caution. Damn kids, anyway.

"Let me see that," he gritted.

Fogerty flipped the off switch on the small but powerful receiver, then turned it back on. A moment later, the tiny light began to blink green and display the western direction that Braxton had read.

His eyes were beginning to reflect his temperament. "Is the damn thing broken?"

"No sir, Mr. Fogerty. We had it tested before da wedding, like ya said ta do. It's working fine."

"What the hell are they up to?"

"Maybe dey come ta town ta get a good meal or

some supplies. It's gettin' dark, but dey got time to get back to da jungle."

"Maybe you're right. If so, we got lucky. We won't have to traipse through the damn trees to bring her rebellious ass home. Plug that location into the GPS and we'll give her and shit-for-brains the surprise of their now-over-with honeymoon." He shook his head with disgust. "Honeymoon, my ass," he said under his breath.

Lighting another Cuban, he reflected on how much this little escapade to San Juan had cost him. Delays, meetings, lessons to be taught, and of course, it all added up to gouging his bottom line. His daughter would pay for his losses, out of her allowance and, if he had a mind for it, out of her hide.

If they were lucky, he'd get back to Barbados before ten o'clock or so, and he could get a few things done before tomorrow's schedule made a twelve-hour day feel like a vacation.

"Sir?"

"What, Braxton?"

"Um. Dis ain't so good."

"What does that mean? Spit it out."

"Dat address where dat chip and Ms. Amanda are ain't good."

"Shit, she's in a seedy part of town?"

"No sir."

Randall's instincts kicked in, and they told him there was a problem. "Like I said, spit it out."

"Da address is in Toa Baja."

Moving faster than men his size do, he grabbed Braxton by the shirt, pulling him within an inch of his face. "I said, SPIT IT OUT, you moron."

"Sir, dat address goes to da city morgue."

CHAPTER-20

"What the hell do you mean 'we're in big trouble'?" demanded Josh.

Chloe placed her hands palms down on the table. "This girl, this Amanda Griggs, isn't just someone who was in the wrong place at the wrong time."

"What does that mean?" asked Manny.

"When I was working the terrorist unit in New York, our caseload diminished a wee bit, so I volunteered to work with the DEA and our own drug-enforcement division. We were working on a huge sting, focusing on the cocaine flow from the east coast to the west coast and how it got into the US from South America. There were plenty of creative smuggling methods, don't you know. The stupid ones always taped the bags to their ribs or some dumb-ass thing; the clever ones, well, let's just say an enema got us the evidence we needed. Hell, we even tracked mini submarines transporting shipments off the coast of Miami. Very ingenious and expensive, but effective."

There was another air bump, but Chloe barely flinched this time. The woman was tough, another reason he wanted her in his life. "Now, that wasn't so bad," smiled Chloe.

"Speak for yourself," said Josh. "Keep going."

She continued. "Anyway, we kept coming up with

a connection from Bolivia, an up-and-coming cocaine producer to the Caribbean, particularly Barbados. We came up with a few possibilities, even arrested two of them, but suspected the big fish had made himself untouchable, and we were right. This big fish, this man, this Randall Fogerty is better at covering his tracks than most. He is as deadly as a cobra and has less of a conscience. He thinks nothing of offing people who try to compete with him, or even his own people. Three times the DEA sent in undercover folks. None of them were ever seen again."

Rubbing his chin, Manny spoke. "Let me guess. This girl is related to Fogerty, right?"

Chloe raised her eyebrows. "Oh, more than related. She's his only child."

"Oh man," groaned Josh. "So this could be a hit job?"

"I think it could," said Chloe.

Alex leaned forward over his paunch, elbows on knees. "And the rest of the killings are to cover up the real purpose for that hit?"

"I suppose that makes sense, but isn't that going way out there to disguise one drug-related murder?" stated Sophie.

"Maybe, but it's not unheard of, given the enemies this asshole has made," said Chloe.

Josh sat back in his seat, frowning at the ceiling. "So my brother may have been just some kind of collateral damage in a freaking drug-war hit that went south?"

Chloe shrugged. "Maybe."

"What do you think, Manny?" asked Alex.

"I think anything is possible, especially with

people who have done what this unsub has done. Having said that, I think there's a slight pattern change with each new victim."

"What pattern change?" asked Sophie.

Manny got up, reached behind Josh's leg, and took the briefcase containing Caleb Corner's file. "I'll let you know in a few. There's something here that we're missing."

He felt every eye follow him as he moved to the backseat, away from the others. Somehow, going off alone made him feel more alive, more in tune with his purpose on this rock. He couldn't ignore the passing thought that everyone had an intention, a reason for being alive. But most people were clueless to it and chose to remain that way rather than seek out that single purpose that put fire in their loins and a tingle in their stomach, like the one he had now.

Popping open the case, he pulled out the blue folder, and let out a deep breath.

Let's see if I'm losing it.

The standard FBI organization of a crime scene file had one report processed on a pre-printed form and stapled to the inside left cover, a forensic report on the right, then pictures usually followed on the next pages. This file had no forensics report, a brief write-up by a Detective Julia Crouse from the SJPD, then five pictures. Five horrific pictures. No one should ever have to see this kind of carnage. He'd seen a few Hollywood horror productions in his time, some that gave him that little tinge of discomfort because the special-effects guy was good. Or maybe the FX man had deep-seated fantasies involving that sort of reality. He wasn't sure he wanted to know, but figured it was a fine line between the two.

There was no fine line here. Caleb Corner had been murdered in the same fashion as the others—except he hadn't been. His face had been hacked from his skull. There was a close up of his Park ID, resting on the neatly stacked ranger uniform. His heart immediately hurt for Josh.

The wounds on the dismembered body had the same smooth, precise edges of the others, and the angle of the blows looked similar, if not exactly the same. The killer had slashed poor Caleb into eight sections, then placed sections in a random order so that the body appeared like a puzzle out of order. What was the reason, the logic? Manny wasn't sure. It could be nothing more than random actions, but Caleb's neatly organized clothes said no.

That wasn't the only difference. This killing had a more violent feel to it than the others, if that was possible; it felt more personal. Very personal. He was sure the unsub knew Caleb Corner, and as more than a passing acquaintance. It seemed as though a possible dislike or hatred had grown to insatiable rage. Scary to contemplate, impossible to ignore.

Manny's mind felt the next thought far too clearly. He didn't know how he knew, but he suspected the killer had taken his own pictures. A form of trophy? Or was it for something else. . . masturbation?

Good God. This one had *really* lost it. And, he suspected, was without any hope of recovering. This individual—and he was sure it was an individual—had gone way beyond any psychotic episode syndrome, but instead had immersed themselves completely into another reality, one that wouldn't end with whatever mission these attacks represented. The killer would create another mission, if or when this goal was completed.

Turning the next page, the last picture displayed a side profile of the flora of the crime scene revealing a few broken branches from the tiny trees and enough blood to paint a small car. No doubt this was where Caleb was killed. Manny ran his fingers through his thick hair. Something wasn't right. There was *too* much blood, *too* much splatter.

What the hell?

Rising quickly from the chair, careful to keep the folder secured, he rushed back to the table where the others were talking quietly.

"I want you all to look at the file pictures again and tell me what you don't see."

Chloe looked up from her phone, green eyes alive, and he couldn't help thinking what a beautiful distraction she was. Good and bad at the same time, like chocolate. He shook off the thought and continued.

"There's something missing at each body display. What is it?"

The others frantically opened the files and turned pages. A few moments later, Alex stood, his hands slapping the air.

"I've got it! This much blade work should have more blood, a lot more blood. In fact, there's almost none on the ground, or around the scenes, at all, with the exception of Dan Griggs. There's some on the body parts, and on the stacks of clothes, but not nearly enough."

"Bingo. That's it."

"Okay, so what does that mean? Other than this killer moved the bodies before setting up the displays," said Sophie.

"Firstly, I think it shoots down the theory of a hit on Amanda and her husband. They *were* in the wrong place at the wrong time."

"How so?" asked Josh.

"I think the killer had one central killing location. He or she, somehow, incapacitated the victims, at least four of them outside the tower, and killed them all in one spot. Then took them back to their individual camps to let the world see the killer's work."

"How do you know that?" asked Josh, his voice cautious, as if he wasn't sure he wanted to know.

Manny bowed his head. "There's a picture in Caleb's file that indicates that it's true."

Josh stared at Manny, regained his composure, then spoke. "That seems like a hell of a lot of work, but say you're right. Why? What purpose?"

"I think I can answer that," said Chloe. "The fact that the unsub brought everyone to one location could mean he's using that particular place as some kind of shrine or altar."

"What? Really?" asked Alex.

"I think she's right on. The victims' campgrounds, outside the tower, were within a quarter mile of each other, so getting the people there and back couldn't have been too difficult, even if he would have had to drag them." His hand was in his hair again, and he continued.

"This one definitely has a different agenda, something else in mind. Also, remember when I said that there seems to be a slight pattern change? I believe this perp is enjoying each attack a little more than the last. The later victims are more mutilated, except with more purpose. He's got bloodlust going along with his perceived purpose."

The plane grew silent except for the sound of air flowing under the wings and the drone of jet engines.

Sophie spoke first. "Let's go back a second. If the killer is about sacrifice and on a mission; what are the sacrifices for and why step out of his norm to attack those people in the Britton Tower?"

Manny shrugged. "I have no idea. The tower episode could have been an experiment. The killer could have just been testing the waters."

"That seems right," Chloe agreed. "He could be more comfortable in the forest, and he may have thought he made his point, whether at the tower or at the other site."

"Maybe when we get to the scenes tomorrow, they'll shed some light on that. But I think we have a bigger problem, maybe two bigger problems, than the why," added Manny.

"The first has to be about Randall Fogerty." said Chloe. "It's just a matter of time before he finds out that his daughter was murdered by some lunatic running around in the rainforest. He'll be less than happy, of course, and for a man like that, revenge is a way of life, and he won't care if the FBI's involved in the investigation."

"Yeah, that's one. The other is theory, but I'm about 99 percent sure I'm right."

He ran his hand through his hair. "I think the reason he murdered Caleb at the altar, or whatever he thinks it is, is that he's done with that area."

"Done? You mean no more murders?" asked Alex, frowning.

"Yes and no. I'm sure the killer's completed this

phase, and unless I miss my guess, he's going to the next level—and it will be far worse than this one."

CHAPTER-21

The doorbell rang, startling him. It was almost eight o'clock, and he wasn't expecting anyone, especially here. Placing his book on the end table, he rose from the recliner, moved to the stereo system, and turned down Paul Hardcastle's greatest hits. He thought briefly of blowing out the vanilla-scented candle that for some unknown reason to him, was one of the all-time greatest scents on the planet. Maybe something from an incident long ago in his childhood, of which he had no recollection, had triggered that eccentric appreciation. He left it burning.

Taking a look in the mirror, he grinned. He was still handsome, in his own way, as his mother used to say.

He watched his grin dissipate as quickly as it had appeared. For a moment, his mind went blank, then recovered. His mother would never utter those words again.

He clinched his hands and stood motionless. He had no need of external reminders regarding his mother's demise. The voice of his rage took care of that.

Walking to the door, he peered through the peephole and saw a young, attractive, dark-complected woman shifting her weight nervously from side to side, glancing at the sky, then the door, then the sky. She was wearing white shorts and a tight, white tee shirt, revealing her assets. It wasn't unusual to have a student knock on his door. It happened several times per month. But classes didn't begin until next week, and never had he seen a student here. He swung the door open and felt the pleasant Puerto Rican air brush against his face. He never tired of how that felt.

"Good evening, young lady. May I help you?"

"Hello, ah . . . professor. Am I bugging you?" she asked, her voice thick with Puerto Rican heritage.

"Well, now that depends on why you're here. Does it not?"

The young woman shifted her feet again, her breasts dancing as she did. She caught his eyes dart to her chest. He smiled even wider.

"My name is Anna. I don't know if you recognize me, but I took one of your classes on Environmental Justice, and I'm here for some . . . advice."

The tone in her voice was casual, yet he sensed a great excitement.

"I really don't recall seeing you, but all right, Anna, what advice can I give you?"

"Can I come in? This may take a few." Her voice was still native, but now seemed more refined.

What is she after?

This could be interesting. He'd had sex with more than one student, but oddly, he didn't think her visit was about sex, and moreover, he only felt a passing interest himself. It seemed his libido was carving new territories into the vast unknown. But his curiosity was more than stimulated. He relented.

Motioning her inside, he closed the door and led her to the living room. He felt her stare, and it made him slightly uneasy. He didn't like the feeling. It gave him a sensation that he hated: no control.

This *will* be interesting.

"Please sit on the sofa. Can I get you something to drink?"

"Thank you. And no thank you, I'm fine."

Her accent had faded almost completely. Clever girl or nervous?

Settling onto the edge of his leather recliner, he gazed at her face. She returned the look, for a moment, then her sparkling, green eyes darted to the floor.

"What's this about, Anna?"

"I'm not sure. It could be about me, maybe you, maybe something more."

"Explain what you mean."

"A question first. Hypothetically, what would you do if you saw something, a crime, so appalling, so barbaric, that it caused you to puke your guts out, but left you so sexually aroused that you had to take care of that arousal right on the spot?"

"That's quite a question. Are we talking about you or a friend?"

"Oh, ah . . . a friend."

Never missing a beat, he smiled. "The first thing I would say, in this hypothetical scenario, is: why wouldn't this 'friend' go directly to the authorities?"

"Good answer, or question. Say they tried, over and over, and all day, but simply couldn't get the total situation, especially the sexual side of it, out of their mind. It was too . . . gratifying."

Leaning closer, he expected her to shrink away, but instead she followed suit. Their faces were less than two feet apart.

Interesting isn't the right word. Fascinating is more

like it.

"Well, we call that a conundrum. Life's full of those. In the environmental arena, it's referred to as a stakeholder's interest. Making or accepting one positive decision and sacrificing another, and then weighing the overall benefit. That's the critical part of these situations: what benefit is the most . . . desirable."

She nodded. Her cheeks were shading red, her breathing shorter, slightly labored. Young Anna was becoming aroused. Interesting didn't cover that.

"Ah. Could I get a glass of water? It's kind of warm in here."

"Certainly."

He left for the kitchen and came back with a bottle of distilled water and a glass of ice.

"Thank you."

Anna poured the water and quickly drained the first helping, repeating the action. She, then, seemed in more control. He wanted to say the same for himself.

"So, young Anna, tell me about this hypothetical crime."

"Okay. My friend was hiking on the north side of the El Yunque trail, when she heard two men talking, then some yelling. She got curious and worked her way over to that area just in time to see . . ."

She took another drink, her eyes wider than ever. He wondered if the girl was going to melt on the spot. His mind was churning, but his emotion had settled down. That deep voice of rage was gone, replaced by a renewed sense of control. He suspected what was coming next.

Anna inched even closer to him, her breath warm and sweet. "I saw you hack that man to pieces, rearrange the body, then take pictures." She swallowed hard. "I was so horrified that I couldn't move. The blood, the sword flashing in the sun, the sounds it made as it struck the body. I wanted to run, but I was mesmerized by my own fear. When I snapped out of it, I started to crawl away, then out of nowhere I was so overcome with . . . desire, I, well, I didn't get very far."

"I see."

He stood and then paced for a few moments, then he sat beside her, taking her hand. Amazingly, she didn't flinch.

"How did you find me?"

"I watched you leave and did my best to follow you. I lost you when you turned off the main road, but I remember the vehicle you were driving. It took me three hours of running through neighbor hoods, but here I am."

"Very persistent, I see. Did you tell anyone?"

She shook her head, her long, black hair swinging back and forth. "No. But before you think about doing that to me, know that I took my own pictures of the place and copied them to a disc. Then I left a coded email message that will be sent to my father, pictures and all, if I don't change the send date every twelve hours."

"It seems you've covered your bases."

Moving quickly, he gripped her soft throat with his right hand. Pulling the small dagger from his ankle sheath, he raised it tight against her neck.

"While I admire your courage and preparedness, what makes you think that anyone will believe what you've said? That it was me? Furthermore, why do you think your story will stop me from getting rid of a witness that has no idea what this is all about?"

Her smile was unexpected. "You're right, it was a gamble. That's why I have a friend sitting in the car down the street. I told her I'd be less than an hour. If I don't get there, well, this was the last place anyone saw me alive."

Pressing the knife closer, she yelped as a small cut began to bleed.

"I don't scare easily."

"Please," she begged, "Just hear me out. I want to be part of whatever you're doing. If you say no, I'll destroy the pictures, delete the email, and you'll never hear from me again."

He doubted that. Easing the knife from her neck, he spun her toward him, his eyes on fire.

"You have forty-five seconds."

Letting out a breath, she locked onto his eyes. "I can't explain how what you did made me feel. I'd never been more alive, my thinking clearer. It's like everything I'd ever been taught was a lie. I struggled with emotions as a kid, and couldn't understand why I didn't 'feel' like others said they did. I faked it with the best. I just didn't get it. All of those huggy, kissy moments were nothing more than a ritual. I never felt a thing. The only thing that ever got a rise out of me was killing a lizard, or even a couple cats—that was amazing. I also loved how fire felt against my skin."

Raising her shirt, she showed him a dozen tiny scars that were probably caused by matches or a lighter.

Her eyes grew harder. "I still piss the bed. Another reason I wanted to kill myself a hundred times over. Do you know what I was doing in the rainforest? I was getting ready to kill an iguana, just for the joy of it. I've read all of the research, all of the profile shit, and I know what I am. Watching you confirmed it."

Her voice had grown detached, but still sincere. She was perspiring profusely and trembling, waiting for him to answer. He frowned. A profile for a killer without doubt, if what she had said was true.

If what she has said is true.

He made his decision quickly.

"You'll have to prove yourself, and I have just the thing for you. If you pass the test, I'll explain everything to you. This isn't about killing, but about a much nobler goal."

"But you enjoyed the killing, didn't you?"

"Let's just say I've grown to appreciate that part of the mission far more than I imagined, and it has . . . certain benefits."

Running her hand down his thigh, she smiled. "I can see that benefit."

"Later. The test?"

"I'm ready."

"We shall see. Call your friend up to the house. Let's see how committed you really are."

She stared at him. "I lied. I don't have any friends, let alone someone who would wait for me this long. Is it getting warmer in here?"

"I see. And the pictures and email?"

She crossed her arms over her chest and stood, her eyes darting back and forth. "Both lies. I was too afraid to take any pictures and I don't use email. You need friends for that. I wanted you to hear me out. To know what kind of help I could be to you. I've lived such a lonely life, nothing but lies and insincere babblings. I've finally discovered what I am and I want to embrace it. I think I need to sit down."

"I suspected so. But you've come to the right place. I can use your help—and help you at the same time."

Anna began to sway and sweat even more. She sat back on the couch and then slid off the front. She was having a hard time focusing.

"Wha—what did you do to me?"

"Oh, a concoction I confiscated from one of my students. It works quite well. Don't you think?"

"Please. I—my dad is . . ."

Pulling the Katana out from underneath the sofa, he gently opened the case.

"I'm going to help you like I said I would."

CHAPTER-22

The coroner's technician swallowed nervously as she opened the door leading to the archaic, stone-front lobby of the morgue in Toa Baja. Randall Fogerty noticed the dank, musty odor that even the air conditioner couldn't mitigate. It mingled with antiseptic smells and one overpowering scent that he was more than familiar with. He wondered, for a moment, if it was really just an odor or something more. Perhaps a feeling or some primordial sixth sense that would trigger a flight response in most people. Either way, death lived here.

"How can I help you, senõr?" asked the attendant. She had a pretty face with a clear complexion and large, dark eyes, but not as large as her waistline. The woman was huge. He never understood that one: young ladies with great looks attached to a chassis that could have plowed fields back in the day.

"I'm here because I think there's been some mistake. I, for some unknown reason, have been led to believe that Amanda Fogerty, Griggs is her married name, has checked into this Godforsaken hotel." His voice was calm, yet uninviting.

The attendant became even more fidgety. She nodded, then closed the door to the outside. "I just came on duty, so I'll have to check the records. I know we had a busy day because the reports are stacked up. Please give

me a few minutes to check, señõr. May I see your identi-
fication?"

He pulled his passport from his pocket. She took it,
glanced up to him, then handed it back.

"Thank you."

He glanced at her name tag. "Colita, is it? I'm not
a patient man and, as you might imagine, a little more
than distressed at this moment."

"I'll hu—hurry."

She waddled away and swiped her card at the
electronic terminal. The stainless-steel doors opened as
slowly as any he'd ever seen.

Once she'd disappeared down the dimly lit hall
and the doors closed behind her, he folded his hands
and stood still. He'd give her three minutes, then he'd
send for Braxton and the others, to find out for him if
Amanda was. . .

Emotion had always been a little strange to him,
but this one was more than strange, more like es-
tranged. And now he knew why. He felt fear. Not the
kind that sent you blubbering to your momma, but the
type that says you've lost something precious, including the control to protect those you care about. Fogerty
hated this feeling. He'd vowed to never experience this
situation again, but vows and reality are always at conflict on some level. Today, the conflict had escalated.

Turning his gold Rolex to the left on his thick
wrist, he stared. Two minutes. He felt like he was ready
to explode. He'd left his .45 in the car, as was his custom
when in public settings like this one, but Braxton could
have it to him in less than thirty seconds, and by God,
he'd use it if Fat Ass didn't get it in motion.

One minute. His hands were clenching to the

rhythm of an unknown conductor, and the maestro was building a serious crescendo.

What the hell is so hard about getting good help these days?

Three minutes expired, and he reached for his cell just as the metal doors swung open. Colita's face was bent toward a file. She glanced up, closed the folder, took a moment to compose herself, and then walked directly at him. One look on the woman's face said everything he needed to know, but never wanted to know, ever.

"Mr. Fogerty. Who did you say sent you here?"

"I didn't say. Is that file my daughter's, Colita?" The words were quiet, but filled with venom.

She took a step back, eyes bigger than ever. "Yes, Senõr Fogerty. There were seven bodies brought in from the rainforest today, and she was one of them."

Out-of-body sensations had long left his repertoire of reactions, but he had one just then, felt it kiss his cheek and remind him that no one is immune to death's circle of influence, not even him. There was a brief flashback of her playing in the sand at an age he couldn't recall, a couple Christmas mornings when she'd been beside herself with the gifts he'd given her. He had even made her high school graduation, at least part of it. And of course, she'd been beautiful as a bride. They even did a superficial kiss and dance at the reception, but that was it. He had been far more detached than attached, and that struck home. Maybe he was in shock, but the thought left as quickly as it had come. His mind raced to the next step.

"What happened to her?"

"Her husband was brought in too and—"

"Do I look like I give a shit about him? Just answer my damned question."

"I'm sorry. I know you're upset, but there's a flag on her file to contact the SJPD if anyone asks about the details. You'll have to reach Detectives Ruiz or Crouse. And please don't yell at me. I hate this part of the job, but I have my orders."

Fogerty had always been able to control his reactions, his emotions, and his intent. It made him what he was. The last thing he wanted was a confrontation with SJPD. Although he had several "employees" there, he didn't have enough to cover his ass in this arena.

If the SJPD is involved and there are seven bodies, this is homicide.

He had to find out for sure if one of his competitors had struck back.

"You're right; I'm not handling this well. I need to see, to make sure this is my girl. May I see her body?"

"Well, I brought out the file with her picture and that's the procedure in this situation."

"Please indulge me, this once," he soothed, "she's my daughter."

He could see Colita's mind was racing, then she motioned for him to follow her. They made it through the steel doors. Twenty feet later, she stopped at the three-by-three cubicle door that matched the texture of the double doors.

"This is unusual, and I've not done my report, so please just identify her, and then I'll do the paperwork."

He nodded, searching for an emotion he'd lost long ago: true love. He felt nothing except a growing desire for revenge for an act that was intended to disrupt the business.

No mourning, no sense of loss, maybe they would come. But at this moment, he was relying on what he always relied on; himself.

Pulling the door open, he watched as Colita scowled. The body under the sheet wasn't positioned like either of them had expected. There seemed to be objects stacked just below the body's neckline.

Colita pulled back the sheet, swore, and quickly tried to draw the covering back over the body. Randall Fogerty's hands were far too quick to let that happen.

He tilted his head to the left, then the right. Amanda's face looked serene, with a few cuts on her graying neck, but that's where her body ended. Below that, stacked on her severed torso, lay an arm and a discolored leg.

Finally freeing her hand from his grip, Colita pulled the sheet back over the body.

Before she could speak, he was through the door, heading for the limo.

Fogerty stopped a few feet away and stared at the dazzling display of sunset and early evening stars jealously vying for top billing. His daughter had been murdered, desecrated in a manner he'd always tried to protect her from. In his way, he'd loved her more than any other because he'd spent such effort. Now someone had gotten to her anyway. It had always been a possibility in his line of work. He felt her loss, that was a given. But he felt an even more disturbing pang: someone had taken something from him, and that wouldn't do.

Braxton stepped close. "I be sorry, Boss."

"Sorry? That's a word to contemplate later." He rubbed his eyes with his thumb and forefinger. "My baby was butchered like a pig."

Braxton shook his head and stared at the cracked sidewalk.

"Whoever did this to her has no concept of sorry, but I'll teach them."

Motioning for Braxton to get in, he followed behind him.

"Take me to the SJPD. I'm going to introduce myself."

CHAPTER-23

Screeching to a halt, like Gulfstream Vs were prone to do when the pilot clamped on the brakes, caused Sophie to scream. Chloe followed suit, both clutching one of Manny's arms. Glancing at Josh, Manny noticed his fingers dig into the leather of his chair, but said nothing. However, if eyes had mouths...

"Damn. I'm glad we're on the ground for a few days, or whatever. Maybe you two can act more like FBI agents than pansy-ass schoolgirls," said Alex.

"Schoolgirls, eh?" huffed Sophie. "It's going to be embarrassing to tell your friends, both of them, that a schoolgirl blackened your eyes and pulled your scrotum up around your neck with one hand tied behind her back."

"Maybe, but that would mean you have to let go of both your purse and Manny to do it. By the looks of things, that doesn't seem too likely."

"He's got a point," said Manny.

"Yeah, on his head, but it won't save him," said Sophie.

The co-pilot emerged from the cockpit, a big man wearing a disarming grin and a pilot's hat that seemed a size too small for his head. Manny immediately thought he recognized him, but the moment vanished. He'd probably seen him when they boarded.

The co-pilot looked at his watch. "Welcome to beautiful San Juan. Safe and sound. It's 10:08, so we got you here a little early. We'll be pulling up to the private part of the tarmac in a few. Just thought I'd let you know."

With that, he squeezed back through the door.

"That's new," said Manny. "Why the speech?"

Josh sighed. "He told me before we took off that he realized he didn't really know the agents he flew all over the world and just wanted to try to connect a bit."

"That's nice. We are all in this together," said Chloe.

A few minutes later, the five stepped off the plane and walked toward the terminal. The co-pilot was right; it was a beautiful night. The first thing Manny noticed was the warm air that carried a mixture of jet fuel and tropical trees. The atmosphere brought back some memories of his first time here for Mike and Lexy's wedding just before the cruise. So much had changed since then. He'd gained much. New friends, new career, but wondered if the price he'd paid to get them had been worth it. Louise was gone. Sometimes he'd wake up at night and still wonder how that had happened, and always why. They'd had everything a couple could want or need. Then, in the blink of an eye, she was on to bigger and better things— at least that's how he saw it. He'd promised himself to not dwell on it. In fact, Louise had told him not to in that dream he still couldn't explain.

As if she knew his thoughts, Chloe slipped her hand into his. He turned to her and let her mesmerizing smile move the memories to the shadows. Chloe would always be a reminder of what he'd gained through the war that was life. Smiling back, he recalled a saying by Ralph Waldo Emerson: *"Each suffering is rewarded, each sacrifice is made up, every debt is paid."*

Chloe epitomized that wisdom, a hundred times over. She was his reward.

"Agent Williams, you started to say something in the hospital room just as Josh came in. What was it?"

"You'll have to refresh my memory. Getting old, you know."

"Getting old my arse, you know what I'm talking about."

True enough. He did know, and now that he considered it again, he was struck with an impetuous thought that wasn't him at all. But times were different these days, especially for this crew.

"You caught me in a weak moment. I thought I'd lost you, and you're way too hot for my own good. So we should. . ." he hesitated.

You really going to do this?

"Should what?"

The terminal door flew open, and as they entered, two people waved them over. A third stood a distance behind them. The first two—tall, attractive woman dressed like a cop and a shorter, muscular man wearing a teal island shirt—both displayed large, golden badges. Partners with the SJPD, he assumed. The third person was *not* dressed like a cop, at least none he'd ever seen. The man looked like an argyle peacock. His long beard and matching hair only added to his milieu of being totally out of place. Always something.

"That's two strikes, Williams. You'll not be getting out of this the next time, I tell ya," Chloe whispered, releasing his hand.

"Out of what?"

She elbowed him and moved ahead to shake hands

with their greeters.

"Come in, agents. I'm Detective Carlos Ruiz and this is Detective Julia Crouse. We're pleased to have you here. I hope your trip was pleasant enough."

He spoke with an accent, but also with an air of melancholy that Manny recognized from his own experience. The man had not only seen too many human-on-human atrocities, but had lost someone he loved.

"Yes. Glad you could make it," said Julia. She scoped everyone in the blink of an eye, hesitating at Josh, then giving Manny far more time than she should've. He returned her smile.

Always good to be appreciated.

Chloe must have noticed too—of course she would —and stepped between them, introducing herself and grabbing Julia's hand.

Ruiz motioned for the walking argyle sock to join them and then turned to Josh. "I'm sorry for your loss, agent. Caleb was a good man and a pleasure to work with, although I didn't work with him all that often. I suppose your earlier flight situation doesn't help, either."

"Thank you for your condolences, and you're right: I've had better days."

The man in the beard reached the group and moved directly in front of Josh.

"Agent Corner? I'm Dean Mikus, the new CSI from LAPD."

Josh stuck out his hand, and Dean hesitated, shrugged, and shook it.

"I don't typically shake hands, disease and all of that. Do you know that at any given moment, you might have as many as six million bacteria on each hand?"

"Ah, well no, I didn't know that."

Alex laughed and put his arm around Dean's shoulder. "I'm Alex Downs, the other CSI on this team. I like you already."

The terminal door opened behind them, and Sophie charged in.

"Damn. I forgot my makeup kit and had to go back to get it. Leaving that behind ain't going to work."

Josh introduced Sophie to the two detectives and, when he came to Dean, he stopped; in fact they all stood in place and watched the new CSI.

Manny had seen a case or two of instant infatuation. The kind that reduces its victim to a brief catatonic state that evolves into worship, possibly accompanied by some kind of private shrine, which if discovered, would cause the worshipper to be sent to counseling and relieved of duty. Dean Mikus was absorbing Sophie that way.

Glancing at his face, Sophie did a double take, then looked him up and down. "What on God's green earth are you gawking at? Ain't you ever seen a hot Asian chick before?"

Silence.

Chloe began to giggle, and Julia joined her.

"Dean? Dean? Shake Sophie's hand," said Manny.

Dean came out of his self-induced coma and stuck his hand out so fast that Manny wondered if he'd hurt himself. Then he pulled it back, dropped to one knee, and kissed her hand.

"You're a goddess and, hell yeah, there are a ton of hot Asian chicks living in LA. I dated some, but, well, none like you."

He jumped up, regaining more of his composure.

He turned to Josh, his face a bright red.

"Sorry sir. Is that sexual harassment? I'll take it back if it is. But she's so—"

Josh laughed. The first real laugh Manny had heard from him since before Cleveland.

"No, agent, particularly given the parties involved, and our unit. But be careful in the future."

"I shall, sir."

"No problem from my side either, Mucus. Hard to be upset with a man who has such great taste in goddesses," said Sophie.

"It's Mikus."

"Yeah, whatever. Besides, you're kind of cute, but you can't wear red-argyle pajamas when you're working. Damn. Who dressed you?"

"Well, I kind of like—"

Ruiz's phone went off, the ring tone mimicking an old telephone ringer that Manny remembered from thirty years past.

"Ruiz."

"What? Aw, *mierda*. We're on our way."

Ruiz put his phone in his pocket and let out a long breath. Manny recognized that one too.

"More trouble?" he asked.

"With a capital T," whispered Ruiz.

CHAPTER-24

Manny followed Chloe and Alex to Ruiz's green-and-white SUV while Sophie, Josh, and Dean rushed to the detective's cruiser.

Some things never change with the BAU. No sleep, no time to eat, a few clothes in a bag, and some sicko who'd lost all sense of how sacred human life is. At least he knew this game, and in a sick way, even embraced it.

Climbing in the back with Chloe, he smiled to himself.

Embraced it, huh?

That fact, and it was a fact, made him wonder who the sick ones really were.

"The morgue is about fifteen minutes away, on a good night, so we'll be there in less than twenty," said Ruiz, his sense of sadness still lingering. The detective careened up the ramp, lights swirling and siren blaring, hitting Highway 26 full out.

"You said there was an incident at the morgue, but you didn't say exactly what that was," said Manny.

"Just a minute."

Ruiz flipped on his radio, hit a blue button, and adjusted the volume to turn down the static.

"Crouse? You got that box working?"

Working came out "wurr-king," revealing his Puerto Rican roots. Certainly not unusual during stressful moments. Chloe did the same thing.

"Yeah, got it. Seems Agent Mikus has a gift with these things because I can't ever get the damned thing to work."

"Good, then all of you can hear me. Okay. Here's the rest of the story. It seems we have at least one body missing—one of the murder victims from the rainforest —and a dead technician lying in the lobby. And it's a sick mess."

"Damn. Those two events could be related. Do we know which body is missing?" asked Alex.

"I didn't get that far. The dispatcher said the caller was in a huge panic. All I know is that someone came in to identify one of the bodies, and they were supposed to be referred to Crouse or me. That didn't happen, as far as we know. I mean, no one told us."

"One situation might lead to the other. Do you have the system flagged to be contacted when someone inquires about a body?" asked Manny.

"Yes. For obvious reasons, we want to talk to them," said Crouse over the radio.

"Of course. I'm wondering if you have access to which records may have been pulled in your system," said Manny.

"Damn. You're right. Should have thought of that. Crouse? Can you get Agent Mikus to access those records?"

"I don't think you'll have to," said Chloe.

Manny glanced her way. "Why?"

"This has Fogerty's MO all over it, and he'd be brazen enough to do it."

Talk about getting your head out of where the sun didn't shine. He ran his hand through his hair. He should have considered that.

"I think she's right," said Josh, his voice sounding more like a robot than a human through the bouncing static.

"Makes sense," said Manny. "But we need to make sure."

"Bingo!" said Dean. "I'm not sure who this Fogerty guy is, but the system was flagged that Amanda Fogerty Griggs had a visitor a couple of hours ago. It says it was her dad."

The SUV swerved into the right lane and headed to the exit ramp leading to Tai Boa.

"Fogerty is suspected of being one of the largest drug lords in the Caribbean. But he's so very good at keeping low. He's like Teflon. We can't get anything to stick to him," said Chloe.

"Wow," said Dean. "Serial killers and drug lords? Great first day on the job."

"I've heard that name, but didn't know how deep he went. I mean, we've got our hands full with homicide," said Ruiz.

"Grief can do goofy things to people, and it might be true in his case. It was his daughter. But if he did this, he'd be putting his whole operation at risk, and from what I know about these guys, that's way out of character," said Manny.

There was a commotion echoing through the short band radio, originating from the other car. Then he heard Dean yelp. "Get out of the way, Mucus," said Sophie.

"It's Mikus," said Dean in the background.

"Whatever. Manny? Manny? Is this thing still working? Okay. Anyway. You might be right, but what about his ego?"

Chloe agreed. "That's a good point. Men like him are used to complete control and something like his daughter's murder would certainly challenge him, but what would he gain?"

"I don't know. It doesn't seem to fit," said Manny. "Still. It would be—What the—?"

He felt something on his thigh, then realized it was Chloe's hand. She giggled softly, then wiped the smile from her lips.

"You okay?" asked Alex, turning to him.

"Yeah. Just snagged my finger on the door handle."

"You've got to stop talking with your hands," said Chloe.

"Yeah. I'll watch that."

Ruiz swung around the corner. The street in front of the morgue was throbbing with lights from at least six SJPD cruisers. To Manny, it looked more like a circus than a crime scene.

They parked just as Crouse's car pulled up behind them. A minute later, Ruiz led them under the yellow-taped entrance and into the lobby.

Manny took two steps inside the building and stopped, trying to get a feel for what had happened. Ruiz made a beeline to the two coroner's techs talking to two blues. Alex and Dean took out their kits and started taking pictures. Josh, Chloe, and Sophie gathered around two other officers and started throwing questions at them. A job for everyone, and this team did it well.

A few minutes later, he continued toward the center of the room where a bloodied sheet covered the murdered tech.

Why?

Glancing back at Ruiz and the two techs, he could see they were having a somewhat animated conversation. The looks on both techs' faces spoke loudly. They'd seen something that would send them to nightmare land for months. Manny shook his head. That meant the rest of them would soon see the same thing.

Moving closer to the middle of the room, he gathered more first impressions. The security window glass hadn't been broken, and there were no signs of any forced entry at the building's entrance so the killer must have been let inside or had access to the morgue.

Searching the ceiling, the walls, even the restroom doors that were propped open, per procedure, he saw nothing out of the ordinary, but that's where Alex and Dean came in, wasn't it? Micro clues could break a case wide open.

The floor, on the other hand was another story. There were streaks of blood running in more than one direction, and it didn't make sense.

What the hell?

Before he could look closer, Ruiz motioned for Manny and Josh to join him.

"These two are a little freaked out. They covered the body, but didn't touch it. They said we'd know why in a minute. They kept saying it was 'of the devil.' Anyway, after that they noticed the morgue door was left open. Two of the blues started to go in, saw one of the drawers open with nothing inside, and decided to wait for us. I guess it's out of their pay grade to get too real."

"We'll let Alex and Dean tell us why the body's weird, but first things, first. I need a minute," said Manny.

He walked back to the first set of blood streaks and

squatted to look closer. The intruder must have taken out the attendant and, according to the bloody shoe-prints, had then entered the morgue area.

Manny frowned.

Why did the killer drag the victim to the middle of the floor, or did she crawl?

After walking around the whole room, his eyes followed the crimson trail to where he suspected the streak had started, then back again. There was another crimson line disappearing underneath the morgue doors. Something was off. That couldn't be right. That would mean this perp dragged the body from two different directions, or . . .

He came back to where he started and kneeled again.

"What are you looking at?" asked Josh.

"Just trying to get a bead on what happened. This is more than strange."

"No shit, there. I mean who in God's name breaks into a morgue and steals a body?" asked Sophie.

"True, but there's something else going on here. I need to see the morgue section and the empty drawer. It's like the unsub is trying to confuse us."

Just then, Alex waved a latex-covered hand at Manny, motioning him over to the body where he had the sheet raised. Dean was crouched beside him, staring. He then began to stroke his beard in the way of someone contemplating great mysteries.

"I guess we're about to find out about the body," said Manny.

Walking in Alex's direction, Sophie, Josh, and the two detectives followed, albeit a bit reluctantly, because no one enjoyed looking at dead bodies. It wasn't easy to disassociate death from the life that had been the vic's just hours before.

The things we learn to live with alter the things we can't live without.

"You got to see this. It's a first for even me," said Alex, a disturbed look on his face.

Manny stood between the squatting CSIs and leaned over.

"The tag says her name is Colita Rodriguez, and she's one of the night attendants," said Alex. "She's been dead only about two hours based on the liver temp, so that checks out."

Her face was round, pretty, and her eyes were closed, looking like she was truly at peace. He looked further down to her bloodied abdomen, stopping at the lower section of her torso. There were several marks through her green smock that could have been gunshots, which made sense.

Then he saw it.

He heard Detective Crouse gag and move toward the pale brick wall.

"What the hell? How can that be?" whispered Manny.

CHAPTER-25

Standing just out of range of the throbbing lights and any inquiring eyes that the scurrying blue-clad officers and suited detectives might direct his way, he leaned against the angled palm tree and wondered how long it would take before they discovered his handiwork. Not the obvious, but the subtle, the masterful, the "design" of his little project. No question it'd been risky, and he'd taken precautions, but not too many, because they weren't needed. Amazing what a little planning and timing could accomplish.

The FBI had arrived to help, and that was good. He'd even wished for it because it opened up a whole new avenue of exposure to his world. In the end, the more awareness he could raise to the plight of his rainforest, the better. However, moving the government into action was like turning a cruise ship on a dime; it simply took more time. He was sure it would take additional "convincing" for the authorities to think more of the public's safety than the revenue El Yunque generated. Fine. Rome was not built in a day, to be sure. He was more than willing to continue to paint the town red, so to speak. He smiled.

Willing? What a great word.

He felt the heat rise in his body and, even now, was getting hard as he pondered the sacrifices he'd made to his real mistress. It had to be done, but he never imagined the pleasure this venture would birth. Never.

Two of the SJPD cruisers pulled out, sirens and lights maintaining a perfect cadence as they headed east toward the Condado area. For a moment, he felt a tinge of sadness that they hadn't hung around long enough to appreciate his genius. And make no mistake, it was exactly that. Young Anna had provided the inspiration, even though she hadn't intended to. The eager, and disturbed young lady thought they shared some delusional kinship that would draw them together in a killing spree to make Gacy look like Tinkerbell. She'd been mistaken.

Shifting against the tree, he wormed his hand into his pocket, touching his full-blown erection.

Anna didn't understand, and in her state, never would, the nobleness of his endeavor. It wasn't about the body count, but instead a purpose larger, more encompassing. One needed to understand sacrifice and had to be willing to risk the very life they cherished the most: their own.

Another cruiser pulled out, heading west, leaving the two vehicles that the FBI and detectives arrived in, along with three other SJPD units and the coroner's wagon. That made at least thirteen people inside. Surely one of them would get it, find the first clue, the first communication leading to his ultimate revelation. But then again, no reason to hurry the progression any faster than necessary. As they say, timing is everything, and no one knew that better than he.

He finally brought his breathing under control and turned to leave, precisely in time to see two men near his vehicle parked at the intersection half a block away.

Hurrying in that direction, he pulled the Katana from his slacks and reached the SUV just as one of them pulled back an arm, tire iron in hand, to break out the front window.

"I don't think you want to do that," he said quietly.

The second man, a burly twenty-something wearing an amused sneer, turned to him and laughed. "What chu gonna a do, eh, gringo?" With that, the would-be attacker pulled out a knife and brandished it in a slicing pattern.

Taking two steps forward, he raised the Katana high. "I believe mine's bigger than yours," he said, moving into an en garde parry, demonstrating that he knew what he was doing.

The confidence of the large man diminished significantly, even more as his tire-iron-wielding partner turned and sprinted down the dimly lit street.

"You loco," the man breathed and quickly followed after his compadre, moving quite well for a man of his stature.

"You have no idea, my friend, no idea at all."

Driving off, he felt more than exhilarated.

He was about to bring all of San Juan to its knees.

CHAPTER-26

"Yeah, I've got to admit, I've never seen three arms on a body, not even in LA. Two heads once, but not three arms," said Dean.

"What?" said Sophie. She grabbed Josh's arm as she, he, and Chloe stepped closer to the body. Ruiz took one look and then put his hands on his hips, his face never changing expression.

Manny filed that expression, or lack of one, away for future reference. Even the most hardcore cop had to have some reaction to something this gruesome.

Shaking off the initial shock of seeing a third arm protruding between Colita's chunky thighs, Manny stooped next to Alex.

"Obviously, it's not hers, so what's going on?"

"Don't know yet. Dean, help me lift the body and pull this arm out."

"Okay, but let me get two more shots of this. Might need a new wallpaper for my laptop."

"Oh, that's sick," moaned Sophie.

Glancing up at her seemed to take Dean into a fantasy world all of his own, and Manny wasn't sure he wanted to go there with the new CSI.

Dean explained, "I'm sorry guys. It's how I cope with this junk. I need to keep reminding myself there are better sides of the human race than we see in this business, so I joke some."

"I get that," said Josh. "But let's exercise a little more control."

"I'm working on it."

He took two more photographs, then slung the camera around to his back. "Ready."

The two CSIs grunted as they turned the body away from them. Dean strained to hold up one side of the hip and a leg, as Alex shone his flashlight underneath the swollen buttocks.

"Hang on buddy, got to make sure there's nothing underneath her that could taint evidence or get us killed."

"I-under-sta-nd. Ju-st- hur-ry."

Satisfied that it was safe to dislodge the arm, Alex pulled, then pulled harder. As the third arm dislodged, Alex fell to his rump, but he kept the arm from hitting the floor, then regained his stance.

"Not bad, Dough Boy. It looked like you'd be sprawled on your ass halfway back to Miami," said Sophie.

"I'm full of surprises," he answered, already studying the arm through his dark-rimmed glasses.

Dean let go of the body and wiped at the sweat on his forehead, turning toward Alex.

"It's definitely female, maybe twenty-two to twenty-five."

"Yes, you're right. Been dead for less than thirty hours, and look at this." Alex pointed to the back of the hand. "A dragon tattoo. I remember seeing that on one of the victim's pictures."

"It belongs to Amanda Griggs," said Manny. "It's hard to forget that one."

"The cut that severed the arm from the body is even cleaner than I saw in the other crime scene photos. Amazing," said Alex.

"May I?" asked Dean.

Dean took the arm gently away from Alex. "I saw a couple of these in LA. This is no doubt a sword cut. I had a little time before you guys flew in so I went back to a case file and matched them up. Very similar, but not exact." He pointed to the top of the arm. "See the striations running away from the cut? That says the killer was behind and above the victim, probably antemortem, but we need a lab to make sure."

Grinning, Alex turned toward the others. "This guy's going to work out fine."

"Okay, we can talk about the details when you two finish examining the bodies and we all get your report. But let's get back to basics first. How was this woman killed?" asked Manny.

"You're right," agreed Alex, moving back to the body. "There are eleven holes in her smock, one in her throat, and two in her uterus. I thought they were gunshots at first, but they're not. She was stabbed."

By now, the others had put on their cop faces and were all business. Turn it off. Turn it on. Manny was one of the best at it, but this crew wasn't far behind. "Stabbed with what?" asked Josh.

"I'm not sure yet," answered Alex. "See this puncture up here, by her shoulder? It looks as complete as any. By that, I mean the thrust was straight on and will leave a complete impression of the weapon."

"It looks similar to the wounds we saw in a couple of the files," noted Manny.

"It does, but not exactly. This could be a long knife

or some kind of dagger, but we'll get it ID'd when we get into our database and compare it with what we have on record," said Alex.

"That's not all," said Dean. "We've got traces of fibers, a few hairs, and God knows what else we have to get collected and analyzed. One never knows what the science will tell us."

"Yeah, we hear that all of the time," said Sophie, smiling at Dean.

Manny thought the man was going to fall over. Dean swallowed hard and could only nod.

"Any theories as to why this was staged like this?" asked Chloe. "If it was Fogerty; why his daughter's arm and what was he trying to say?"

"There's some sick symbolism here. Maybe it was a way to say we screwed up and let his daughter die," answered Manny. "I'm not sure yet, but it'll come to us, or . . ."

Stepping back, Manny's eyes followed the blood trail on the floor for a third time. Turning to the morgue, he pointed. "Your people said there was a body missing?"

Crouse pulled out a notepad. "Yeah, it was in drawer twenty-four."

"These streaks are bugging the hell out of me. Why drag her around, then take her into the morgue, then drag her out again?"

"Only one way to find that out. Let's see what's going on in the morgue," said Josh.

Detective Ruiz walked to the yellow keypad, typed in six numbers, pulled his weapon, and hit the "open" button.

"Your weapon?" asked Manny.

"Hell, I don't know. This is creeping me out."

"The coroner techs were already in there, so I think you need to relax."

Ruiz sighed, reholstering his Beretta Px4 Storm. "You're right. Damn, I need a drink."

"I'm in," said Sophie.

"Make it three," added Dean.

The door swung partially open, hesitated, then continued. As they took two steps inside, Manny heard a muffled pop, then a crash just as the fluorescent lights in the morgue blinked out.

CHAPTER-27

The headlights blurred past as residents of San Juan drove to their nighttime destinations, oblivious to any other world but their own. Randall Fogerty understood that—in fact, better than most. If one's world wasn't the most important, then what was the sense of being alive? He'd never understood the "die for my loved ones" bullshit that people espoused. When the rubber met the road, they'd choose to save their hypocritical asses. He'd seen it up close too many times to think differently.

His thoughts turned to Amanda, again. He'd avenge her death because that was how it was done in this world of his, and not just because she was family, but because it was the way.

There wasn't much else a man of action like himself could do. He had an empire to run, which, over the years, had become his real family, his most important interest, his only true love.

Amanda had spent most of her time away from him over the last three years and that had led to an out-of-sight, out-of-mind mentality they both secretly enjoyed.

In a way, he almost felt relief. Since the day she was born, he had been waiting for this shoe to drop, and now it finally had. One of his competitors—no doubt one of them was the responsible party—would pay. Then the scale would be balanced.

His competitors.

Maybe it was time to take over another one, to build the kingdom even more. The rest already feared him, he knew that. Once word got out that his daughter had been murdered, the men who ran the other cartels would get messages to him that they had nothing to do with it. But one of them would be lying, and he'd figure it out.

Braxton brought him out of his thoughts.

"Sir, where would ya like us ta start?"

"Straight to see the detectives. Then we'll do a little investigation of our own. We need to take care of this pronto."

Ten minutes later, they pulled in front of La Uniformada in the Hayo Rey area of San Juan.

The night duty officer looked up from his computer as Fogerty passed through the tinted lobby doors of the old, five-story building. He watched as the thick officer quickly slammed the laptop's cover down and put his wire-rimmed glasses back on his chubby face, all in one motion.

Damn. Is everyone on this island a lard-ass?

And this one, no doubt, was watching porn on the job. Fogerty shook his head. Cops like this one made it easy to do what he did with minimal risk.

"How can I help you, senõr?" asked the officer.

Randall glanced at the officer's name tag and smiled, knowing if he didn't force the smile, he might kill the man just because he felt like it.

"Officer Malaga, I'm here to see Detective Ruiz or Crouse. I've just been to the morgue and was instructed to visit here for details regarding the death of my daughter."

Malaga's eyes narrowed as he scanned Fogerty up and down.

"Is there a problem, officer?"

"There's been a disturbance at the morgue and the detectives you asked for, along with some of those FBI assholes, won't be back for a few hours."

"What kind of disturbance?"

Standing, the large man folded his arms. "I can't go into that, but I know the detectives would want to speak with you, Senõr Fogerty."

Fogerty moved closer to the desk, and the officer flinched.

"Is that so? I've not even told you my name or why I went to the morgue," his voice became quieter. "So how did you know it was me?"

Fogerty watched as a pudgy finger hit a red button just to the left of his computer. Almost instantaneously, six officers rushed into the lobby from three different doors, all with guns pulled and pointing them at his head. He slowly raised his arms.

"What is going on?"

Malaga waddled out from behind the desk, cuffs in hand.

"There is an APB out for you, senõr. It seems you were the last one at the morgue before the call came in— now the attendant is dead and a body is missing."

Fogerty gritted his teeth, fighting for control as Malaga reached for his wrists.

"If I'd done such a thing, why would I march in here to speak to your detectives?"

Malaga snapped the cuffs shut.

"I don't know and don't care. You can explain it all to the detectives and those Feds when they get back."

"You're making a terrible mistake, officer."

"Yes? That's what all of you muchachaus say." He laughed.

Bending close to Malaga, Fogerty whispered in his ear. "Yes, but not all of them are going to rip out your throat when they get released."

Malaga's face went from smug to shocked in a nanosecond.

Before the officer could respond, the sliding door opened, letting in the warm night air, as a huge man entered the room.

Braxton strolled directly toward his boss and Malaga. "Sir, is everyting okay?"

Three of the officers turned their weapons toward his number one. He needed to defuse this now, or there'd be seven dead cops, all caught on video, no doubt.

"It's fine, Braxton. Go back out to the car and wait. It's a misunderstanding. I'll make a call and be out shortly . . . after the detectives and I have a heart-to-heart."

Braxton scanned the room and broke into a wide smile. "Dat will be a conversation for sure."

Then he was out the door.

"What the hell did that mean?" asked Malaga.

Randall smiled. "I'll let your boss tell you. I believe I'll make that call now."

CHAPTER-28

"Damn it! What the hell was that?" yelled Sophie. "And why the blackout?"

"I don't know, but maybe pulling your weapons isn't such a bad idea," said Manny.

He didn't have to say it twice. Everyone except the two CSIs held their weapons steady, pointing at the now darkened morgue.

Manny went over the sound in his mind trying to figure out exactly what he'd heard. His first, and re-occurring thought, was that a stack of packages had been pushed over. But by who or what? The perp? Fogerty? Not likely. Whoever had done this was gone.

Rats? It wasn't uncommon for that to happen, especially in big cities with a large daily body count. Particularly in areas where the standards for rodent control weren't high. He had read an article just last month of that same problem in India. Rat's had eaten and destroyed several corpses, including one that had been integral in a murder investigation.

"Could it be rats?" he said.

"Oh shit. Really?" strained Crouse.

"Yeah, what she said," said Sophie. "I hate them."

"He could be right. We had that problem a couple of years ago," said Ruiz.

Chloe moved beside Manny, Josh a step behind.

"If that's a rat, we'd better find bigger guns, because it'd be a big one," said Chloe.

Her voice was all her own and he couldn't help thinking how much he loved it. It was just one more reason his heart couldn't keep steady around her, especially in these situations. She helped him *live*. Maybe the bureau was right; when she was this close to him, he didn't always think straight, and that could be a problem.

Shaking off her influence, at least for the moment, he walked to the keypad, found the light switch with the round timers attached, and turned it clockwise. The lights flickered back to life.

"What the hell?" asked Ruiz. "How did you do that?"

"I suspected they were on a timer and motion detector. Most late night offices are. But that's not the issue here. Let's check this out."

"You first," said Sophie. "We got your ass, er, back."

"Thanks, I hope," said Manny.

"I'll go with you," said Josh.

"Not afraid of rats?"

"Only if they're packing Uzis or armed like the Three Musketeers."

"If they are, just run like hell."

Manny moved to the right side of the opened doors as the last bank of lights regained their full brightness. The silence was broken by the subtle buzzing released by the lights. Scanning the room, he saw four steel tables. Each equipped with all of the necessary tools to complete an ordinary autopsy. It was hard not to think of how many people had that jagged 'V' carved on their chest in this room. He understood that the people were no longer there, but still . . .

Damn. A little morbid, aren't we?

His eyes moved slowly from right to left, looking for anything, or anyone, that could explain the noise they heard. He stopped at the small, opened, three-by-three door on the left bank of body storage units and noticed the rack that had held a body was still fully extended. He frowned. The perp had propped it open with something.

"Shit," he sighed.

"What?" asked Josh.

"Come to this side."

Josh shuffled cautiously to Manny and looked where he was pointing.

"Another arm?" he whispered.

"Yeah. The perp jammed that door open with it."

Taking another step deeper into the room. Manny noticed a door marked SUPPLIES, a gender-neutral restroom, and a triple sink, dressed with small hoses and soaps and disinfectants. But nothing living appeared to be around.

The morgue was clean, and he recognized the smells of antiseptics and soap, except there was an underlying odor.

"No rats or Uzis," said Josh nervously.

Pointing to the supply closet, he motioned to Josh. By then, Ruiz, Chloe, and Sophie had entered the room. Crouse stood outside, gun raised, per procedure. He made eye contact with Sophie. She nodded and then guided the others over to the restroom door.

Manny was struck with a déjà vu he'd thought long buried. This was the same situation when they'd found Christina Perez hanging from the closet on the

Ocean Duchess, her pretty face missing eyes that they'd later found in a jar on the patio. She'd been a victim of the now-deceased Fredrick Argyle. He felt his heart rate climb. He wasn't sure he'd be ready for something like that again, ever.

Josh gave him a look. Manny nodded and opened the door an inch. A second later, sure there was no booby trap, he tore open the door.

He watched Josh's eyes grow wide, then he let loose a pent-up breath.

"Nothing but plastic bags and latex gloves," said Josh softly.

"That'll make Dough Boy happy," whispered Sophie.

"It made me happy, too," said Josh, relief painted on his face.

"Not like Dough Boy," she replied with a wink.

Manny watched her turn to Ruiz and Chloe who were waiting at the restroom door. Ruiz placed his hand on the door as Chloe backed up, widened her stance, and raised her Glock 19. Sophie moved forward to within a foot of the door's opening radius and waited. No one was breathing as Sophie motioned to Ruiz to open the door a crack, like he'd done at the closet. Good girl. She was making sure there were no wires that would blow them all into the next life. Ruiz caressed it open an inch. The odor that had been subtle became more prevalent. Sulfur, but not as intense. More like a rotten egg, but sweeter.

He raised his hand for her to stop, but to her credit, Sophie wrinkled her nose, waved him off, and nodded to Ruiz to open it farther. The detective took a breath and swept the door open in one motion.

Sophie took one step inside; gun raised high, and stopped so fast he thought she had run into something, or someone.

Manny had seen Sophie at her best and, once in a while, at her worst, but never had he seen that look as she turned to find his face. Talk about dead eyes.

Not wasting any time, he busted through the corridor of the room and felt his heart sink. No, that wasn't right: his heart *fell*.

From behind, he heard someone ask God for help. A good idea.

"I'll take that drink now," whispered Sophie.

CHAPTER-29

Alex walked boldly into the restroom, Dean at his heels.

Is this for real?

He quickly turned back to Manny. "Are you shitting me with this?"

Manny raised his hands to the ceiling.

Alex had been with Manny and Sophie for a long time, and they had weathered Argyle's take on modern art, but this abomination was subhuman. He closed his eyes and recited a mantra he'd concocted in grad school just for a situation like this one.

It's only biology, only tissue and bone, not a person. The person is gone.

Dean touched his arm. Alex gave him a quick glance, then a nervous grin, and went to work . . . almost. He hesitated one last time and looked to see if he really saw what was there a moment ago. It was.

The first open stall of two was open and sitting on the stool was what looked like a ravaged body, but looking closer, it clearly wasn't just one body, but a conglomerate of several bodies. All different races, ages, and in different stages of decomposition. The head—that of a young man with long hair and a beard—had been partially destroyed, apparently from the inside out, and now rested in the "lap" of this grotesque statue.

Blowing a breath, Dean took three pictures, then let the camera dangle around his neck.

"Wow, what a mess," said Dean.

"No denying that, but they were already dead so the unsub just rearranged them. He or she must have used that sword or whatever on all of them," said Alex.

Bending close, Dean squinted, then began to nod. "The cuts were made so that they would fit together to make something entirely different."

Alex felt Manny and Sophie over his shoulder and turned to face them.

"Josh and the others are pulling open each drawer and making a list of each body part that's missing in the drawers that have been. . . disturbed. Maybe that'll help give us a lead or two," said Manny.

"Good. It'll take us a couple of hours to process this room and then we can get the parts back where they belong. But that's not why you're standing here, is it?"

Manny shook his head. "The obvious question is why? Then there are a few million other situations running through my head. For instance: how is this related to the body in the lobby? What was the sound we heard just before the lights went out? And since I'm about 99.9 percent sure Fogerty had nothing to do with this, who did it?"

"I've said this before, but you almost never ask a question you don't know the answer to," said Sophie.

"Let me interject something here. I'm not sure about the who and why questions, but I can tell you about the sound we heard before we got in here and that will explain why the head looks like it does," said Dean.

"Have at it, Mucus," said Sophie.

"It's Mikus."

After what Alex thought was a brief blush, brought on by a slight smile that Sophie probably didn't even realize she showed, Dean put his hands in his pockets and then spoke.

"The smell, the one kind of like sulfur, but sweeter, is nitroglycerin, or some close derivative. It's worse once it detonates. It can hang in the air, especially in a closed area."

"What? Nitro?" asked Manny.

"Yeah. I'm kind of a geek when it comes to explosives."

"You? A geek? No way," said Sophie.

"Let him finish, smartass," said Alex, frowning.

"Okay. Damn. Still touchy, I see."

"Anyway, I had a case in LA where the killer, a stripper in one of those high-priced clubs where anything goes, was working her way through grad school as a chemistry major, and she had offed one of her clients after he beat her up. She managed, somehow, to place nitro on the inside of his cell phone, right on the battery, and then when she dialed his number, the electrical charge ignited, or I should say detonated, the nitro. It blew his weenie to Long Beach along with half of his guts."

"I know that stuff is deadly, but it's so unstable. How did she manage to keep it from blowing up in her face?" asked Alex, feeling more and more comfortable with his odd, but talented, new partner.

"She wouldn't say, but I think she got lucky. Besides, although that stuff's scary, it can be handled safely. She could have mixed it with gun cotton, dissolved it in an acetone and created a thin cord, which is more stable, but will still explode with the best of those mixes."

"What's that got to do—?" Alex watched the light go on in Manny's face and knew this investigation was now hitting the next level.

"Show me what you're thinking," said Manny.

Dean shuffled into the stall, wearing blue latex booties, matching hairnet, and latex gloves. Alex glanced at Sophie and almost laughed out loud with her. He snapped a picture from his own camera and knew they'd "discuss" Mikus's dress code at a more appropriate time, but he did feel some of the tension leave his body. Always a good thing for a science guy.

Picking up the head carefully, Dean reached into the expanded mouth and brought out what was left of a small cell phone. He reached into his back pocket, pulled out a new evidence bag, and dropped the phone into it. "Looks like a cheap pay-as-you-go unit."

"Good God, that's gross," squirmed Sophie.

"Oh, I've done worse. Like the time—"

"Later with the war stories, we've got a lot of work to do. But helluva job with that one, Dean," said Alex.

He blushed again. "Thank you, just trying to earn my check."

"Can you get the number that was used to detonate the nitro from the memory card?" asked Sophie.

"Maybe. It's pretty bad, though."

"The killer probably used another pay-as-you-go phone, so I doubt it'll do any good. But it might help us figure out where the perp called from," said Manny.

"You're right. You are learning about this tech world, aren't you?" grinned Sophie.

"Don't hold your breath on that one," answered Manny, moving closer to the human statue. He scanned the stall with those blue eyes of his burning every detail into his brain. Alex thought Manny would have been a hell of a forensic man too, but that hadn't been his long-time friend's calling.

"What are you looking at?" he asked.

Manny didn't answer, but bent even closer to the killer's version of Frankenstein's monster.

"Hey, you trancing again?" asked Sophie.

"Trancing? Does he do that?" asked Dean.

"Oh yeah. Big time."

"I don't trance. Like I said before, you got to pay attention. Come in here, Sophie, and tell me what you see."

Whenever he did that, Alex knew it was important. He squeezed close, too.

"I see a lot of body parts put together by some homicidal lunatic who probably wanted to hump his mother."

"That might be true, but what else?"

"Hell, I don't know, Manny. It looks like a jigsaw puzzle, that he cut the pieces to fit—oh, I get it. It's a puzzle, isn't it?"

"Yes. Each piece was intentional. Each body part came from someone that he specifically chose, so that means something in the killer's mind. I'm still trying to get my mind around what he's trying to tell us."

"You mean like the twisted messages Argyle sent?" asked Alex, not sure that he wanted to hear what was coming next.

Josh, Chloe, and Detective Ruiz came up behind him and Dean, crowding the entrance of the restroom.

"No, not like that. Argyle *wanted* us to react, to have fear. He thrived on it. This one is telling us something different altogether."

"How in hell are you getting that from this mess?" asked Ruiz.

Standing, Manny ran his gloved-hand through his hair. "Let me guess. The only body parts that you all found missing came from the rainforest victims? Right?"

"That's right. Except for Caleb—I had him flown to Miami. All of the other victims have something missing," answered Josh, never batting an eye.

Alex was impressed with the way Josh was holding it together. It had to be tough, even for Special Agent Josh Corner. Alex didn't think he could do it. But you can never be sure of what you're capable of until it becomes necessary.

"That confirms what I thought. We're dealing with the killer that murdered the people in El Yunque. But there's more to this one."

"More?" asked Chloe.

It grew so quiet that Alex thought he would be able to hear a drop of sweat hit the gray-tiled floor.

"I think this unsub is planning to shock the world, and this is the first test."

That's when the scream erupted, causing the hair on the back of Alex's neck to reach for the ceiling. The hair reached even higher the next second as a gunshot exploded throughout the morgue.

CHAPTER-30

"Parting is such sweet sorrow," he said out loud, relishing every word as if he'd uttered the most profound phrase ever spoken. Then he smiled. "Well, at least for me."

Anna had provided him with unexpected pleasure in an evening he'd set aside for reading and enjoying a few glasses of wine while listening to music that no one seemed to appreciate these days, after he'd returned from his "appointment," of course.

Too bad. As usual, the masses remained clueless regarding pleasures from another place in time. Music, literature, paintings, and sculptures from the masters. They were lost on a world filled with electronic gadgets for every purpose. People missed so much. Take his swords for instance, particularly the Katana. No question about the pleasure it had brought him, and he didn't even have to plug it in.

He poured more wine and reflected on his new guest, again. From the moment Anna had knocked on the door until he'd left the morgue, his heart hadn't really stopped racing. Instead, it thumped with a life and rhythm he hadn't experienced since he stood in front of his first classroom and delivered that lecture on habitat destruction. Not that any of the adolescent shitheads had appreciated or, for that matter, understood the wisdom he'd shared, but standing behind that clear, acetate podium had been a culmination of a dream. And what is life without dreams?

"A little too philosophical for this late in the evening, I think," he whispered.

Philosophy.

Kingdoms were built and destroyed on philosophies, and everyone seemed to have a different one. His was quite different than the prevalent take, especially when it came to law enforcement, or the lack thereof. He was more than positive on point that of view.

He wondered how the authorities were doing, sorting out the morgue scene. Had they figured anything out? He guessed not. When he considered the tiny explosion that had set his handiwork into motion, he smiled. He hadn't begun this journey to save El Yunque with the thought of playing any kind of game with law enforcement. Not really. Only a fool would think that his work would go unnoticed. But he and his methods had evolved, just as Darwin had predicted, so he needed to create diversions, such as his display in the morgue. And it wasn't only a diversion, but a message, a puzzle that the SJPD and Feds had to solve. He wasn't even sure, at first, why he had taken that step, the one that said *I'll help you understand my purpose, if you're intelligent enough.* He did appreciate intellect. But it was becoming clearer that, in the grand scheme of things, he was special. In fact, hadn't his mother said so? More than once? It had taken time, but he had accepted the assessment, and deep down, he knew he deserved it.

Special.

It sounded so . . . perfect.

Tasting his wine again, he contemplated his newly

discovered gift for games. Even in nature, there were certain advantages that the weaker species possessed to stay alive and even thrive. So offering the opportunity to discover him and his intent to the investigators seemed natural, almost instinctive, because they had no chance otherwise. And he was still fair-minded, was he not? Besides, the thrill level went up about a million-fold at the thought of encountering worthy opposition who believed their sole, narrow-minded purpose in life was to protect the lives of others, and at any cost. How archaic.

Once, he understood that life was sacred, and still did. But the life, the total living organism he was concerned with—El Yunque—had taken on an elevated importance. What were a few human lives compared to her? One thing he'd learned, and eventually accepted in the world of science, is that sacrifices were unavoidable and necessary. Over the centuries, people had died for the good of the species. Individual humans succumbed to groundbreaking research that could save someone in their very own future generations. Sacrifice was a commendable attribute that many humans shared, and at the ultimate price of losing their lives. He simply helped some of them make that decision, knowing full well that not everyone would agree with him. In fact, he was a member of a very significant minority.

Thus the cops, the FBI, relatives of his supposed victims, and even the Park Ranger staff no doubt wanted his ass out of commission, in jail, or, he guessed, more likely, on one of the same slabs in the morgue that he'd just visited.

Finishing the glass of wine, he rose, inserted his CD of Tchaikovsky's greatest compositions, and returned to his chair, more serene, more confident than when he'd risen. There would be a full-fledged investigation, of course, and he'd have to be more careful, at least a while longer. As much as he hated the coming conflict, he also welcomed it.

What is living if each breath has no purpose?

Purpose he had, no question about that. But this other "feeling" he hadn't considered.

Loving, almost needing, the sound and sensation of the sword slicing through the air, and through living flesh, had more than surprised him. It was a by-product of doing the right thing. Was there something to the thought that God gave people the blessing to enjoy the calling of a special destiny? He brushed the idea out his mind. This was pure biology. Personal gratification isn't divine but discovered through trial and error. Random genetics, not some intelligent design fairytale, explained deviant sexual behavior, why some people preferred steak over chocolate, and his new, special lust.

Again his mind focused on Anna. She was a perfect example of his theory. Would a God create such a soulless, uncompassionate, unfeeling individual?

I think not.

A moment later, he heard a tiny sound coming from his spare bedroom. His smile grew wider as he rose from the comfort of his chair and strode to the room's door, putting his ear close to the thick mahogany. There it was again.

Grasping the antique brass knob, he turned it slowly and entered the almost dark room. Moving to the nightstand, he pressed the switch of the teakwood lamp.

Glancing at the bed, his eyes grew wide. His prize,

his inspiration for the evening—young, beautiful Anna —was not how he'd left her. If fact, she wasn't there at all.

CHAPTER-31

"Where's Detective Crouse?" asked Manny.

He pushed through the others, rushing in the direction of the scream and accompanying roar of gunfire that had the same effect on him as stress test, the jackhammer rhythm in his chest said so. He pulled his Glock, looking for Julia and what she was firing at.

Turning left, the others close behind, he heard the second shot, then the rush of hard shoes on tile as the blues ran from the front of the morgue in the same direction Manny was headed.

Damn it. Have we missed something, or someone, again?

He exited the morgue's double doors and immediately smelled the expended gunpowder prancing through the air. A second later, he saw Julia Crouse in the far corner of the lobby facing away from him at a slight angle. She was on her knees, hunched over someone, blood staining her khaki slacks at her right knee. The detective had her gun raised high in the air, ready to bring it down like she was pounding the last nail of a casket. She was speaking Spanish in a loud, panicked voice. She brought the gun down, hard, and the thump of metal against flesh was intense, then she raised it again.

"Muere hijo de puta, muere! Muere hijo de puta!"

Manny understood a couple of the words, but he couldn't see who she was screaming at, this son of a bitch that she wanted to see dead. He ran faster.

To his right, three blues stopped ten feet short of Crouse, weapons pulled. A moment later, the first one lowered his, and the others did the same. All three began to laugh.

Crouse turned to the three, an intense snarl on her face.

"What the hell are you laughing at?"

The first blue spoke. "Sorry, Detective, but isn't that a little extreme? I mean it's only a—a"

"I'll let you know what's extreme and what isn't. Get your asses back to the front door," she ordered, a combination of anger and fear in her voice.

The men turned on their heels and did as they were told, pronto.

Swearing, she brought the gun down again, releasing more of that sickening sound.

Taking one more step, Manny saw the object of her rage: the biggest black rat he'd ever seen. His mind went back to the alley in Lansing where he'd found Detective Ross's body. The rats scurrying around there had been half the size of this one. Startling, no question, but. . .

"Julia! What the hell are you doing? You freaking shot a rat twice and now are beating it for good measure?" said Ruiz, shaking his head. "There's enough damned tension in this place without you pulling that shit."

Detective Crouse stood, wiping at the blood on her knee. "You don't know, Ruiz, you don't know—"

"I know this. You gotta file a report on why you discharged your gun, especially in this morgue, and in the midst of an investigation that makes Jack the Ripper look like a ballet recital."

By now, Sophie was giggling. Chloe had turned her face, then blurted out a laugh. Alex was staring at the ceiling, trying not to explode. The only face showing the same emotion as Crouse was Dean's. There are looks of fear, then ones of pure terror. Dean apparently carried the latter contemplation for rats, particularly one the size of a large tomcat.

After cleaning the blood and hair from the butt of her handgun with a gloved hand, Crouse holstered the gun, regained her poise, and got into Ruiz's face.

"Listen, peckerhead. That rat jumped out of the ceiling and ran right over my feet. You know I have a thing for them anyway, so what part of that brain of yours thinks I'd let this bitch live?"

Chloe, Sophie, and Alex laughed again, with more gusto.

There was a rush of commotion, and suddenly Josh was in between Ruiz and Crouse, a look on his face Manny had only seen one other time. Rage wasn't his MO, usually.

He grabbed Detective Crouse's arm and brought her face so close to his that Manny thought he was going to bite her.

"You're the peckerhead, detective. I don't give a shit about any of your damned phobias. You just disrupted a crime scene investigation that has at least eight people dead. Not to mention, you're shooting your weapon in a closed area. A damned rat? What the hell's wrong with you? People die from ricochets, not to mention you flat out scared the living hell out of every one of us. For what?"

There was an abrupt end to the laughing. It was replaced with shock and silence.

Been waiting for this.

"I'm sor—sorry. I—"

"I don't want a freaking apology. I want you to act like a detective, not a damned schoolgirl who is petrified of rodents, for God's sake. You could have killed someone. If you pull anything like that again, I'll make damned sure you're writing parking tickets on the streets of Old San Juan so fast, you'll think you were riding a time machine. You get what I'm saying?"

Walking up to Josh, Manny reached for his arm, intending to pull him away from Crouse. Ruiz beat him to it.

"Agent, she screwed up. We're all feeling the—"

Josh whirled around and bumped Ruiz before Manny could intervene.

"You keep her together, or the same thing goes for you. I'm tired of this local incompetence shit. Got me?"

Ruiz took a step back, surprise registered on his weathered face.

Josh spun on his heels and strode away from the detectives . . . and confronted his team.

It's catching up to him, all of it.

He opened his mouth to speak, glanced at Manny, then slowly dropped his head to his chest. Tears glistened in his striking eyes.

Manny walked over to his good friend and leaned close. "Let's go to my office and talk for a minute, okay?"

Josh nodded, and they headed for the men's room.

"You guys get organized, and please get rid of that rodent disguised as King Kong. We'll be back."

Standing with his back to Manny, Josh held both

hands on the marbled countertop, looking deep into one of the stained sinks. Manny leaned against the wall, folded his arms, and waited.

"So, was I a little harsh?" Josh asked, not looking up.

"Oh, hell no. Everyone's used to you losing it, especially on a couple of the locals. It helps with the public relations part of our job."

"Screw you."

"Ah well, you're not my type. Besides, that was a pretty good bend job without any of my help."

Josh's shoulders sagged. "Yeah, I suppose it was."

Manny shifted his weight. "Remember when we were in Ireland, and you told me I was in denial, and you'd be there when I wanted to talk?"

"I do, and we talked later."

"Your turn."

Josh nodded. "I've got other . . . pressures right now."

"Not to mention, you looked at Caleb's file, right?"

"Couldn't help it," he whispered. "But I couldn't get past the first picture."

"It's always different when it's someone you know and love," said Manny.

His thoughts went back to Liz Casnovsky and Lexy Crosby on the cruise ship. He felt his gut tighten. Another way this job sucked the life out of you like some new-born Succubus feasting on its first kill.

"That's not all, Josh. I know you were freaked out by the crash too, but what else?"

He let out a breath. "Oddly, the crash didn't bother me all that much. I figured with all the other shit going on in my life, maybe a quick trip to the afterlife wouldn't be all that bad."

"Spill it. What else?" he asked softly.

Josh held Manny's eyes and then slowly sank to the floor; the tears were no longer hiding behind the tough exterior.

He spoke in a voice that hardly sounded like a confident, organized leader, but instead a broken, lost man.

"Losing Caleb is bad enough, but Manny, I don't know if I can do this, this assistant director's job. They've been grooming me, and I jumped into the fire, but I'm really feeling it. Making decisions that could get people killed isn't where I want to be. What if I mess up and someone does die? Maybe even one of you."

He licked his lips, and kept going. "The stress is insane. I've seen this job kill better people than me. The AD they want me to replace tried to commit suicide. He said he couldn't take it anymore. You've talked to Dickman; you know what he's like. I don't want that. But if I say no, put a fork in me, I'm done. I'll get assigned to the mail room."

He shook his head without looking up. "Some of the things that go on . . . well, you have no idea. Not to mention, it's more time away from Nikki and the boys. We're already fighting about that."

In a split second, Manny felt what Josh was feeling—a hopelessness that batters you when your rock, your reason for living, is suddenly jerked from your life. Josh's job had become that.

They call me a workaholic. . .

He stood quietly and waited for Josh to find solid ground. A few minutes later, after the tears dried up, he watched part of Josh Corner's famous resolve return to his face. It was time for one more question.

RICK MURCER

"Is that all?"

"Is that all? Hell, ain't that enough?"

"No, I mean is there anything else?"

"Let's see. I almost die in a plane crash that almost killed two pilots with families. I lose my brother to a freaking lunatic with a slaughterhouse fantasy, my wife and I are fighting, and I want a job that might destroy my life, killing me in the process. I guess that covers it."

He reached down to help Josh off the floor. "You forgot something."

"I think I'd remember anything else, but since you're the damned profiler, what'd I forget?"

"Remember that line in that old movie that's says something about love means not having to say you're sorry?"

"Yeah, I do. It's one of Nikki's favorites, so?"

"That doesn't work here. I don't think Crouse and Ruiz are loving your ass right now."

Sighing, he smiled a weary smile. "I don't suppose they do. You're right. I owe them an apology. Let's go. And Manny, thanks. I just couldn't—"

"Hey, that's what I'm here for."

"Ever think about throwing up a shingle?"

"A counselor? Hell no, this job gives me all of the problems I need."

Splashing water on his face, Josh took a deep breath, and pushed through the door, looking a little more like the man Manny had come to know.

Once back in the lobby, Josh motioned to his team and the two detectives.

The six gathered round him, everyone looking at the floor, faces tight. Manny stood behind Josh, a little to his right.

"Detectives, I . . . listen, that's not my style, and I apologize. It's been a hell of a day and I'm tired. No excuse, but it's the best I've got." He stuck out his hand.

Ruiz shook it right away, wearing a grin. "You could be Latino with that temper and a few of those looks."

Crouse reluctantly reached for his hand, a cold stare shining in her big eyes. "You get a pass on this one," she said. "But not again."

"Fair enough. Don't shoot anymore rats in a tight area like this, endangering my team and others, and we won't have another problem. Deal?"

Her stare intensified. Then she nodded, lips tight and arms folded across her chest.

Josh returned the nod and then did what he does best: took charge. "Okay. Here's what we're going to do. Alex, you and Dean will have to process this place tonight. You can get some help from the night crew from our local FBI ERT group. Remember, you won't be waiting on the CSU report—you'll be doing it. You're now a Fed, so we'll be waiting on you."

"Got it. We'll need access to ViCAP, IAFIS, and CODIS to run any prints and DNA we might find."

Reaching into his pocket, Josh handed Alex a small, sealed envelope.

"These are your very own access codes and logins. You won't need to wait on anyone, at least for the ViCAP information. You'll need lab reports for the DNA, but CODIS has a new process for the field. If you find a good print, or even a partial, download the picture and the scanner at the database in Quantico will do the rest. Something about high resolution scanners that are a hundred times more sensitive than the last ones we had."

"I read about those. Awesome," said Dean.

Sophie rolled her eyes. "You science guys are all alike. If it has circuits or latex, you don't need a date."

"I don't know, Agent Lee, I like dates, just don't get many," answered Dean.

"Well, shut my mouth. I'm shocked," grinned Sophie.

Was that a little more than grin?

Manny thought it was.

Josh picked up the focus. "We can talk about your love lives later—ah, never mind. I don't want to know. The rest of us are going to interview anyone who's willing to come in to talk to the cops and the FBI at 10 p.m. We also need to find this Fogerty character. He could be a key, even though Manny thinks not; we still need to make sure. Also, I want everyone at the hotel and in bed—alone—by two a.m." He glanced at Chloe who had moved closer to Manny. She was touching his arm with hers.

"What?" she asked. "My intentions are honorable. Sort of."

Ruiz's phone rang, and he stepped closer to the large windows on the south side of the room.

He then snapped the phone shut and returned to the group. His body language was less than encouraging.

"We got good news and bad news. The good news is that Randall Fogerty is awaiting us at HQ. Seems he made a call, and he's no longer in cuffs, but wants to talk to us about what happened to his daughter."

"Well, we get to put one theory to rest, or not, tonight. What's the bad news?" asked Manny.

The SJPD detective shifted his weight. "It seems there was a package delivered to my desk a few minutes ago."

"You get those all of the time," said Crouse.

"Yeah, but this one's leaking blood."

CHAPTER-32

Standing in the soft light emanating from the lamp, he scanned the room slowly, listening intently as he did. The window was still sealed and remained unbroken. He'd locked the door from the outside so there was no way she could escape, especially in her condition. She was still here.

Another game to play?

He was beginning to enjoy that part of his crusade far more than he would have suspected.

"Come out, Miss Anna. Come out wherever you are," he sang.

The room was large by any standards. It included its own bathroom with a Jacuzzi tub, two separate closets, and a mauve motif. He'd designed it just for his mother, and she'd loved it. She had used the tub nightly during her short visit. He recalled the loud, unrestrained laughter each time she stepped into the bubbling, steamy water.

You won't hear that anymore though.

That dark, inner voice was in the house.

The remote for the Blu-ray player sat on the dresser untouched for all of these weeks. He remembered his mother turning on the forty-six-inch HDTV only once. That was to catch up on a couple of game shows she loved to watch.

Running his hand over the bed, he began to circle toward the first closet. It occurred to him that this room also doubled as the last place his mother had slept. In spite of the good things he wanted to dwell on, the truth was large; it always is.

Again, he wondered how his life, and hers, would be today if he hadn't come to visit his island, and if he hadn't introduced her to his mistress.

You know how things would be, don't you?

Anger was building up a little steam, and he felt his pulse pound in his head. He closed his eyes and pushed it away. It worked, but it was becoming harder. The rage simply had to have its say.

Reaching the first door, he noticed the blood on the door knob. His smile returned. He thought his Anna brighter than to leave a trail a blind man could follow. But maybe she just wasn't thinking straight. Intense pain can have that effect.

Gripping the brass knob, he bent low and pulled the door open in a fluid motion. Expecting to see her wielding some sort of weapon, he jumped back and waited.

Nothing.

He searched the floor of the closet, feeling both left and right. His newly discovered friend wasn't there.

"Clever girl," he said out loud.

Moving slowly, he stepped away from the open closet door and moved around the antique oak dresser, catching his reflection in the old, wavy mirror.

Still looking good.

Rarely had he had thoughts like that in the past, at least no more than others, but it occurred to him lately that it was part of "the gift," the complete package needed to attain his destiny.

No one would listen to an unattractive crusader.

Standing before the closed bathroom, he noticed more blood, much more, on the floor and on the door, just beneath the glass knob and lock.

"What are you thinking, young Anna?" he asked quietly.

Pressing his ear tightly, he listened for any sign of her. It was a heavy oak door, matching the others in the room, but certainly not impenetrable. Thirty seconds later, he moved away. She wasn't in there either.

Obviously, she was running out of hiding places. For the first time in this little game of hide-and-seek, he felt a twinge of nervousness.

Could she have somehow gotten out?

"Where are you Anna? I grow tired of this. Come out now, and I'll make your contributions to this grand scheme less painful."

Then he heard it. A delicate rustling from underneath the bed, near the foot. Circling around to the bed's left, his feet scarcely touching the Oriental rug, he lowered himself to his knees. He grasped the island-designed comforter, felt its soothing texture, then jerked it up. He immediately noticed the string attached to the small storage box, running along the floor just as the closet door burst open behind him.

His days as a fencing addict served him well. He spun out of the way of Anna's desperate charge and nudged her as she passed close to him, the sound of her hand swooshing far too close to his face. She landed heavily on the bed. The odor of perspiration and fresh blood attacked the air, then seemed to settle on his shoulder, at least figuratively. He loved it.

She lay on the bed, breathing harshly. Her eyes were clear, but moving back and forth like a caged animal looking for any escape route. She thrust her hand at him again, and he caught it, wrenching the six-inch dagger from her. She must have found the dagger on the shelf of the second closet, because that's where he'd left it.

"Here, here. That's certainly no way to treat a host. You might have hurt someone with that. And after I've been so kind to you."

"Please. I ne—need a doctor. I'm bleeding."

"That you are. But I'm all the doctor you'll need. If you'll do what you're told, you'll play an important role in this tragedy."

Her face contorted. "I could have helped. I could have—"

He watched as her eyes rolled up in her head and she passed out.

"You are helping, my beautiful Anna."

Glancing at the right arm that was missing its hand, he smiled.

"Piece by piece, you'll help more than you could imagine."

CHAPTER-33

The second-floor interrogation room at SJPD Headquarters was smaller than Manny had expected. There were only six chairs and a long, worn-out maple table that wobbled when he leaned on it. Add a small, barred window about six feet up on the south wall and the faded one-way mirror and that was it. Except for the pointed graffiti that remained strangely untouched. He smiled to himself.

Isn't it physically impossible to do that to one's self?

The stale aroma of old cigarettes and spilled coffee added to the claustrophobic feel, and he wondered if the room's setup was intentional to make the subject of any intense questioning more uncomfortable. He thought so. Good ploy, for most perps, especially the local garden variety B&E or assault offender, but not for the man sitting across from him. This man was confident, and his smug expression showed more than Randall Fogerty wanted to say. And Manny had a feeling Fogerty didn't care, not one iota.

Detectives Ruiz and Crouse were trying to track down the source of the package that had ended up on Ruiz's desk. They were talking to the delivery service and the young woman employee who had dropped off the box. So, that left him and Sophie to "talk" with Fogerty. Josh and Chloe stood outside the room to observe.

Not a bad idea, more eyes and ears never hurt in this business. Besides, Josh was looking a little beat, and he and Sophie worked well together.

Added to that, Chloe didn't want to run the risk of being recognized by Fogerty, but that wasn't the only reason for her absence in the room. The distraction she caused for Manny was on the rise, more than he'd ever imagined, and she sensed it.

Each time she touched him, or whispered something just for them, or smiled that Galway Bay smile, he fell deeper. That included the physical. How could he not? She was knockdown, drag-out gorgeous, and it had been a long time.

"Hey, Williams, you gonna start this story or you want me to?"

"I'm sure Mr. Fogerty won't mind, either way," answered Manny, glad that Sophie had taken him off that other horse.

"You're right, Agent Williams, but Agent Lee seems like a woman who gets right to the point," smiled Fogerty.

The man didn't sound like someone who had just seen his daughter in the morgue, appearing like a butcher-shop mistake. His hands didn't shake; his crossed legs indicated that he was more than relaxed and willing to talk. But his eyes . . .

"Okay. Let's get to it. First, let me say I'm sorry for your loss. I can't imagine."

"Thank you, Agent. And you're right, you can't."

"What time did you leave the morgue, Mr. Fogerty?" asked Sophie.

"I'm sure you have that on record. I'm assuming the security video will verify my statement, but I'll humor you. I left around 8:05."

"Thank you. We don't have working video yet, and our records need to be verified."

Sophie sat back in the chair, her eyes narrowing. "Did you return to the morgue after you left?"

Her voice was calm, professional. Manny gave her a quick glance just to make sure it was her.

"Now why would I do that, Agent? Once was all I needed."

"Yes, I understand. It must have been tough on you. I mean, seeing your daughter like that, right?"

Fogerty didn't flinch. Incredible. But that look in his eyes reappeared, then disappeared just as quickly.

Cold bastard.

"It's not something I'll forget, Agent, ever."

Leaning forward, she spoke in a low voice. "You didn't answer my question, Mr. Fogerty."

"No, I suppose I didn't. No. I did not return to the morgue. Why do you ask?"

Manny waited for Sophie to go forward. He didn't have to wait long.

"It seems there was a terrible disturbance there. One attendant was brutally murdered and several of the bodies were desecrated."

In one smooth motion, she floated the picture of his daughter's arm sticking out between the legs of the unfortunate Colita. She'd circled the tattoo that identified the arm as his daughter. Manny braced for the reaction Sophie was trying to evoke.

It never came.

Fogerty stared at the photo, inhaled, exhaled, then leaned toward Manny and Sophie. "Is it normal FBI protocol to attempt to enrage, embarrass, or stimulate some kind of emotional response that serves no purpose? Unless, of course, your reasons are veiled under some sick need to look at my daughter's severed arm shoved up some fat woman's crotch. In that event, you both should be fired and forced into an asylum."

That look waltzed into his eyes as he spoke with perfect control. It dawned on Manny what Fogerty's eyes reminded him of: a shark. Dark, unfeeling, bent on nothing other than satisfying the most basic of needs. The difference was that sharks only wanted to eat. Fogerty had a much deeper agenda, and it was psychopathic, no doubt. He believed there would be a blood bath that would never reach the papers. They seldom did in the drug world. But if that's what Fogerty suspected, he was dead wrong. This had nothing to do with the drug realm; these murders were committed by a killer with a purpose. This had nothing to do with a drug-war hit, or whatever the hell term people like this scumbag used, but instead. His daughter was a victim of a killer whose game was afoot.

"Damn. You really have control over your disgust switch, or maybe you just don't have a bit of compassion in that heart of yours. So which is it?" asked Sophie, not backing down.

"My emotional state is none of your business. Could it be that I'm still in shock?"

"Yeah, that's it. You look like the type who shocks easily. Should we call one of the department's counselors? Or you can talk to Manny here; he's a great listener."

"I don't like your tone, Agent. But I will say we all grieve in our own way. Like the way you grieved over your divorces."

Meeting Fogerty's resolve, Sophie stayed on track.

"I don't know, and don't care, how you know about my divorces, so we'll keep my personal life out of this, but I guarantee we'll be finding out a whole lot more about yours."

"Excellent. I've nothing to hide."

"Then you won't mind if we dig into your income sources. I'm sure the treasury officials in Barbados, after we employ certain Bureau policies, will help us figure that out," she smiled.

His lips tightened as he leaned back in the chair.

A reaction. Good girl.

"I've cooperated fully, yet you threaten me. I don't care for that, Agent Lee, especially from loser dykes like yourself."

Before Manny could stop her, she grabbed Fogerty by the shirt and pulled back her hand. "Dyke? Dyke? Loser . . . maybe. But a dyke? I'm going to kick your ass," she roared.

Manny grabbed her hand, picked her up by the waist, and carried her to the door. She was pointing at Fogerty and opening her mouth to speak, but he whispered into her ear.

"Great job, let's see if we got his number."

She stopped struggling and Manny set her on the floor. She slowly opened the door, gave Fogerty the sign that she'd be watching him, then left the room.

Walking back to his seat, Manny sat down and stared at Fogerty. "That wasn't very nice. Particularly for an upstanding citizen like yourself."

"Was she offended? I thought it was part of the good cop, bad cop routine that you Feds screw up with the best of them. Besides, I just call 'em like I see 'em."

"I see. Now I think we're getting somewhere. What

do you see in your daughter's murder?"

"I don't know; that's why I'm here. I want to know what you know about Amanda's death, and I expect you to tell me. You owe it to me."

"Really? Owe it to you?"

Manny looked to the opened window and listened as a few Coqui frogs revved up the mating call that sounded more like a bird than an inch-long reptile. He also heard the car as it passed slowly by the window, again.

"Maybe you're right. And I suppose your lackeys are tired of doing circles around the building. That's at least eight times since we started this enlightening discussion, so maybe I *should* clue you in."

Fogerty said nothing, but the shark was back.

"Your daughter and son-in-law are just two of seven people murdered in the rainforest in a twelve- to-sixteen-hour stretch. The attacks appear to be random, as in *the wrong place at the wrong time* kind of random."

"I see. Do you have any leads?" The shark was swimming faster.

"We're working on it, and of course, we'll let you know when we have something more."

"Pretty stand-pat answer, Agent. I don't suppose you want to go deeper than that?"

The man was asking the right questions, but Manny knew what he was really thinking.

"No, I don't. But let me explain something to you. This is an investigation of horrific murders involving a killer that I believe is not finished. The SJPD and the FBI are hard at work and won't appreciate any interference."

Fogerty pulled his chair up to the table and put his large hands on the surface. "Do tell, Agent Williams."

"Furthermore, let me tell you what these crimes are not. They are not an attack on you and your way of life."

"My way of life? What, pray tell, is that?"

Fogerty's stare had immersed completely into the dark side, and he reveled in it.

Time to drop the hammer.

"That of a piece-of-shit, drug-lord gig that has ruined lives and killed countless all in the name of what you think you deserve."

"Really?"

Manny leaned closer. "Maybe there is something to this karma thing .Maybe you get what you give. What do you think?"

The man's hand left the table and shot towards Manny's face, but he was ready. He grabbed it in midair and twisted and pulled at the same time. Fogerty yelped in pain as his face jarred the table.

"Assaulting an FBI agent, a Special Agent, could land your ass in a cell, but lucky thing for you, I'm in a good mood. So here's the deal. You're going to walk out of here, make arrangements to get your daughter's body released, and head back to whatever deep, slimy hole scum like you crawl out of. This isn't about you. If I see you where you don't belong, I *will* throw your ass in jail, got me?"

There was a slight nod, and Manny let him up. Fogerty straightened his shirt and moved toward the door, wiping at the small trickle of blood oozing from his lower lip. Hatred danced in his eyes.

The shark is ready for a meal, an FBI meal.

As Fogerty brushed past Manny, he stopped, then leaned close and whispered. "Know that this isn't over,

Agent."

Then he slipped through the door.

Taking a deep breath, Manny rested his backside against the table, knowing what Fogerty said was true: this was a long way from over, for all of them.

The intercom flared on. It was Sophie. "Shit. Why can't they put the damn talk button on these things where you can find it? Hello? Manny? Manny you need to come quick. We've got bigger problems than Fogerty right now."

CHAPTER-34

"Damn, this is a real piece of work," said Dean. The trace of admiration in his voice was undeniable. Alex turned in his direction, and his first reaction was of disgust, but also . . . veneration . . . same as Dean, though admitting it would be like a married woman saying she was waiting for Mister Right.

"That's kind of sick, you know," Alex said.

"I get that and you got to be a bit touched to do what we do, *si*? But this guy, and I'm pretty sure our butcher is a guy, was as precise and intentional as any killer I've seen, in any class, anywhere, online or in living color. It's like he played it out in his head, then executed with no concern for making mistakes. I also—"

"Go back a second," said Alex, leaving the second stainless-steel table in the row of four. He walked to where Dean had just separated the last leg from the torso of the gruesome, eclectic body from the bathroom stall.

"What?"

"You said you were sure this killer is male. Make your case."

Dean stripped off his blue latex gloves, pushing his glasses up on his nose.

"Ever notice how these new gloves come off so much easier?"

Alex grinned. "Hell yeah, they're the best yet. Don't chap my hands either." He glanced at the floor and shook his head. "Oh shit. Sophie's right: latex makes me tingle."

"Hey, you're not alone."

"Somehow, that doesn't comfort me much."

He motioned to Dean to continue.

"Right. Well, first thing is that ninety-eight percent of all serial killers are male between twenty-two and forty-five."

"Nothing new there. Keep going."

"Another issue is the strength it would take to cut these folks the way he did. Cutting through bone, even with an edge as incredibly sharp as this one, is no easy game. The blade still needs to be brought down with true force. Unless the killer is some exotic female Ninja with years of training and wears boxers instead of lace."

"You mean like the kind of woman you might see in the movies or read about in comic books?"

"That's it, boss, like that."

Alex watched Dean finger-rolling the edge of his unkempt beard, He'd receded into his own world. There was no other way to describe it; he'd checked out.

"You okay?"

Dean's eyes snapped back to this dimension and he gave Alex a weak grin. "Yep. Just thinking this through."

"Well, think out loud."

"All right. Like I started to say before, it's like he planned this piecing of the bodies together. The cut-angle on each body part was no accident. The bastard had to be planning this from the moment he felt the hilt of that weapon in his hands, otherwise the limbs wouldn't have fit together so precisely."

"I'm glad you're sticking to the science. What else?"

"If what I've said about the strength that's needed to take these people out didn't convince you this perp is male, how about the width of his hand?"

Alex raised his eyebrows. "What the hell are you talking about?"

Raising the mangled head off the table by the hair, Dean spun the left side of the face to a forty-five-degree angle and pointed to two oval, intensely dark bruises.

"These are thumb and forefinger marks, I believe. You know how this works. Sometimes these kinds of marks don't show up for a day or even a few days post-mortem. The distance between the two fingers is almost eight inches, not a large male hand, but too wide for most women, since the average distance between those little piggies for women is somewhere around five-and-one-half . . . well, you do the math."

Déjà vu was a sensation Alex hated, even worse, hated to acknowledge. There'd be no ignoring it this time, however. His mind immediately flashed back to the *Ocean Duchess* and the marks on the heads of the victims Eli Jenkins and Dr. Fredrick Argyle had butchered. He could see Liz Casnovsky's face like the murders had been seconds ago, instead of going on three years. Manny had broken that case open by observing the bruises on the crime-scene photos, and they looked eerily similar to these. Argyle's postmortem marauding had created deep purple blotches that sang and danced to music that had been written by Satan, if one believed in that sort of thing. Right now, Alex was real close to singing *Amazing Grace*.

It was Dean's turn.

"Are you okay, boss?"

Alex sighed. "Yeah. I think you're right about having to be a little 'off' to do this kind of work. Some days . . ." Walking back to the second table, Alex went back to work on Amanda Griggs's body, hoping to find something, anything. He had taken the arm that was between the legs of Colita, and Dean had brought over a foot and hand that looked like they were Amanda's as well. Alex pieced them together and felt like he was assembling the world's most macabre puzzle.

She's not here. It's just flesh and bone.

Her flesh was a gray, hopeless color, and the thirty-nine wounds on her body were difficult to look at, even now—but they told a story, and he needed to read better. Josh's words came back to him. He and Dean *were* the FBI file report. They had to get it right.

Damn. Nothing like a little more pressure.

He'd do what he knew best, that's all he could do. But he was good at it, and Dean was every bit as good as his old CSI associate, and friend, Max Tucker, maybe better.

Taking a step back, Alex took several more pictures. As he got to her calves and then her Achilles heels, he noticed the deep, precise slits on the back of each heel.

"I think he sliced her Achilles tendons to incapacitate her," he said, frowning.

"I noticed those cuts. She wouldn't have had much of a chance," answered Dean.

"Bastard," breathed Alex.

He squinted, setting the camera down. He reached for his magnifying glass and zoomed in closer. The faint aroma of decaying flesh massaged his nose, but he was virtually oblivious. He bent over the left cut, located an inch above her ankle. Closer still, the lens almost touching her cold skin, he repeated the process on the other side.

Something was different.

"Dean, come look at this."

Dean dropped the small, polyethylene evidence bag onto the metal table and moved to Alex's side.

"What?"

"Take this and get real close to the wounds on the Achilles tendons. Tell me what you see."

After following Alex's actions to a tee, he glanced up quickly, then did it again. Thirty seconds later, he did it a third time.

"There's something imbedded in the right cut. Is that what you mean?" asked Dean. "It could be just a piece of dirt, or even an insect egg."

Alex didn't answer. Instead, he pulled his smallest set of tweezers from his kit and took the magnifying glass from Dean's hand.

Slowly, with the steady hand of a surgeon, he teased at the dark spot near the middle of the lower part of the wound. Eventually, he was able to get a firm grip on the sliver-like object immersed beneath the epidermis. By this time, Dean had retrieved a microscope slide. Alex placed the fractured material on the glass. Dean put the thin slip-cover atop the slide, one side first, then let it drop into place so not to jostle the sample. It fit like a glove.

"Nice work, for someone from California."

"We don't all do drugs and surf, you know. But there was this time—"

"Later. Is that microscope ready?"

Saluting like an awkward cub scout, Dean nodded. "Ready for action, Sir."

"Well done, Private Smartass. Get out of the way."

"What do you think it is?"

"We're going to find out. You might be right on the dirt particle, but unless I miss my guess, we just got a break."

Guiding the slide under the lens, Alex adjusted the light and magnification until he finally grew still. A small, triumphant whistle escaped his lips as he stood back and motioned for Dean to take a peek.

Moving with more enthusiasm than a thirteen-year-old finding his first real whisker, Dean almost pushed Alex out of the way.

A few moments later, Dean mimicked Alex's whistle. He stood, frowning and smiling at the same time.

"Do we have a database for this?" asked Dean.

"Not too sure on that one." Alex heard the excitement in his own voice. "But maybe we'll start one. There are a dozen ways to analyze this. At any rate, that *has* to be metal from the murder weapon."

CHAPTER-35

As Manny rushed through the dingy, white door, he wondered what could be worse than what they had. A deranged, motivated serial killer getting ready for stage two of his mission and a drug lord that wasn't about to sit still and wait for the FBI to do its job. Throw in the fact that they had no freaking clues worth a tinker's damn . . . it had been a wonderful night for the bad guys.

He turned the corner, and Chloe met him head on.

"What's going on? Did Fogerty and his lackeys do something stupid?"

Chloe shook her head, her red hair framing her face. He had to remind himself to breathe. She saw his expression, maybe even felt same. Chloe tilted her head to the left and gave him a quick grin, then reached up and kissed him full on the lips. That now-familiar electric shiver rattled up and down his spine, and for a moment, just a brief moment, he thought of nothing but making her his wife and what came next—a lot of what came next.

An instant later, she was all business, almost.

"No, not Fogerty," said Chloe. "Sophie went ahead of us, so we have to hurry. Follow me."

He watched her hurry away and couldn't help gluing his eyes on her shapely backside. No doubt about it now, she wasn't making this part of the trip any easier. And just maybe he didn't want her to.

Chloe stopped on a dime, turned his way, and gave him that look women have that says *I know what you're thinking and it's about damn time.*

The accompanying grin was even worse. Or better. Yeah. Better.

Manny reached for her and pulled her close, then whispered in her ear. "Soon, very soon."

"It better be, or I'm going to have to make a quick buck on one of those lovely side streets in Old San Juan."

Exhaling, he did his best to arrest those images and remove them from his head—the ones with her dressed in nothing but a birthday suit and a smile.

"Okay. Where are we going?"

Pulling open the door to the next floor, she led Manny down the first flight.

"Remember the box that came for Ruiz? The one that was bleeding?"

"Of course I remember. They were going to have the bomb squad make sure there was no problem, then have the CSU take a look."

"Well, Ruiz got impatient, then pissed that it was making a mess on his desk, so he started to open it."

"Did it blow?"

"No, not that. Detective Crouse was with him, waiting for the two squads to show. By the way, I've been noticin' how she looks at your arse. I don't like it, and if she doesn't stop, we'll be talking. Anyway, Miss Roaming Eyes stopped him, but only temporarily, until about the time the CSU and bomb squad got there. He couldn't take it anymore. It's almost like he had a premonition."

"What does that mean?" He thought he already knew.

They reached the door that lead from the dilapidated stairwell to Detective Ruiz's office and burst through it.

They made the next bend in the narrow, dimly lit hall. Sophie was standing outside a small row of cubicles that meandered left toward an enclosed glass office that belonged to Ruiz and Crouse's boss. She was talking in a low tone with Josh and Crouse, who had, at least for the moment, forgotten her less-than-pleasant encounter with the FBI man.

As he and Chloe got closer, his heart-of-hearts told him he'd been right. Ruiz was sitting in a worn, brown, leather chair behind the glass in his boss's office, face in his hands, shoulders heaving.

When Manny reached Sophie's side, she looked up at him, a sheen of moisture in her beautiful, almond-shaped eyes. Somehow, they were larger than he'd thought possible.

"Chloe filled me in. What was in the box? What body part?"

Josh shook his head. "The box hit the floor when Crouse tried to stop him from opening it."

Nodding, Crouse's tears made small rivulets down her high cheek bones.

"It's—it's unbelievable."

Josh took over. "The body part was a hand. The CSU guys said it was severed no less than three hours ago."

"Let me guess. It belonged to someone he cares about."

Sometimes you can see a heart break, other times you can hear it. Still other times, you can feel it. Manny thought Crouse was going through the full gamut as Josh spoke quietly.

"There's a ring Ruiz gave her on the fourth finger. The hand belongs to his daughter."

CHAPTER-36

Climbing into the white limo, Randall Fogerty had already decided what agenda he would pursue. In fact, he'd even run most of the details through his mind, more than once as usual. *The devil is in the details.*

His grandmother, the only member of his miserable, nonfunctioning, pathetic excuse for a family he'd ever remotely cared about, had said that a thousand times if she'd recited it once.

Braxton handed him a pearly-white handkerchief. He blotted his mouth, the corner of it blotching into a crimson cloud. .

When his granny had died, he'd even cried real tears no less. She'd gotten sick from the damned cancer sticks that the tobacco industry still maintained weren't as harmful as the research indicated. But life is full of choices, and one of hers was to rock in that aged, red wicker chair sitting at the corner of their small, sagging veranda. She'd roll her own and smoke unfiltered tobacco all day, every day. Even on most winter days, she'd venture out to smoke. She did it for some forty-five years and paid the price. After she was diagnosed, she even laughed a little, saying she was surprised she'd gotten away with it as long as she did.

Granny had been hard as nails, no mistaking that, but every once in a while, those old, dim, gray eyes would soften, and she would hand him a candy bar and tell him to do right.

Up until she passed, when he was twelve, he'd tried to do what *she* told him was the right thing. For her, just for her. But when she checked out, so did his reason to respect anyone else. He quickly discovered that the world was full of assholes, and all of them wanted what you had, no matter how little that was, so you had to guard it with whatever you could.

"Hotel, boss?" asked Braxton, from across the seat.

"Not just yet. Circle the building a couple more times."

His voice did not reflect the pulsing volcano ready to erupt from the lack of respect he'd just endured at the hand of that son of a bitch Agent Williams and that little Asian bitch.

Respect.

There was that word again. It seemed he wasn't getting any lately. First his daughter, then the cop at the front desk, then the hour waiting in that pigsty of a interrogation room, then the two Feds and the rest of their little crew, whom he knew more than a little about, thanks to his "friends" in the department. Williams had dared to touch him. And not just touch him, but made him bleed.

He squeezed the kerchief and felt his manicured nails dig into the meaty section of his palm.

No one does that to me. No one.

They made the next turn and rolled unhurriedly past the steps of the pale entrance to the SJPD building. He cracked his window, rolled it back up, and waited. Fifteen seconds later, his cell phone rang.

"Did you get what I needed?"

Fogerty's face contorted into what may have been a smile, though anyone could easily mistake it for a snarl of rage. "Excellent! Please send the rest of the files to Braxton's laptop and keep me abreast of what I need to know, and I need to know *everything*, yes?"

He listened for a moment, shifted the phone to his left ear, and began to nod.

"Why thank you for asking. There is one more thing: where are they staying?"

He listened then hung up the phone. Blotting his lip again, he saw the bleeding had stopped and stuffed the kerchief in his front pocket.

"Boss, I'll tak' dat one and git you anoder one," said Braxton, holding out a hand the size of Detroit.

"Thank you Braxton, but no. Let's just say I'll keep it as a souvenir for the next time Agent Williams and I talk."

Braxton smiled.

"Let's go to the hotel. It's been a long day, and tomorrow will be busy. Of that, I have no doubt."

"Yes, boss."

Turning to the driver, Braxton gave him instructions and turned back to him.

"You know, old friend, come to think of it, there is one more thing we need to do."

His number one bodyguard's smile grew wider.

CHAPTER-37

Alex and Dean entered the fairly modern conference room as Manny leaned on the wall outside the entrance staring at Ruiz who was sitting in his boss's windowed office, down and across the hall. Alex had called to say he and Dean just typed up the rest of the details on the crime scenes in the morgue and got the pictures transferred to Alex's computer from the cameras. The team could go over the findings before they went to the hotel.

All of that had been accomplished except for a new complication, and for a change, it didn't have anything to do with Chloe.

He shifted his gaze, for about the hundredth time, to the office where a distraught Detective Ruiz was still sitting. But there was something else–almost a sense of resigned relief and Manny wanted to know why.

"We made it, but this fat boy is tired," said Alex, grinning.

"I think we all need a good night's sleep. Glad to see you an hour early. It's only twelve fifty-eight," answered Manny.

"Dough Boy, not Fat Boy. Dough Boy," said Sophie as she stepped from the room and stood near Manny. "And Mucus still needs a freaking tailor."

Dean's eyes lit up, and a quick smile came and

went, mostly aimed at his Asian tormentor and fantasy princess. A quick smile came and went from his face.

"It's Mikus, Agent, *Mikus*."

"Okay, but that outfit needs a firing squad."

"Yeah, well, I've got a couple more outfits just like it, but different color, so get used to it—please," he said, lowering his gaze.

"You're kidding me? Really? I hope not. You'll blind me, and I'll have to panhandle to make a living. Not to mention, you'll be arrested for impersonating a freaking peacock in heat. They might even bring you in to see if you're assaulting peacocks. You don't do that kinky stuff, do you, Mucus?" asked Sophie.

"Not birds, princess. But there was this one time—"

"Okay. TMI, even for me," said Sophie. "Come on in, the gang's all here."

Following Sophie into the conference room, Manny caught Josh's eyes, then Chloe's. He didn't know how those two were even able to sit up, let alone be coherent. But adrenaline is a drug—in fact, the drug of choice for workaholics and this BAU world.

Sophie leaned close. "It's going to get longer, isn't it? The night, I mean."

Training his eyes back to the glass office, he answered without looking. "For me and you, yep. We have to talk to Ruiz about his daughter."

"Why the hell do you want to do that? The rest of his department thinks this is some kind of revenge thing and doesn't have anything to do with our case. Not to mention, they've got half the nightshift out looking for her. I know it's gotta be tough on him, and the rest of us ain't too thrilled about seeing his daughter's mitt whacked off either, and— Damn it, Williams. I know that look."

"What look?" asked Manny.

"Is it the trance thing? Cause I want to see it," said Dean, stepping closer.

"No trance this time," answered Manny, almost absentmindedly. Again, he couldn't control the need to look in on Detective Ruiz.

"Manny? You paying attention?" asked Josh.

He ran his hand through his hair and moved away from thoughts of Ruiz, as difficult as that was.

"Yeah, I am. Listen. Let's meet in the morning. It's one a.m, we're all beat, and it's been a hell of a day, especially for you and Chloe. None of us are in a great frame of mind to discuss the evidence, the murders, and you can kiss goodbye any hope of putting a great profile together until we see more of what Alex and Dean have found, plus the reports from the SJPD aren't totally ready. Especially since Ruiz has other things on his mind."

Josh was stroking his stubble, then rubbed his face with both hands. "You're probably right. Besides, these two don't smell like roses," he added, tossing a thumb at Alex and Dean.

"Good. Detective Crouse can get you to the hotel. How about we meet in the lobby at nine a.m.?"

"What do you mean 'you'? What are you going to do?" asked Chloe.

"Well, for starters, I thought I'd go learn the flamenco and show you all how it's done."

"Pink dress?" asked Sophie.

"You know me. I like the red dresses with a little lace."

"As interesting as that sounds . . . what the hell are

you really up to?" asked Josh.

"I want to talk to Ruiz, talk *with* Ruiz, and see what's going on in his head. His body language doesn't match the information he's giving us. I don't think he's lying, so much as we aren't asking the right questions."

"Maybe he's just unhappy because they won't let him go out and join the search. That would make me a little nutty," said Crouse.

Her eyes did a quick tour of the scarred wood floor when Manny looked her way. That told Manny more than anything else she could have said.

"You think something's not quite right too. Don't you?" he asked.

Crouse sighed and locked onto Manny's face with those striking, brown eyes. He heard Chloe clear her throat.

"I know him better than the rest of you, and yeah, I have some history about his daughter. But that was always off limits, his *hija* and he, I mean. But I recognize that look too. He's stressing, and not just about the obvious."

"He thinks she's involved in something?" asked Chloe.

"Maybe," said Julia.

"Or maybe it's more than that. Maybe it has to do with who she is. I have a seventeen-year-old and think I know her pretty well, but everyone hides something," said Manny.

"True enough. I'll get them to the hotel, the Puerto Rican. It's down at the Port where the cruise ships come in," said Julia.

"Deal."

Manny offered a lingering look to Chloe, she accepted, winked, and then followed Crouse down the hall.

He took Sophie's elbow and headed to the glass office holding Detective Carlos Ruiz prisoner. As he opened the door, Ruiz's drawn, bloodshot eyes blinked at Manny. He barely acknowledged Sophie, took a puff from the cigarette smoldering in his hand, and then he spoke.

"You're a profiler, Williams. I know that, but you ain't no mind reader. Still, you know about her, don't you? You know about my Anna."

CHAPTER-38

Ruiz crossed his legs, then seemingly as an after-thought, crossed himself in the Catholic tradition, as he turned away from Manny and Sophie, staring at everything and nothing in the same fracture of time. There *was* far more going on than the fact that his daughter's hand was delivered in a bloodied box. It was torturing this man. Manny had known something was more than amiss, but the closer he got to Ruiz, the more he realized that something had to do *with* his daughter, not about her. It was completely separate from the fact that she'd been dismembered. He was haunted by something more.

In the interrogation room in Lansing, Manny had seen men and women who'd hidden secrets all of their adult life, maybe longer. Some as disturbing as anyone could imagine, and many times, it had nothing to do with the crime they were being questioned about. It was like the first time, the very first opportunity they'd ever had to share, or confess, that particular secret. The stress, the pressure, and even the relief, at having a captive audience brought courage to their spirit and the words to their lips.

Some had killed the neighbor's cat, stolen money from sick, old people, cheated on their spouses, and killed another human in another place in time. A drug addiction, a sex addiction, a fetish that would curl your hair had it been confessed in a different setting. You name it, he'd heard it all. Except, looking at Ruiz, he was now sure he *hadn't* heard it all, had he?

Ruiz looked up from the floor, dried tears painting the corner of his creased eyes. He smiled a faint, exhausted, humorless smile, put out his cancer stick, and moved to the edge of the black leather sofa, hands folded together. Manny sat in the matching office chair as Sophie leaned against the metal desk.

"Did you know Christina Perez was my partner?"

Surprise registered on Manny's face as he and Sophie exchanged glances.

"I didn't. She was a good cop and a good woman."

He smiled sadly. "And I loved her. I should have been on that ship with her, with you. Maybe I could have saved her."

"Maybe not," said Manny softly.

"I'd like to think so, but I'm sorry I wasn't there, just the same. I've not slept a full night since."

"You loved her as a woman, not as a partner," said Sophie.

"I did. But it seems everyone I love— Anyway I wanted you to know that I have normal emotions. I love, I feel, for my Anna."

"Tell me about Anna," said Manny.

"I've already told the rest of the damned department everything I can think of about where she might be, where she hung out, her school address, everything. I'd tell them her best friend's info too, if I had it," said Ruiz, doing his best impression of a cooperating witness.

"You mean you don't know it, or she doesn't have

one?" asked Manny quietly.

"Like I said, I think you know there's more to this, too her, than just what I'm feeling. You strike me as that kind of cop."

Manny shrugged. "Maybe, but no close friends isn't always an indictment of something gone haywire."

"No, but in this case, I think it is," said Ruiz. That tired look returned.

"You say I know about your Anna. Truth is, I know about how you're reacting to this situation, and it's pretty normal, mostly. What isn't normal are the flashes of relief I'm seeing, followed by serious guilt, that comes and goes from your face and eyes, your hand gestures, and how fidgety you become when anyone comes near this office into the office. It all means you're hiding something that could help, doesn't it?"

Manny waited for him to react, to get pissed. Hell, maybe even throw a punch. Most men would when you accuse them of hiding something that could save their daughter's life. But none of that happened.

Sighing, Ruiz lit another cigarette and cleared his throat. "She was never normal, not like I expect kids to be. She was fascinated with . . . things. Morbid, sickening things. I remember when she was barely two, and one of those programs came on that show how an operation procedure goes. I think it was like an open heart surgery situation. I never watched that shit, so I don't know how the TV got there, probably her fruit-for-brains mother. Anyway, they'd nicked an artery. There was screaming, yelling, total chaos, plus all of that blood. It's the kind of thing that would send most toddlers screaming and crying into their daddy's arms. But not Anna. She stood fixated, and I swear by the name of

Jesus, she had a smile on her face before I finally got the damned television turned off."

Sophie must have felt the same kind of uneasiness that Manny was feeling, because she crossed her arms, giving him a nervous glance.

Rubbing his face with his hands, Ruiz continued. "I chalked it up to my imagination, but as she grew, she never did the cute little things kids do to show their parents they love them. No real hugs, and there sure wasn't any intentional kisses, at least from her end. By the time she was eleven, she was still having trouble wetting the bed. So much so, that I took her in for some counseling. I know that most bedwetting is about deep-sleep syndromes, but it was the excuse I needed to get her in to a counselor. Not to mention, my ex and I had divorced, and I'd gotten full custody. I think her mother was relieved by that, especially since she hasn't seen Anna since the judge said I was free. She knew something wasn't right, too."

"The first doctor said she was a little detached, but he didn't think there was any real issue. But there was. About a year later, she came down the stairs and, in the calmest voice you ever heard, said her room was on fire. She'd been playing with matches, and I'd grounded her for doing that same thing the day before. She just ignored me, or just had no sense that she might get her ass kicked."

The relief was beginning to flower on Ruiz's face.

"The day she turned fifteen, I came home from work early to surprise her. She'd seemed to be coming around some. She was smiling more and even told me she loved me before she went to bed most nights. I was going to take her over to Arecibo, the Observatory, and then a nice supper in Old San Juan. A daddy-daughter night. But it didn't happen. When I walked through the door, she wasn't there. I checked in her room—still no Anna. I searched the whole house—still no baby girl. I finally went out the back door and then saw her out near the far corner of the garage. It was hidden from the neighbors because of the weird-ass angle the builder had constructed the building. I called to her, and she didn't respond. So I walked out there and just as I got there, she heard me and tried to cover up what she was doing."

Ruiz shivered and lit another cigarette. His eyes were dry, but ever so distant. Manny knew that look. He wore it for months after Louise had died.

"Detective, you don't have to finish..."

"No. I do. Not just to help find her, but . . . I *need* to."

"Okay, Carlos, tell us what she was doing," said Sophie.

"I know you know. My little girl was watching an iguana die. It had been carved to pieces; blood and guts everywhere. The knife was still in her hand. Like I said, at first she tried to hide what was going on, then she sliced it again. It was like she didn't give a flying frog's ass for what I thought. She only wanted to watch that lizard bite the big one."

"After that, I took her to more counseling, lots of it. She seemed to get better, but I'm a cop. A detective. I knew. I read up on the Macdonald Triangle thing. By the time, she went away to live on campus, I was relieved and terrified at the same time. Every murder, every weirdo killing that happened on the island scared me. Because I knew."

Standing, he stared out the glass facing the conference room. "I spend most of my time thinking about how I could've stopped this, but no one seems to know why the switch flips like it does, at least not completely. I don't know. Maybe something happened to her when I wasn't around . . ."

Looking back to Manny, he was broken. But glad to get his story off his chest. Ruiz was right—one day, the odds were good that she would evolve into something worse. Rare as it was, a woman serial killer, especially a non-Caucasian, wasn't out of the question. But Ruiz would always live with the guilt that dads harbor when their children didn't turn out a certain way.

"Detective. I'm sorry you're going through this. But how can this help us find your daughter? I mean, why would you think that your story could help us?" asked Manny, running his hand through his hair.

"I think she'd try to find this killer. Maybe even try to partner up."

Manny raised his eyebrows. "Why would you say that?"

"Because the last two serial killers caught in San Juan both had visits from my lovely daughter. She said it was research, but I knew better. The last one, Jorge Munoz, the guy that had stalked and killed four nuns at the school he'd attended, actually sent for me saying he wanted to confess to more killings. But he didn't do that. Instead, he told me to put Anna down. Imagine that, a serial killer telling me to kill my daughter because she was going to join the clan. My God. It was like she was drawn to them."

Manny let the silence have its way. It seemed right. He wondered if Anna Ruiz could be the one they sought, but dismissed the thought as fast as it came. Mostly because of the hand in the box, but not entirely. Self-maiming is not an unusual trait for some killers. Most serial killers start small, test their plan, their method, their preferences. They didn't run like this one was running.

One of the CSU techs knocked on the door, waving a file. Sophie retrieved it and handed it to Manny. He opened Anna's file and saw that it contained information about the hand, and maybe more important, about the amputation tool. It was a sharper-than-normal blade, and the cut was very precise, a perfect north-to-south slash. There were no jagged edges, and it appeared to be a one-swing cut, consistent with their perp.

There was a note in the preliminary toxicology report saying that there could have been a sedative in her system, but they didn't know which one, yet.

Closing the file, his mind was racing a mile a minute. Why send Anna's hand to her father? Was he escalating the game aspect? Exerting control? Trying to muddle up the investigation or maybe delay it? Was that it? Random? Or was Anna in the wrong spot at the right time? But if she did seek this killer out, and somehow found him, how did she do that? He's obviously clever. She was just a second-year criminal justice major, but a complete psychopath in the making, according to Ruiz. He'd read that some psychiatrists theorize that this type of serial killer actually have some sort of subconscious kinship with each other. That by their subconscious actions and habits, they actually might recognize one another.

He ran his hand through his hair again and felt Sophie looking at him, waiting. Most of these killers are also opportunists. It's how they reach the high road to satisfying their urges. Maybe his plan mandated sending body parts all along, and the fact that the victim was Anna was a pure coincidence. Again, right place, wrong time?

Or, if what Ruiz said was true and Anna had tried to partner up, had she been an unwelcome guest? The problem wasn't just that she'd seen the killer, but given that the vast percentage of these men worked alone, she'd be just another body to him. That couldn't be good for anyone because it meant things were going to get even more complicated than he'd anticipated. Much more.

Multiple messages from one killer displayed supreme arrogance and confidence, narcissism at its finest.

"Agent? You all right?" asked Ruiz.

"No. I don't think I am. This is far worse than I thought, even two hours ago. Finding your daughter may be the key to all of it."

CHAPTER-39

Running his hand over Anna's wrist, the one that was missing its hand, he admired his work. Remarkable what a red-hot iron could accomplish. He'd cauterized the wrist right after he'd cut it off, but it hadn't been as effective as he'd intended. After all, he wasn't exactly a doctor—at least that kind. But after he'd gotten her back on the bed, tied spread eagle and much more securely than before, she was, once again, his. He'd repeated the cauterization. She'd screamed, despite the new dose of sedatives. The tang of burning flesh hung in the air. It was one that he found less than unpleasant. In fact, it wasn't bad at all.

I wonder what it would be like with a spice or two . . .

He was amazed at the human body, and what it was able to undergo when the situation commanded it. Anna should not have been conscious, but there she was, fighting to survive. That was more than interesting, but in the end, she just didn't have what she truly needed to survive.

His guest had lost blood, had been traumatized past what most people could ever imagine, and moreover, had experienced a disappointment that rivaled no Christmas presents under the tree by not being able to team with him. Yet her heart rate seemed fine, and her breathing was even and steady. She had a slight temperature, and perhaps could use a bath, but all in all, was doing well.

His eyes shifted to the rise and fall of her chest, fixing on her breasts. After a few breaths, he felt that sensation again. The one that said he could do anything he wanted. That he was entitled to anything he wanted.

It rose from a place he hadn't been familiar with, until recently. The instinctive and primordial urges that society, and the church, over the centuries, had taught mankind to submerge into the realm of the unacceptable and perverse, were now *right* for him.

Running his hand along Anna's bare thigh, his mind wandered deeper into what he wanted as opposed to what he needed. He ran his hand back and forth over her soft skin and speculated on how many people knew the difference. How many really cared? Just feed the beast.

He unexpectedly felt her eyes on him, accompanied by a humorless grin.

"You *are* a sick one, aren't you," she rasped. "But do it, if you want. I'll even moan and groan, it you need me to. Maybe I'll even feel something."

"Sick? Is that what you think? Not sick, Anna: driven. And soon the whole island, perhaps the world, will see what's really important. What's really at stake here."

She laughed, one of those haunting kind. "You make it sound so noble, but you're no different than me. You got the fever, and that's all that matters. A dog always recognizes another dog."

He moved very close to her face, smelling her coppery breath, and grabbed her throat, squeezing.

"Whatever fever I may have has to do with justice,

not murder. These deaths are a tool, that's all. Exactly like you, you're here to serve the greater good, my greater good."

Anna's eyes grew large as he tightened his grip. A moment later, he released it and stood. She caught her breath, coughed, and repeated it, all the while, that peculiar smile never leaving her face.

Fascinating.

He bent to her again, putting the rag back in her mouth and then squeezed her face as he whispered into her ear.

"Let's see how long that smile lasts when we send another package to the authorities bright and early in the morning."

CHAPTER-40

Detective Crouse pulled up in front of the neat but not overdone hotel and let Sophie and Manny out, promising to be back at nine a.m. sharp. The plan was to go over the case files at headquarters and develop a profile for their blade-happy perp that could be released to the entire force. Six hours of sleep, maybe, but he knew in his gut it'd take some time to unwind. Then again, exhaustion was a harsh dictator. He'd been there more times than he wanted to recount.

Thanking Crouse for the ride, he and Sophie pulled their travel cases out of the car and watched her speed off. Sophie looped her arm through his, and they headed for the front of the hotel. They had taken only a few steps when he stopped, jerking Sophie to a halt with him.

"What the hell, Williams? You tired of walking?"

"Exhausted, but look." He pointed to the two ships in port and how they were lit up like the proverbial Christmas tree, even at two a.m.

"Yeah, they were hard not to notice when we went around that other hotel and ended up in front of this one. You'll excuse me if I don't gush. That cruise thing hasn't been the best experience for me, and God knows, you either."

"True. But I have some good memories from the

first one. Like when we found out Louise didn't have cancer, and that night we danced ..."

Suddenly the past was gripping his throat, making his words stick. He looked to the dark brick sidewalk and slowly shook his head.

"You okay, Big Dog?" asked Sophie, squeezing his arm.

"I will be. Sometimes those memories, the ones that are kind of carved into your soul, come around for a visit."

"Well no shit, Sherlock."

They took a couple of steps forward and Sophie stopped him.

"I don't get that whole dream world you and Jen went to, or think you zoomed to, but Louise was right, you gotta move on. But having said that, if you think she's not going to hang out in things that you see, places you visit, or food you eat, every once in a while, then you really are tired and a little goofy, too."

"You haven't been this nice to me for a couple of months, what's up?" he grinned.

"Hey, everyone likes a little ass, but no one likes a smartass, and I know that one."

The almost-full moon seemed to catch the twinkle dancing in her eyes, and his appreciation for her climbed another notch. He couldn't have done better in the partner department.

They went through the large brass doors and straight to the check-in counter. A few minutes later, they were riding the elevator in silence heading for the fifth floor, and sleep that he hoped was waiting for both of them.

Yeah, and people in Hell hope for ice water.

They got out of the elevator and moved down the west wing.

"Okay, 509, this is my room," said Manny.

"I don't think so," said Sophie. "I've got that key and you're SOL. You can have 513. I hate that number anyway."

"A little too old to be superstitious, aren't we?"

"You got a mouse in your pocket? You can't be talking to me. We Chinese don't call it superstition; we call it not tempting the gods into some little bullshit prank."

"Seriously? I never knew that about you. Is that another way to say chicken shit?"

"Just go down the hall and plop your blue-eyed ass into bed before you get hurt."

"Yes ma'am."

She waved him off and got half way into the room, and turned back to him.

"Manny?"

"Yes?"

"I'm not so good with some things. Like I kind of like this new guy, but I don't really know how to be nice to him."

"You'll figure it out."

"I'm also struggling to try to piece all of this case into something that makes sense, even in my convoluted way," she said, biting her lip.

Every picture of each of the victims exploded into some ungodly collage in his mind's eye. He sighed. "You ain't alone on that one, Missy, but it'll be better in the morning. You're not standing here because you want to talk about this case, so what's really on your mind?"

"I don't do *thank you* and *I love you* very well, never have, but thank you for believing in me and recommending me for this FBI gig. You're the closest thing, well, you're like a big brother and I, ah, love you."

Then Sophie ducked into the room, pulling her bag behind her. She moved through the door so quickly that he laughed out loud.

"I love you too, Sophie," he whispered.

Manny stepped down the hall, still grinning about his partner's confession, slid the keycard into the slot, and pushed the door open.

The high-pitched scream raised the hair on his arms and caused the goose bumps to come so fast he felt like he just had gotten out of cold Lake Michigan. It took a second to realize where the scream came from.

His pulse pounded in his head as he ran down the hall. The scream had come from Sophie's room.

CHAPTER-41

As he reached Sophie's door, pulling the Glock 22 from his holster, Manny vaguely, somewhere in the confusion, heard at least two other doors open, but that was the least of his concerns. Whatever had happened, whatever had caused Sophie to scream, had been meant for him because he was supposed to be in 509, not her. His mind sprinted to one name the way those intuitions do until you acknowledge them to be pure truth.

Fogerty.

"Sophie!"

The door swung open as he rattled the door knob, pulling his hand away.

After one quick glance, he wondered where his willpower not to laugh came from. Even without knowing for sure what had happened, he knew his partner was pissed. That meant she was okay.

Her long, black hair was mussed, and her bangs were partially on her forehead, dripping down to her eyes. Her blouse was untucked on the left side, and there was a smattering of blood on her tan skirt. All of that added to the priceless expression that was displayed on her face. Her eyes were flaming arrows that were directed at everyone and no one. The scowl on her face wasn't really a scowl, was it? It was a snarl gone wild. That small vein above her right temple was throbbing a beat that would make any doctor nervous.

"What the hell is so funny? You ain't that good, Williams. I saw that asshole smirk when I opened the door."

"Sorry about that, but what the hell were you screaming about? You gave me a freaking heart attack and—."

"Let me guess," she interrupted. "You thought it was your fault. Well, this time, damn you, it was, and I'm not lettin' you off the hook."

She shivered, shook it off, and then grabbed his shirt. "Come on in, I'll show you why I screamed. And you can put the gun away. I took care of it."

By then, Chloe and Dean had bracketed the door, and he saw Alex staggering down the hall.

Dean was garbed in blue silk Captain America pajamas that were a tad too small and bare feet. Manny wasn't sure Alex realized he was standing there in the hall in just a tee shirt and red boxers. Chloe wore a robe, covering something lacy, at least that's what it looked like near her soft neck. But they all had their weapons drawn. Manny wasn't sure if that was good or bad.

Sophie pulled at him and he followed, after taking a second look at Chloe.

The bright-orange suitcase sat askew on the king-sized bed, a few clothes were scattered near the pillows like she'd been startled and tossed them in the air. Her black loafers were sitting exactly where she'd slipped them off. Nothing too distressing; until he saw the dots of blood splattered against the pale wall. Sophie was standing, arms folded and tapping her foot, starring at something below the crimson pattern. The rest of the team came in behind him. Manny took two more steps, then felt his mouth drop open. Pinned to the wide base-board was a small, slim, brown animal, maybe two feet long, adorned with a long tail. Its eyes were staring at nothing. Just below the animal's head, right at the base of the neck, shined two points of a Chinese throwing star. Three inches below that was another one, showing less steel through the critter's brown coat.

"What the hell?"

"What the hell is right. Damn. A girl can't even un-pack in peace."

"What is it?" asked Chloe.

"It's a mongoose. Bigger than the ones I saw grow-ing up in the city, but it looks like the same freaking spe-cies," answered Sophie.

"A mongoose? In your room? How?" asked Alex.

The blood dripping from Fogerty's mouth came into full view as Manny pondered the shark eyes the drug lord wore so well.

"It was Fogerty. I'm guessing he didn't like his re-ception at the SJPD headquarters," said Manny.

"But why Sophie?" asked Chloe.

"I was supposed to be in this room, but we got the keys mixed up so Sophie took this one."

By then Dean had bent over the animal with a curi-osity that reminded Manny of an eight-year-old who had just picked up his first frog. He poked it with the pen he lifted from the desk, and then turned his attention towards its mouth; the razor-like teeth, still looking like they could do some serious damage.

"You did this?" asked Dean, not even attempting to cover the admiration in his tone.

"Of course. I told you, I'm bad. When that little peckerhead jumped at me, I tossed my clothes at it. I guess that's when I screamed. I jumped on the table. He tried to follow, but hit the edge of the chair, like he hadn't seen it, and it seemed to stun him. He didn't look too steady. Then I pulled a couple of stars from my garter, flicked them at him, and it was all over but the bitching. And there's going to be more of that, just hang tight."

She gave Manny one of her evil-eye looks.

"You wear garters?" stammered Dean.

"Yeesss," she said slowly. "Would you like to see?"

The CSI swallowed hard and turned away. Manny thought that was a yes.

Josh came into the room, looking a little more harried than the others. God knew he needed the sleep even more than the rest of them, but he was here, and that's what Manny loved about his new boss.

"Did I hear mongoose, Fogerty, and garters in the same conversation?" Josh asked.

Manny expected Sophie to run to Josh and say something totally off color and act like she needed him to protect her. It didn't happen. Instead, she'd fixed her gaze intently on Dean, watching his every movement. In a sense, maybe she thought she was protecting him, or . . .

We're going to talk about this one later.

"Yeah. I think Fogerty meant this little reception for me."

"But why? Mongoose attacks aren't deadly, at least as far as I know. It'd hurt like hell, but that's it," said Alex.

Before Manny could answer, Sophie and Dean began to speak at once. Dean stood, doffed an imaginary hat, and deferred to Sophie. She accepted.

"I know a little about these rodents. They catch and carry rabies with the best of them. My mom almost died from an attack back in the late nineties. She got a nasty bite from one when she went to the market. One had escaped from a vendor who didn't know it was sick," she said.

Running his hand through his hair, Manny spoke. "I read that. They were brought to San Juan to control the black rat population, I think."

"Maybe they can team up with Detective Crouse and do a real job on those rats," said Alex.

"Good one, Dough Boy, good one," grinned Sophie, regaining most of her old verve. "But what I'm saying is that maybe this one has rabies."

"No need to speculate on that," said Dean. "It definitely had rabies."

"Let me guess; foaming at the mouth? That could be several other disorders." said Alex.

"That's true, but combined with the erratic behavior it seemed to display while going after Sophie, I'd say it was a sure thing. Of course, the tag on its ear that says 'Rabies Virus,' clinches it."

Squinting, Manny looked to where Dean was pointing and noticed the round white tag clipped to its tiny ear. He glanced at the teeth again and a thought flashed about how bad this could have gone. But then again, the mongoose had no clue with whom he was dealing.

"Great. That brings on a question or two. Not the least is; where in hell did it come from and how did Fogerty get his hands on it?" asked Manny.

"I'd say some research lab, and, a guy with his connections, well it's not hard to put that one together," said Chloe.

"We're not going to be able to trace this animal, are we?" asked Josh.

"I'm guessing no, but we'll get this thing boxed up and check it out. Most research viruses have a genetic identifier specific to their lab. Maybe we'll get lucky. I mean, how many labs can there be in San Juan?" said Alex.

Somewhere, Manny could swear he heard Fogerty laughing.

"I know there's a series of shots to treat rabies, so I don't think his point was to kill me, just to cause some pain and give me a scare. To show me who was really in control, but we can deal with that later. There's another question, maybe even a bigger one," said Manny.

He looked at Sophie, and she puckered her brow.

"Who put the damn thing in the room?" asked Sophie.

"That's the one. It could mean connecting Fogerty with some criminal intent. We'll see if we can get a security shot of anyone going into the room, in the morning," said Manny.

"Good idea, but my bet is that it was an employee, or an employee who conveniently lost his keys, or some shit like that," said Sophie.

"Sounds like a good theory, but I'm tired of those today. I'm going back to bed," said Josh.

"Okay. Let's pick this up in the morning. I'll call security and make sure the animal gets sent to the lab, and they'll want to clean this room up," said Manny.

Dean folded his hands together and glanced at Sophie. "Well, if you want, you can take my bed and I'll sleep on the floor, unless you need me to hold you. You know, because of how traumatic the night's been?"

offered Dean.

Rolling her eyes, Sophie looked at Dean. "Don't be stealing my lines, Mucus."

"It's *Mikus*."

"Yeah, yeah. Whatever. No worries there. Williams is going to give me the key to his room, right after he checks it out for mangy-ass critters, so I can get some beauty sleep. But it was a nice first shot."

"I'm a little hurt," said Josh. "Does that mean the thrill is gone?"

"Never gone, just trying to control myself, but . . ."

"You can have the key, but I'll need a place to crash, and soon," said Manny. "The problem is that the manager said the hotel is full."

Glancing at Chloe, then back to Manny, Sophie raised her hands to the ceiling. "Damn Williams, you really don't get it sometimes, do you? I'm going to bed. Figure it out."

"Me too. Tired don't cover it," said Alex. "And she's right. Figure it out."

Manny handed Sophie his key and watched as the others left the room behind her, leaving Chloe and him alone. She slipped her hand in his and led him into the hall.

"I'll take care of the room part," said Chloe. "You can bunk with me, don't ya know?"

He pulled at the collar of his shirt. It was definitely getting warmer.

"I'm not sure that's a good idea. I've been thinking about you way more than I should, and I'm only human."

"That's always good to hear, especially the human part," she whispered.

Wrapping her arms around his neck, she kissed him gently, then again, with more purpose. Much more. For a moment, however short, he let himself go, falling deep into the essence that was Chloe Franson, God's gift to him. The kiss was—brilliant. He scrambled for control, and for the first time since he'd met her, had none. He scooped her up and headed for her room.

"Why Mr. Williams, whatever are you doing?" she laughed.

Manny didn't answer because he didn't know what he was doing. He only knew that he wanted her, in every way. Not just the physical—God knew that was overpoweringly true— but the intimacy. It was the final step in making a relationship what it should be: permanent.

Why Mr. Williams, whatever are you doing?

The question ran around in his head even as he pushed the door open and laid Chloe on the bed. He bent over her and kissed her like men in love should. But it wasn't just love. The desire for her was somewhere between a roaring fire and a super nova.

Opening her robe, he saw that she was wearing a short, white negligee that shadowed her curves in such detail that it forced him to take another hungry look. He couldn't help himself and didn't want to.

He cupped her breast and heard the accompanying moan, as she unbuttoned his shirt. The sound cheered him on like the crowd at Comerica Park rooting on the Tigers. He kissed her again and again. Small little butterfly kisses that raised the temperature even higher and caused Chloe's cheeks to burn red.

A moment later, she spoke to him, softly, lovingly. "Manny?" she breathed. "Is this what you want? God knows ya can have me, you always could, but I love you and don't want any regrets."

Her words struck home. Not just the "rethink this" part, but the fact she was willing to give up what she really wanted—for him. To make sure this wasn't going to be something he'd regret.

Maybe he would have gotten there on his own, maybe not. Doubt clouded his thoughts as he stared at Chloe. She was so beautiful and was in need, but doing the right thing, at least sometimes, carried a deep cost. He was about to indulge in that conundrum.

"You're right. This has to be perfect and I *would* regret it tomorrow, mostly."

"My mum would think her daughter crazy. I finally have you where I've been dreaming about for two years, and I spoil the moment. You must be rubbing off on me, Agent Williams."

"Good thing, I don't know if I could have stopped," he sighed.

It was Chloe's turn to sigh as she ran her hand through the hair on his chest. "You better make me an honest woman soon, or I just might go mad."

Flopping over to the other side of the bed, he grinned. "I'm going to need a cold shower, but it'll be a minute before I can stand up."

She laughed and poked him, then laughed again. "I'll go with ya."

Her laughter forced the idea he'd had, just before they'd left Cleveland, to come roaring back. He reached for the phonebook on the desk, thumbed through, and tore out the page.

"What are ya doing?"

"What I should have done three months ago."

Pulling out the cell phone in his pocket, he dialed

the first number on the page and waited for an answer.

CHAPTER-42

Braxton rolled down the window of the limo, feeling the warm Puerto Rican night caress his face. It was late, but it was part of the job, and he didn't actually mind being away from the boss for a few hours. The man was crazy, but so was he.

He turned his focus on the\ front of the hotel and strained to see what he needed to.

It seemed his work was never done, but it would be soon, then maybe he'd get some real sleep. But then again, he wasn't paid to sleep, just to take care of what he was told to take care of. Something he was damned good at, always had been. He grinned a toothy grin.

Ask Agent Williams and his sad sack group of friends.

Agent Williams.

The white boy had touched the boss. That was never supposed to happen under Braxton's watch, even when the boss made decisions that put him at risk. His grip grew tighter on the door handle. He heard it groan.

No one was to get into Fogerty's shit unless they'd gone through him first. He hated that he'd not been able to stop the FBI wimp from doing what he'd done. In all of his years at taking care of the boss, that hadn't happened. The silver handle gave way. He hardly noticed. That couldn't happen again. Years of training had led him here, and another mistake like that would cost him his life.

The door of the hotel spun open and his contact walked out, smoking a cigarette and casually blowing the smoke into an endless, starry sky. A moment later, he scanned in the limo's direction and nodded. Then he flicked the smoke onto the cobbled brick street, reached inside his pocket, and pulled out a cell.

Braxton's phone vibrated and he answered.

"Done, mon?"

"It is."

Braxton snapped the phone shut. He resisted any temptation to smile, for now. But the message had been sent, and that was all that mattered. The results weren't even really important. He wondered if the agent was covered with bites. Who knew, maybe the mongoose had torn his throat out, and the man lay bleeding to death.

There was tinge of disappointment at that thought. If anyone tore out Williams's throat, he wanted to be there. But most likely, the FBI prick had been bitten a time or two and would have to go through all of those shots, and they hurt—he was aware of that pain.

The phone rang again. "Yes?"

"We just got the call. The animal's dead. Killed by that female agent, Lee. No one was harmed, but they're pretty pissed. Rumor has it they think it was Fogerty."

"Lee?"

"Yes. They switched rooms."

He released a long, deep belly laugh. "A wom'n sav'd his ass?"

"Looks like it."

"And dey tink we had something to do wid it?"

"That's the rumor."

He laughed again."Good. Dat's what da boss wanted."

For the second time, he flipped the phone closed, then for good measure, reached his long arm out through the window and tossed the phone over the roof into the bay.

Waiting another minute, he motioned for the driver to roll. It was time for sleep because the next day was going to be a big one. The boss had said so.

He was also relieved. Williams was unharmed and that made his night. He'd be there personally the next time, and things would be different.

Who said there is no God?

CHAPTER-43

He handed the sealed box to the young man seated on the old bicycle and stuffed the twenty dollar bill in his shirt.

"You know what to do? *Si?*" he asked.

"You just want me to leave it on that bench in Ocean Beach and take off, and not look back. I got it, *Señor*."

The youth hurried off, and he climbed into his SUV and entered the ramp leading to Highway 26 East.

Phase one of the day was accomplished, and it was only 6:30 a.m.

Despite his dark glasses, the bright Puerto Rican sun was dazzling heading east, not to mention warm and comforting. But he'd consider those things in a few days. Today was today, and it'd take care of itself, with his help. He'd be in El Yunque a few minutes after he crossed the Highway 66 detour and then begin the next act of this play.

I can hardly wait.

As he surged into the passing lane, Anna's words came back to him, at least some of them, and, of course, she was right. He did look forward to this part. And why not? You can't make a cake without breaking some eggs. The thing is, he'd never enjoyed cake like this.

Fifteen minutes later, he turned at mile marker

191, wound through the village's narrow streets, and began his assent up the north side of the mountain. A bright-green iguana scurried across the uneven pavement, and he barely missed it. Maybe he shouldn't have. The population was going crazy, but that wasn't really their fault, was it? Man continued to scramble the delicate balance nature had managed to maintain for thousands of years. Experts, like him, were right: humans *were* the biggest threat to their very own extinction.

Rolling past the Visitors Center, he climbed toward his destination. The excitement nudged his mind, and he could hardly control his anticipation.

Cake.

Winding past Coco Falls, glancing at the stunning water-on-rock display, he drove a few more minutes, finally reaching the La Mina Trail. He parked on the east side of the road, facing north, heading back down the mountain. He left the keys on the floorboard and the door unlocked, slinging the backpack over his shoulder. This wouldn't take too long, unless he wanted it to.

As he reached the head of the four-by-four steps, the rainforest's sounds and smells embraced him like a lost lover. The birds talking in the green canopy and the waterfall's echo combined to form the most remarkable natural orchestra. But the hikers had ruined all of this for him, hadn't they?

Bad timing for my mother.

That's what the authorities had said, more than once: "Unfortunate, but there was no crime, just an accident, and you have our condolences."

Tell that to your mother, whispered the furious voice in his mind.

He swung down the steps, like he had a thousand

times before, but faster. Five minutes later, he heard what he was hoping to hear: voices. But not just any voices. If the paper had been accurate, there would be four members of San Juan's travel counsel camping in one of the small rest huts about forty yards away from the steps to the south. It was something they repeated every quarter, under the guise of showing the island their dedication to making things better.

"But they are making it worse," he whispered.

His hands clenched as he veered from the trail, honing in on the voices. A moment later, he saw one of them, half dressed and doing a sponge bath on his fat, sagging body. He'd seen women with smaller tits, much smaller.

Pulling the Katana from the sword sheath on the inside of his khakis, he moved quickly.

In another life, he might have known this man's name, but then again, in another life, he would have cared.

The world is your oyster, take it!

He did. The first swing of the blade connected just under the jaw as his target turned in his direction. There was a moment of recognition in his eyes, then it was gone, along with his head.

Moving on pure instinct, he reached the back of the small lean-to and saw two others. A moment later, ruffled sleeping bags were covered in lines of blood as the heads of dark-skinned man and the thin woman rested near the small fire pit, facing each other, but never seeing.

"Julio? Katrina? ¿Qué pasa?"

The thirty-something woman crept around the corner, wearing a look of caution and a red towel around her head.

She blinked at the carnage on the floor of the hut, then slowly raised her eyes in his direction. Her mouth had dropped open as in a ridiculous cartoon.

Too easy. Three strides later, just as she spoke his name, it was over. Her fate sealed, just as the others had been.

His heart rate was somewhere near two hundred, his body quivering with pure adrenaline. Each time had been better than the last, no denying that now. Better for his mistress, no doubt, but better for him too.

Closing his eyes, he relived everything in his mind's eye. The looks on their faces, the feel of the blade on flesh and bone, the smell of blood and rainforest as they mingled eternally.

The bulge in his slacks confirmed his state of mind. But as difficult as it was, that would have to wait this time. Survival was still the name of the game, and he had no time to waste.

Still . . .

Bringing out his camera, he recorded the scene for future indulgence.

Moments later, he wiped at the blood sprayed across his shirt, cleaned his sunglasses on the red towel, then finished making the murder scene his.

Six minutes later, after snapping a few more pictures, he was back on the trail.

He stopped at the edge of the steps, some ten feet below the entrance to the trail. He scanned the parking lot and the area leading to his SUV equipped with stolen plates. He saw no one. Then again, he hadn't expected to. It was still only seven fourteen a.m. and his island wasn't one for early risers, especially on the weekend.

Still, he used caution. He was too close to fail now.

Two minutes later, fresh shirt on his back and the Katana under the seat, he stepped into the vehicle and was driving down the mountain.

It was simply a matter of time before their bodies were discovered, and his plan could move forward. He looked at the clock on the dash and wondered if the SJPD and the Feds had gotten his gift.

Grinning, he thought they had.

CHAPTER-44

Manny waited in the lobby for Chloe and the others. It was still early, but he was up anyway, checking for messages.

Looking at the picture of Jen on his phone reminded him that he hadn't talked to his daughter since early yesterday, a rarity for them since Louise had died. He could count on his hand how often that had happened. Maybe it was a sign that they were moving forward. He hoped so. Maybe last night was too. He prayed moving forward didn't mean giving up the relationship Jen and he had developed.

He called, and her voicemail came on immediately. Her voice was sounding more like her mother's every day. He was okay with that, most days.

"Just checking in, honey. I love you. Call when you get some time. Oh yeah, no snow storm here. How does eighty-two degrees sound to you?" Then he laughed and clicked off the phone. Nothing like a jab to the young one once in a while.

His smile faded to a contented half-grin. She was a good kid. She'd be proud of him for not falling on his moral compass last night. Not that they'd talk about that anytime soon, but they would.

Last night. That had been close, far too close for a man who'd made promises to his daughter, and more importantly, to his God. Chloe had been the voice of reason. He loved her even more for it.

He'd left Chloe's room and come down to the desk to see if the hotel had been totally sold out, as the clerk had indicated. He had been in luck. The clerk, George, said it wasn't entirely true. They always held a bank of rooms aside in the event there was a problem. He said a rabid mongoose qualified.

Manny had gotten a few hours sleep—enough—and that's where the rubber hit the road.

Glancing at his phone again, he saw that he still had no responses from any of the five calls he'd made from Chloe's room. Disappointing, but it was still early, and he was hopeful.

Standing at the base of the double spiral stairs, he watched the other hotel guests head to the restaurant, guided by the enticing aroma swirling from the hot breakfast buffet. It caused his stomach to rumble. They hadn't really eaten since yesterday on the jet, and it suddenly struck him just how famished he really was.

Needing to get his mind off food until the others put in an appearance, he scanned the lobby for something to do. That's when he noticed the pretty young woman sitting at the concierge's desk, twirling her long, black, curly hair, studying the computer screen. He was struck with the thought that she could help him maybe. These folks always knew more about the local scene then he'd ever learn. It was worth a shot.

"Hello. I was wondering if you could help me?"

The young lady looked up, did a brief double take, and smiled one of those engaging grins that forces one to smile back.

"Well, helping is what I'm all about and, just for the

record, my name's Tina Martinez and I get off work at four."

"That's the best information I've had all morning," he smiled.

Pulling the page of the phone book from his pocket, he spread it out on her desk. "I need one of these and thought you'd know the best place to find one."

Tina's eyes got big and her grin bigger. "I guess this means you'll not be picking me up for dinner," she joked.

"Pretty and smart, a great combo. As nice as that sounds, you can see how hard that would be."

"I have a couple ideas that would help. Give me your phone number, and I'll call you when I have something. Are you going to need anything to go with this?"

"No, I think I have everything I need."

"Okay, then. I'll call you. And are you sure you don't want one—"

The elevator opened, and the rest of the BAU emerged, almost in unison. Dean brought up the rear.

"Let's eat," said Alex. "I'm starved."

The CSI didn't break stride, walked past Manny, and led the others directly into the restaurant.

"I saw you in your skivvies last night. I'm ordering your breakfast. Fruit, oatmeal, and coffee, decaf. That's it," said Sophie.

"Sounds good. That'll go great with the bacon, sausage, and eggs," said Alex.

Manny shook his head and looked back at the concierge. "That's my cue. Thanks, Tina. I appreciate your help."

Walking just behind Sophie, Chloe fell in step with him, looking a little tired, but ever so stunning.

"What were ya doing there?"

"Just passing some time waiting for you all."

Awkward wasn't usually part of his experience, but there it was. Manny bowed his head as he was rushed with a million memories from Chloe's room.

"Listen. About last night. I want to thank you—"

She put her finger on his lips, caressing them with her, soft touch. "You'll be thanking me soon enough, several times, I might add."

He let out a breath. "I hope I'm up for the challenge."

She grinned. "I'll help with that."

Looking directly in his eyes, she touched his hand. "Just so you know. I didn't look inside the phone book to see what you tore out. It was hard, ya know, but I did it. So are you going to tell me what you're up to?"

"Soon, Chloe, soon."

After they finished breakfast, they entered the lobby, and Manny noticed Detective Crouse, hands on hips, waiting for them. The look on her face was even more indicative of her mood.

"I hope you're all ready for a big day because, as of seven thirty-one this morning, it got bigger."

CHAPTER-45

"What the hell does that mean?" asked Josh.

Manny thought he knew. "Was there another package?"

Crouse raised her eyebrows, almost surprised that Manny had guessed, then nodded. "It was found on a bench in Ocean Park by one of the bike cops. It looked suspicious, and when he approached it, he saw it was addressed to Ruiz. But the officer had no idea where it had come from, and no one seems to have seen anything. We did a little canvassing of the area, without any luck, but we'll try some more when people are up."

They walked out the rotating front door and into the famous Caribbean sun.

Manny asked the question no one else really wanted to. "What was in it?"

"A foot, a left foot. They're not sure it's Anna's yet, but it probably is. The CSU's only had the box and the foot for about an hour. They'll give you what they have at the meeting."

"Does Carlos know?" asked Josh.

Bowing her head, she sighed. "No. He's under guard at his house so he'll behave and not get involved in the investigation. But someone will let him know. He's got a lot of friends."

Trying to grasp the thoughts making a circle dash

in his brain was next to impossible. What the hell did the killer expect to accomplish from this? A diversion? Divide and conquer? Neither seemed right. Again, why Anna? Every time the killer did this, it gave law enforcement a better chance to zero in on him—or maybe that's what he wanted them to think. Did doing this to Anna even have anything to do with the other murders this deranged pimple on society's ass had committed; even worse, was it starting to reveal what the unsub was truly about?

"Let's get you back to headquarters, and we can talk some more," said Crouse.

"I think not, especially now," said Josh, sounding like his old self.

"What?"

"We're not going back to the SJPD headquarters," said Josh.

Detective Crouse put her hands on her hips, standing at the front of the blue Chevy Traverse. The quick frown, followed by a momentary look of uncertainty, grabbed Manny's attention. No one likes being told what to do, especially by someone you don't like and who's not your boss. He understood that, who wouldn't? But the look puzzled him just the same. Almost as if she knew something they didn't.

"Why? We've got things set up for a briefing with our CSU people, and a group of our best detectives want to be involved in the brainstorming. Not to mention, you were going to offer up that famous BAU profile. You're here to save the damned day, remember?" said Crouse.

"We can still do that, after I get a list of all of the people you want to be involved in this investigation.

We'll run a background check, and if things look good, they'll be allowed into the meeting—at the FBI offices in Hato Rey."

"Background checks? Why?" She shifted her feet, her eyes turning dark, angry dark.

"Last night's little incident was not just some lucky guess by a scumbag drug dealer. No one knew where we were staying, except your office and mine. Standard operating procedure for the FBI. Then knowing which room Manny was supposed to be in took it up a notch further."

"Yeah, I heard about that this morning. So that makes you think someone from my office is in bed with Fogerty?"

No hiding her pissy mindset now, but that wasn't what really bothered Manny. The fact that Josh had put it together, and he hadn't really thought that way, made his stomach tighten. He ran his hand through his hair. It was right in front of him. Fogerty certainly had a contact in the hotel, but he'd missed the other connection, and it was obvious. Shit. He threw Chloe a side glance and let the truth slap him one more time. She was good for him in every way, except when they were on a case. No doubt about that now. Even that glance had changed how his thoughts were bouncing around in his brain.

Better get it together, Williams.

"I know it, Detective. This is a pisser of a case and we have no idea who, or what, we're dealing with, and I'm sure as hell not going to let a revenge-crazed asshole like Fogerty complicate things. I'm not going down this road with people that I don't trust, and frankly, could get us killed. So there's no debating my decision."

That infamous folding of the arms across her chest

came quickly, but he could see she'd resigned herself to the logic and the decision.

"So what's next?" Crouse asked, lips tight.

"You're going to drop us off at the Federal Building, go back to your office, get me the list of people that asked to be part of this investigation, including your CSU people, text or fax it to me, then we'll go from there. Any questions?"

Detective Crouse got into the front seat, gripped the top of the steering wheel with both hands, her long fingers turning white, and stared straight ahead.

Sophie nudged Manny as they climbed into the back of the SUV. "I think she needs a man, maybe worse than Mucus needs a woman," she whispered.

"That could be true, but I'm not offering my services."

"Yeah, that could be painful."

The others climbed in, Dean and Alex carrying their crime scene cases. Dean was toting a large brief case that Manny hadn't remembered seeing before.

After Crouse got the SUV in motion and turned onto the four-lane, Manny pointed at the case. "What's in that?"

"Oh, that," answered Alex. "It's our report information. I had it printed at headquarters last night, and Dean volunteered to carry it."

"Volunteered?" said Dean. "I was drafted."

"I guess your initiation is complete. Welcome to the party," said Josh.

"Let's see, a lunatic running around killing half the island with some kind of sword, body parts put together like some life-size puzzle, a mongoose with rabies, killed by Chinese throwing stars, and a possible security leak to a piece-of-shit drug lord: yep, I think that qualifies as a party. I guess I should say thanks. So thanks for the invite," smiled Dean.

Manny wondered if Dean would feel the same when this one was over. Hell, would any of them feel like that when this was over, and would they all make it through? That train of thought made him think past nervous. A quote he read a long time ago came rushing back.

No war worth fighting is without sacrifice.

Shoving it away, it decided to stay.

CHAPTER-46

"Your services have proven to be invaluable. There'll be a little more in the envelope next month."

Fogerty pressed the disconnect button on the pay-as-you-go phone and tossed it on the lush leather seat.

"Dey go som place else, boss?" asked Braxton. "Like de Feder-ral buildin?"

"Very astute, my friend, very astute. Possibly they put together that we had a little inside help locating the Feds' hotel."

"Dat, or maybe dey be more comfortable in der."

"Perhaps. But contrary to what some folks think, the FBI is not an organization riddled with idiots. Most of them can add two plus two. I think someone came up with four. They also know that there wasn't any real danger of Williams dying, just inflicting some pain, and at the very least, scare his pretty-boy ass."

"Yeah, dat's true, but dat little vixen, Lee, got our message, not him."

Stroking his chin, Fogerty nodded. "They, no doubt, think I had something to do with it. There's no way to prove it, but they'll be trying."

"Already sent one of da boys to take care of dat little problem. He won't be reportin' ta work at da hotel tonight. It'll be a heart attack dat da doctors will tink happened."

He smiled. "When was the last time I gave you a raise? You're always on top of these situations."

Braxton's bold, white smile broadened across his face. "I don't do dis for da money, boss. Besides, you pay me too good already, and da benafeet package is perfect, ya know?" Then he threw back his head and laughed. A gesture, no matter how many times Fogerty watched him do it, made him ever so slightly nervous. There was an extremely fine line between what Braxton was good at and insanity, very fine. But he supposed they could say that about him, as well. In the end, wasn't everyone insane? Everyone crazy-stupid for something?

If the Feds were right, and he was starting to think maybe they were, and this wasn't a hit message aimed at his little girl and her dumb shit husband and ultimately him, then their killer was a prime example of someone who'd gone deep and would never come up.

Crazy is as crazy does.

"We'll give them a few minutes to get to the FBI offices, then wait for them. I suspect we'll need another vehicle. This one could be starting to be recognizable."

"I'll get one of dos big SUVs."

After a moment, he held up two fingers. "Get two. If they stick with what they do, they'll probably go in at least two different directions trying to follow up on any leads, whatever those are, and we don't want to be on the outside looking in. Hopefully, our contact won't allow that, but one never knows."

A moment later, the phone he'd tossed on the seat began to vibrate. He picked it up and read the text, then calmly put the phone in his pocket.

Braxton nodded. "Any ting else?"

"Just one, for now. Which one of our people made

the contact at the test lab?"

Braxton pointed to the large man riding shotgun in the front seat. "Domingo."

"What a coincidence. Just the man I wanted to speak with. Open the soundproof partition; I want to thank him personally."

Braxton fidgeted, blinked twice, then did what he was told.

Fogerty left his seat and moved to the one facing the rear, directly behind Domingo. He then tapped him on the shoulder.

Turning in Fogerty's direction, he smiled. "Yes sir?"

"Good job last night, Domingo."

"Tank you sir. Dat's what you pay me for."

"Indeed. Do you have a family, Domingo?"

"I do. Wife and two kiddies."

"Extra money in your pay would help, yes?"

"Mr. Fogerty, I—"

"No need to thank me. You earned it, and this."

In one motion, he grabbed Domingo's neck and with a seemingly harmless flip of his hands, snapped the C1 and C2 vertebrae. The loud crack said so. The big man shivered, then slumped against the door, eyes open.

He tapped the driver on the shoulder. "After you find a place to dump this son of a bitch, let's get a couple of different vehicles, shall we?"

Then he settled back in his seat and drew on his cup of vanilla latte.

Braxton whispered something to the wide-eyed driver. He put the car in gear and moved into the street.

"Boss?"

"I'll tell you more later, and there will be some heat, but it appears that Domingo, with his wife and two kiddies, wasn't exactly what he said he was."

A look of apprehension crossed Braxton's face as he glanced at the floor, then back to Fogerty.

He waved his hand to dismiss Braxton's concerns.

"I know you hired him. We'll have to review that process when the time is right, but those mistakes are the kind that can ruin us all, maybe worse."

Braxton nodded, more fear than anxiety creeping into his bloodshot eyes.

He would deal with that later, but right now he needed his number one on his game.

He leaned forward, putting his hand on Braxton's knee. "If I were going to dismiss you, my friend, you'd be dead already, yes?"

"I tink dat'd be true."

"All right then. Let's get to what we need to get to."

There was a quick smile. "I be sorry, boss. I tought he was a good mon for us."

"I know. We'll talk about how the DEA was able to get him into our camp soon enough."

And you'll have plenty of time to be sorry, my ebony giant. Plenty of time.

CHAPTER-47

"Get some more of this coffee, will you?" asked Sophie, batting her eyes at Josh, and rattling her cup on the oak conference table in the FBI's third-floor conference room.

The infectious grin that Josh flashed, the one that had become a bit of a trademark for him, made Manny smile too. Something had changed in the last ten hours, and he was looking forward to finding out what.

"It is pretty good stuff, isn't it? I'll send for some when the pot's empty."

"That won't be long the way Mucus is draining it."

"It's Mikus, Agent. Mikus." said Dean patiently.

"Whatever, just save some for the rest of us."

Fingering the file and the stack of reports in front of him, Manny felt his smile fade. Josh's next statement didn't help to resolve the churning in his gut either.

"Coffee issues aside, we need to get to work. It doesn't look like this perp sleeps much and he's busy, and yes, I do agree with Dean. This; is definitely a man," said Josh.

"You're probably right, at least statistically speaking, ya know? But what makes you so sure?" asked Chloe.

"Manny said so," grinned Josh.

Sophie snorted a laugh, coffee spraying from her

mouth and nose. "Well, that works for me, but care to share why you think that?" she coughed.

Chloe's eyes came alive as she scanned his face. "You're the best I've seen, but I gotta go with Sophie on this one."

"Fair enough," said Manny. "And for the record, Dean put most of the logic to it."

"Dean! Maybe you'll get to stay after all," said Sophie, winking at the CSI.

Dean blushed, fidgeted with his hands, and nodded. "That'd make my day, maybe my life, Princess."

"Did you hear that, Dough Boy? I love this guy."

"Anyway, Dean had mentioned the force it would take to do what this perp did, plus the intricate purposes for each cut. Not typical for a woman serial killer, but still not out of the question. The required training for a woman to accomplish this would be at the very least, an anomaly."

"Yeah, but say it was someone like me," said Sophie. "I've had training from my dad and brother for over fifteen years."

"That's true, but the last part of this has to do with a bit of evidence found in the morgue."

"Evidence? What evidence?" asked Chloe.

"The footprint in the blood at the mortuary was ten and one-half, 3E, in a man's shoe."

"How did you know that?" frowned Sophie.

"I'll answer that," said Josh. "Manny pointed it out at the crime scene, and the SJPD's CSU took it from there because Alex and Dean were going to have their hands full. They accessed the TreadMark database, it has about twelve-thousand shoe types and treads, and they sent me an email showing me what they found."

"Damn, I forgot about that one. Can I get access to that? You know, for shoe-shopping purposes?"

"Shopping? Really?" asked Josh.

"Just messing with you."

She looked at Manny. "Is that why you were in your own little world, again, studying the blood streaks across the floor?"

"Partially. I'll get into that in a minute, but we need to go over Alex and Dean's report, plus the other files from the SJPD, and then—"

"I know, you need to have some alone time with them," said Alex.

Manny sighed. How many times had he done just that? Countless occasions he listened as the dead spoke, or at least tried, and watched the evidence make enormous efforts to conceal itself. It struck him as a classic battle for control. The dead knew the truth, and the elusive evidence wanted to keep it hidden.

"That depends on what we can figure out this morning. I think we've got good old-fashioned leg work to consider first."

"Manny's right, but let's take a quick look at what Alex and Dean came up with. Then we can talk about it."

A few minutes later, Sophie stood up, walked over to Alex, kissed him on the balding area above his forehead, and sat back down.

"What the hell was that for and do I need to know about any diseases?"

"Great first report. I can actually understand half of the words, and I got rid of that one rash thing a few weeks ago, so I'm good to go."

"Thanks, I think."

"You're welcome, I think."

Alex stood at the table and adjusted his glasses. "Okay. Let me go over this so we're not wasting time. Most of the info here you already know about and saw firsthand so I don't have to go over the body-part display and the crime-scene generalities. Just the juicy parts that might lead to something."

"First thing is to send traces of the nitro we found inside the head and mouth of the vic to the lab. Like I said before, lots of those chemicals have genetic markers that might ID where it came from. We've also sent every hair, stray tissue, and all of the clothing from the victims, including the morgue tech, to the lab, along with all of the out-of-place material we bagged, to have analyzed ASAP. All pretty routine, but sometimes routine makes a big leap for us. One of the FRTs is taking pictures of every tire on every vehicle and any possible tracks within a two block radius to run through Tread-Mate. I know, lots of shots in the dark here, but maybe something will come up in more than one of those searches and give us something to go on."

"Dean and I also went over every severed limb, noting age, gender, and even severity of injury compared to the others. If the time frames are right, as a side note, he seemed to be getting more aggressive with the later victims because the cuts were smoother, more precise, like he had more confidence."

"We're in touch with SJPD's work regarding both boxes and Anna Ruiz's severed limbs. They're working as fast as they can to nail something down, but they have no idea who put the second box on the bench and, except for the blood and the foot, the rest of the box seems clean. Still, they'll go over the print-pattern on the box and see if that shakes anything loose. They are sure it was the same printer for both boxes, so maybe that'll lead to a manufacturer ID, but my guess is that it'll be a printer that anyone can buy at any department store."

Making a few notes, Manny leafed through several more pictures, then, holding his finger in one place, he went back to another picture of the man killed in the Britton Tower.

"I know you haven't gotten there yet, but was everyone attacked by the same weapon?" asked Manny.

Shaking his head, Alex grinned. "You're on track. It apparently is so. Just like in Miami, when you discovered that Chief Richardson's cuts had been inconsistent, thus two killers, we compared the cut patterns with samples of all of the victims under the microscope and discovered a true consistency with the edge patterns. Definitely the same weapon, but that's not all. We'll let you know on the other reports, especially if we get a cross-match hit with CODIS or ChemFinder, but we had one test put to the top of the list."

"What was that?" asked Sophie.

"Look on page six of Dean's report. Right under the blood splatter info."

Manny let out a low whistle. "You got a sample of the metal from the weapon?"

"Yep. Alex found it, but I had to take it out. His hands aren't that steady. Getting old," grinned Dean.

"Bullshit. I was just tired," said Alex, returning the smile. "Anyway, we rushed that metal analysis and got some preliminary information that's not in your files. Judging by the number of folds and the way the metal was processed, it appears to be from a very old sword, maybe German, like a rapier, but since the FBI doesn't have such a person, we need to get a real expert to take a look at it. So I had them send the sample results to one of my old buddies at the University of Michigan, who not only is a mineral and metal expert, but just happens to be an old sword and knife freak. I think that's why he went into that field; he loves the old weapon shit more than his real job. We should know something today, as long as he's in."

The room grew quiet. Manny suspected each one of them was focused on the implications of Alex's discovery. He was.

"So what does that mean to us?" asked Chloe.

"It means leg work, like I said," said Manny. "An old sword has a ton of inferences. All the way from collector to slightly deranged enthusiast."

"What do you want to do?" quizzed Josh.

"The way I see it, we've got three things to check out, pronto. A good place to start with the sword angle is any fencing clubs on the island. If this guy is an expert, and a collector, then maybe someone will be able to help put a profile with a name. And given his penchant for being bold, he just might stick out as an arrogant asshole. We also need to check out the crime scenes in the rainforest, just to see what we can see."

"Sounds like a good approach," said Josh. "What's the third thing?"

"As long as Fogerty's decided to throw his scumbag ass into the mix, we need to check out any animal, or disease research labs in the area and see if we can nail down where that mongoose came from and who might have gotten it to the hotel. If we can nail him for that, it gets him off the streets and out of our hair, at least until some bribed official lets him out. Which brings us to the next point. There are six of us, so teams of two works, but we should have a local with us. Did you get that info from Crouse?"

Josh shook his head. "Not yet. But when she sends the list, it won't take long to go over it. It seems this office anticipated my request and has pulled all of the background checks, including bank account numbers, for the detectives and their bosses, all of them."

"Done it before?" asked Manny.

"Apparently."

"We can't wait all day for that, so maybe we'll have to handle this on our own," said Manny. "I want the rainforest crime scenes. Maybe something will talk to me."

"I'll take the fencing club angle," said Sophie. "I know a little about the moves and positions for fencing, and some of those guys have great asses."

"I'll go with her to keep her out of trouble. Also the men in those clubs may not want to talk to a woman, and any women might feel more comfortable talking to her, great asses aside," said Josh.

"That'll be fun," said Sophie.

"I'll take the lab assignment," said Chloe. "I hate those damned places anyway so maybe we'll find something to shut one or two down."

"I know you'll probably want to take Alex to the rainforest; I would. So I'll go with Agent Franson. I hate those research pricks too," volunteered Dean.

"Okay. Before we go talk to the information officer and see if she has information on any fencing clubs and any research facilities, we have one thing to finish," said Josh.

Handing him a piece of paper, Manny stood and

ran his hand through his hair. "This is the profile for this unsub, as I see it."

Studying the paper, he glanced quickly to Manny. "Are you sure about this?"

"As sure as I can be. He's not like Argyle, or even that damned Murder Club. I think he's got a bigger agenda."

"Read it to them."

Releasing a breath, Manny nodded. "This guy is a white male and a little older, probably in his thirties. He's obviously very bright, but I think past just bright. He's brilliant, could be an academic. He's not afraid of anything, but cautious, when he needs to be. Certainly an opportunist, like most of these men are. He'll use whatever he can to his advantage. The thing about this one is that he has the ability to take that opportunity to a level that fits his plans. Not just a momentary sense of satisfaction, but he'll use it to enhance his circumstance. I think that's where the game kicked in for him."

"What the hell does that mean?" asked Alex.

"I think Anna was a situation he wasn't counting on, but instead of just killing her, he's used her to expand the premises of his goals—sort of like evolving and devolving at the same time."

"Good God, Williams. You're making my head spin again," said Sophie, "but I think I get it. Kind of like playing chess a certain way, then your opponent makes a move you didn't anticipate, and you go another direction."

"That's it. Same goal, but different decisions along the way."

"Makes sense," said Dean.

"He's single. Lives alone, and had a trigger event in

the last three to five months. I don't think he's typical in the sense that he tried out his fantasies, then dove into them full bore. He decided, maybe based on that trigger event, that he needed to go to work right away. So he did."

"I also think he knows the rainforest like the back of his hand and, like we discussed, knows the business end of a sword almost as well. He's arrogant, but not haughty, at least in public. I can't get a bead on his sexual appetite because I don't think that was a thought when he started. But given his progressive enthusiasm, he's getting off on this, and in more than one way."

Frowning, Chloe twisted in her chair. "You didn't mention why the sword. Could it be that's some kind of sexual representation for him, maybe even subconsciously?"

"That's a great point and it may explain why he could be a collector or a member of one of these clubs, but I think it says something else."

Josh shifted his weight nervously. "That's why you wrote the last line?"

"It is."

"What last line?" asked Chloe.

"I think this guy would do anything to reach his intended goal. Adding in the fact that he's enjoying the killing and the game."

"Define anything," said Alex.

"I think if he doesn't get what he wants, whatever in God's name that is, and very soon, he's going to pop his last thread of decency and state his case by killing a lot of people all at once."

CHAPTER-48

"Who knew? I mean I followed a couple fencing competitions in the Olympics when I was taking lessons as a kid, but a Puerto Rican organization for fencing?" said Sophie.

She glanced over at Josh, whose knuckles were turning white, gripping the handle above the passenger's door, and grinned. "What's the matter with you, Corner, don't you trust me anymore?"

"It's not that. It's just taking me longer to remember how damn crazy you are behind the wheel."

"I prefer the term necessary aggression."

At that moment, a rambunctious cab cut her off. Sophie swung to the right, cut between a Mercedes and an SUV, and pulled up beside the cab, rolled down her window, and yelled. "Hey! Hombre! Watch what the hell you're doing." Then she flipped him off.

The cabbie gave her a lazy glance, smiled, and returned her gesture.

"I should pull him over and kick the shit out him, just out of principle."

"I'm glad you've whipped the road rage thing. Damn. How fast are you going?"

"Hey, no one likes a smartass . . . and only about eighty."

"The speed limit is fifty-five and you just left a

forty-five. That old saying that it's me, not you, might apply here," smiled Josh.

"Maybe, but I've never had an accident and no one else could get us to that blue-nose fencing club faster than me, right? Besides, cabbies need to be taught who in the hell runs the road: me."

"Okay then. Do you feel better?"

"Come to think of it, I do. Really good."

She hit the accelerator again and watched the speedometer creep toward ninety.

"The exit is just up there, the one that says State, you better—"

Darting back to the right, she cut in front of another SUV, hammered the brakes, turned through the next lane, exited the ramp, hit the brakes again, skidded to the left, spun the wheel into the skid, then cramped the truck right. The Traverse shuddered, did what it was told, and saddled up between the other occupied two lanes, lined up perfectly in the middle lane.

"Hey, Hoss, you can breathe now."

"That's what you think," whispered Josh.

"I told you I had this."

Exhaling, he released the handle. "You did. I still don't know how we're not buried under five thousand pounds of SUV."

"Manny says it's because God looks out for fools and drunks, and I don't drink too much, so . . ."

"He is a wise man. And you're a helluva driver: scary, but good."

"Thanks, and not just for that, but for taking a chance on me. I still don't know how to deal with some of the shit in my past lives, but I can do this agent gig."

She felt the warmth as he put his hand on her

shoulder. "Sophie. As much as I have grown to care for you and Manny, and as much total as crap he's gone through, I didn't do it for either of you. I wouldn't have let the Bureau bring you on if I didn't think that you could do it. Your attitude doesn't always fly with some of the situations we get into, but I'll take it over the agents who don't care and just want to put in their time and go home. So, you're here because you can be a good agent. I pay attention. Some of the questions you've asked have led to the next step in our investigations. As good as Manny and the rest of this unit are, no one thinks of everything."

Gratitude and Sophie weren't always on the best of terms, but they were kissy-facing right now. It felt good to be thought of as important.

"It wasn't because of my new boobs then?"

Laughing, Josh shook his head. "Well, maybe a little, but you didn't hear it from me."

It was her turn to laugh. "Then if I do that butt enhancement surgery, I should get your job in a couple of years."

"Let's not get carried away. God knows I wish I knew what was going to happen with all of that job mess. But we can talk about that later; we're here."

Sophie pulled in front of the flat, stucco-designed building common to San Juan and parked in the handicapped space to the left of the door.

"What are you doing?"

"Parking. How many handicapped fencers do you know?"

He shrugged. "Good point."

They entered the building, Sophie taking the lead. After getting inside, they stood in the tiled foyer, and she bent her ear toward the sounds coming from the back of the building. The clash of metal caused by foils and épées in fervent battle flooded her with memories of the school in San Francisco that she had attended back in the mid-nineties. It was where she learned about handling such weapons. And for a change, those memories didn't haunt her, but lent nostalgic excitement—one of the few commands her father had made that she didn't rebel against.

Josh touched her elbow. "You okay?"

"Yep. Just remembering how much I liked the club where I learned to flash the steel."

"Any good at it?"

"Hell yeah. Won the club championship my last year there."

"Last year?"

"Long story, but I beat a boy who everyone thought was going to be some Olympic champion. He didn't like it that a little Asian girl whipped his butt so, after the match, he pushed me a couple of times, and I decked him. They tossed me, but that was okay. I was ready to move on."

"Can't figure out why that anger part of your psych exam didn't throw up red flags," he grinned.

"Playing the game, just playing the game," she said. *And who knew that better than her?*

Just then, a short, svelte woman with long, black hair appeared from the office door behind the half-moon counter and smiled. "May I help you?"

"All yours, Princess," said Josh. She glanced at his face and saw encouragement and confidence in those blue eyes. She felt nervous, then didn't.

She flashed her ID and went to work. "We're from

the FBI, and we have some questions for the owner."

The warm reception grew cooler.

"Doctor Donald Flores, But Doctor Flores is busy with a class." Her low voice was heavy with Latino accent. "Can I tell him what this is about?"

"Yes. You can. It's about seven murders."

Her mouth dropped open as her eyes widened. "You mean the ones in the rainforest? I read of them in the paper this morning. You think—?"

"Just go get him. Like I said, we have some questions."

The receptionist recovered her composure. "That class will be over in about ten minutes. Would you care to go watch the end of it and then speak to Mr. Flores?"

She shifted her feet and considered walking back to the back and pulling him out of the class, then remembered something Manny always talked about. Give and take. Give a little and take a lot. That man knew his shit.

"Okay. Deal. Take us back, and we'll wait."

She led them through a hallway smelling like mold and sweat as Josh moved beside her and whispered. "Good control. Good call."

There was that damn gratitude thing again. She could get used to it.

"I freaking hope so."

They entered the wide, metal door escaping to a mid-sized gymnasium. About twenty-five feet to her right stood a tall, thin man in his forties dressed in fencing white with his mesh mask under his arm talking quietly to a group of ten- or eleven-year-old kids, maybe twenty of them. She quickly noticed there were only four girls in the group. Some things never change.

A few minutes later, he demonstrated a touché move that Baryshnikov would have been proud of, spoke to them again, and then dismissed the class.

The receptionist strode over and spoke to him. He frowned, then nodded, handing her his foil and mask, and approached Sophie and Josh. His stride was confident and probably held the blue-blood mentality that sometimes permeated sports like fencing.

"Good morning, agents. I'm Donald Flores, owner of this establishment and head instructor."

He carried an American accent, definitely not Puerto Rican born and raised. Midwest maybe.

"I'm Agent Lee, and this is Agent Corner. That was an impressive move at the end of your class."

He raised his thick eyebrows, making his brown eyes seem smaller than they were. He definitely had a charm and a sense of who he was.

"Do you know this leisure pursuit, Agent?"

"I do, or at least did. I was no Mirtheska Escanellas, but I didn't hurt myself either."

"Ah. You know of our Olympian. But I suspect you aren't here to discuss the highlights of Puerto Rican fencing."

Flores shifted his feet, and Sophie made a mental note of his nervousness. It could be nothing because most people get nervous when they talk to the Feds.

"You're right. We have questions regarding murders in the rainforest."

"Yes. I saw the paper this morning. But they didn't really go into much detail on how the people died."

"We didn't release much information," said Josh.

Dr. Flores nodded, his thin lips keeping a straight line.

"Okay. Let's get to it. The people murdered in El Yunque were butchered, Mr. Flores. Someone used a sword, apparently an old one, and had a slash-and-dash party."

"Oh my," he answered. "That's awful."

"It is. So you understand why we're here?"

"Yes."

"I'll be blunt."

"I can see you're good at that, Agent Lee," he smiled.

"This person is accomplished at the game, as you call it. They're in good shape, bright, and may have a hobby for collecting old swords. Do you know anyone like that, Mr. Flores?"

He shrugged. "Well, yes. Half of the male members in this club could fit that description."

"I didn't say male, I said 'person'. Why did you assume the killer's male?"

Flores never hesitated. "It was just that, Agent Lee, an assumption. We don't have many female adult members, so if your suspect is female, that would narrow the search."

"And ..."

"And I teach criminal justice at the University down the street. I know about percentages and profiles, that's all."

"Interesting. So you'd be familiar with forensic processes?" asked Sophie.

"I also know how to apply counter-forensic measures," he added. "But since I just got back from the States about two this morning. I'm not your guy."

"Fair enough, and of course, you won't mind if we check that out."

"Not at all. See Rachel on the way out, and she'll give you my itinerary for the last three days."

"Thank you, we will. Mr. Flores, who is your current club champion?"

"The open club champion is Dr. Royce Major. He also teaches at the University. But he's not really the sword collector that some of the others are. He loves the competions, and he regularly beats me, especially with a saber in his hand."

"Anyone else that might fit that profile?"

"Like I said, there are several who could. I'll have Rachel get you a list of members who fit that bill, if you think that would help."

"What? Not asking for a subpoena?"

"Heavens, no. I—we've nothing to hide, as far as I know. These are all upstanding men. If they're not, then I don't want them here anyway."

"Anyone here get real pissy when they lose a match, or at least frustrated?"

He opened his hands. "There is always a high level of energy in practice and the weekly matches. So again, I'd say that's most of us."

Sophie moved closer to Flores, looking up to the man eight inches taller than her. She scowled. "Listen, Flores. I don't give a shit about club politics or how much money any of these people pay to keep this dive in the black, but you're not telling me everything I want to know. So, one more time: who are the hot heads that come here and swing swords at the other members? Now."

His eyes darted at the floor, then back to Sophie. "There are two men who hate one another and get 'pissy' as you say when they lose to each other, and to anyone else, for that matter. Charles Johnson and Dr. David Collins. I've had to suspend both of them at least twice, and they are on probation and unable to participate in any events regarding Puerto Rico's Fencing Federation sponsorship. Their information will be on the list we'll provide. Now, if you're done, I have another class."

"For now, and don't leave the island. We may want to talk again," said Sophie.

He nodded, smiled, and turned back to the gathering class.

"I'll get the list from Rachel, you get the ride. We still have another club to visit," said Josh.

Flores stopped and moved back to them. "That one closed last week and most of the members transferred here. But you can check with Rachel on that too. I had part ownership, and we decided to put all of our resources here."

"Kind of convenient," said Sophie.

"Actually, it wasn't. It was quite inconvenient. Closing a business isn't good for anyone."

"Thanks again," answered Sophie.

Watching him walk away, she wondered if she'd asked all the right questions. She saw Manny's face and wondered what he'd do, then it hit her.

"Mr. Flores? I have one more question."

She met him halfway. "Is there someone, a member that recently had a tragedy in their lives? Lost a job, divorce, death of a loved one?"

"Not many divorces. Wait. One of our members lost his mother in a tragic accident in the rainforest four months ago."

"Did his behavior change? Like from outgoing to

Mr. Lonely?"

"He was always pretty much to himself, but come to think of it, he got into a shouting match with one of our members over the price of an ancient Japanese Katana. That was about three weeks ago, and he's not been in since."

Josh came up beside her, wielding several pages of printed paper.

"He's close enough. What's his name?"

"He can't be your man. He's world renowned for his environmental research and an absolute pillar in the academic community."

Josh's phone rang. He looked at the display, rolled his eyes, and handed the papers to Sophie as he moved away. She didn't like the look on his face.

She turned back to Flores. "The name?"

Exhaling, he tapped the paper in her hand with a long finger. "He's the first one on the list, Samuel Crouse. His ex-wife is a detective, I believe."

CHAPTER-49

He tossed the smoldering cigarette onto the warm sidewalk and flipped the next page of the paper as he leaned against the squat palm tree, all the while never taking his eyes from the security entrance of the Federal Building.

He'd watched the Asian bitch and her pretty boy boss leave, but that wasn't why he was here, was it?

Watching the Irish tart leave with the stupid-looking LA boy had got to him a little and he wondered if it would have been the right time to start this journey, but decided against it. The grand prize hadn't made an appearance, and that's why he'd come to San Juan—to see firsthand the object of his attention, then destroy him, in every way possible.

Karma, Agent. Karma.

The door swung out, and two men stepped through it. The first was the overweight CSI; the second, well, the second was the mother lode.

He watched as Manny Williams clapped Alex Downs on the back and then climbed into the white SUV.

"So good to see you, Agent. So good to see you," he whispered, unable to wipe the smile from his face, and caring to even less.

CHAPTER-50

"This sure beats the hell out of Michigan in January, even if we are chasing after some deranged prick who may have a big project on his agenda," said Alex.

Manny watched as Alex held his face out of the window, reminiscent of his big, black Lab, Sampson, on a summer day. Funny. He hadn't thought that much about it, but living in this climate could most certainly taint the place that he called home. Lansing was a good area to live, but warm wasn't on its resume.

"Good point. But there's the whole hurricane season."

"Yep. There is, but life's full of tradeoffs. Freeze ass nine months or stay warm and meet an oversized rainstorm once in a while,"

Just then, a police cruiser, lights flashing, honked. As Manny pulled over, the cruiser zoomed past as fast as a vehicle could zoom on the winding road. He frowned.

What the hell was that?

Before he could speak, two more came around the bend, sirens blaring, blasting by on his left.

"Shit," whispered Manny.

"Shit what? Oh, man."

The sweet sound of Celtic Woman's rendition of one of his favorite Irish ballads told him his phone was open for business. He pulled it out of his pocket and saw that Detective Crouse was calling.

"Hello?"

"Agent. We've got—"Then she was gone. The bars on his phone explained why. Damned dropped calls. Even though the rainforest was remote, he'd noticed several towers on the way in.

"That was Detective Crouse, and I lost the call."

A second later, Nat King Cole was singing one of his all-time greats as Alex's phone came alive.

"You're the one taking those CDs out of Gavin's office, aren't you?"

"Hey, he was one of the best ever, and I always put them back. And you should talk. Celtic music isn't exactly mainstream."

"Yeah, but they're hot and talented; and Chloe loves them too. Better answer that."

"It's Crouse."

"Downs here."

"What? You're breaking up. . ."

Alex listened for a few more seconds and swore. The resignation scribbled on his face said that he was hearing her loud and clear.

"We'll be there in a few minutes, hustle ass and bring at least one more of your CSU teams. I'll see if we can get another from the office. Okay. I'll tell him," said Alex

The CSI dropped his phone in his lap, shaking his head. The small beads of sweat on his forehead and lip sprayed in both directions.

"How many, this time?"

"Four. They were members of some tourist committee for San Juan."

"How bad?" asked Manny, running his hand

through his hair.

"Let's just say you were right; he's gone on to a new creepy high. He decapitated all four of them, then lined up the bodies and switched heads with them."

This shit was getting old. "I suppose it's worse than I can imagine?"

"I'd say that's right."

"Where?"

"Off that La Mina path thing that leads to some waterfalls."

"Do Josh and the others know?"

He nodded. "Josh told her to call us since we were already here, and they'll be showing up as soon as possible."

Manny hit the lights and gas pedal. For the second time on this case, his mind was grasping at the killer's intent. The actions in the morgue were gruesome, yet there was symmetry to the display, and he expected nothing less at this one. He was also taken aback by the closeness of the attacks. He knew this killer was accelerating his agenda, but even Argyle didn't do it this quickly.

The uneasy feeling that this killer was up to something big gnawed at Manny's gut. But what? And that was the million dollar question, wasn't it? They'd better find out, or things would never be the same in Puerto Rico, of that he *was* sure.

They pulled around the sharp curb and Manny hit the brakes. The road was blocked by two cruisers and a small orange barricade between them that said POLICE.

Steering to the side of the uneven, dirt parking area, they got out. Alex's forensic kit in hand, they showed their credentials and moved down the steps.

They finally reached the juncture in the trail leading to the small, faded hut already taped off with the obligatory yellow, crime-scene plastic.

As he got closer, he noticed that the four blues, one posted on each side of the tape, were facing away from the carnage inside.

Fewer nightmares that way.

One of them crossed himself and seemed to be praying. A moment later, Manny knew why. He heard Alex gasp beside him. Manny bit his lip and bent his head to El Yunque's lush canopy. He closed his eyes reaching for that famous, or maybe infamous, cop mode that caused everything emotional to leave and be replaced with a *Just the Facts* mindset. It wasn't going to be that easy.

The rainforest was eerily quiet, except for the eternal rush of water to La Mina falls. The sound seemed out of place and the dichotomy was too ironic not to notice. Death and beauty had always existed side by side, and even tolerated one another. Between them, they represented almost every facet of life, but this was an extreme capturing of both ends of the spectrum. The place that he and Alex stood and the horrifying scene in front of them said so.

Releasing a breath, Alex snapped on his gloves, handed Manny a pair, and ducked under the tape. Manny waited another moment, took several mental notes, and then followed his friend into hell.

CHAPTER-51

Sophie and Josh left Flores's fencing club, stepped into the heat of San Juan's late morning, then quickly sought shelter in the SUV's air conditioned interior.

Sophie swung out into the traffic. "What's first?"

"Let's drop this list off to the office and get our butts up to the rainforest," said Josh.

"You're the boss. Ah, how bad is it?"

The trepidation in Sophie's voice echoed his own.

"Bad. I've called Chloe, and they're going to meet us at the Federal Building."

"I know it's kind of low on the totem pole, but did they find out anything on that damned mongoose?"

"They hit two of the three labs. One was closed, and the others had a few employees off because it was Saturday so that might have to wait. But I want to find a link between that drug-pushing creep and that little critter gift in your room, so we'll get some of the other agents involved."

It'd been some time since Josh's mind had operated like this. Too many pans in the fire and not nearly enough cooks, as usual. But then again, these situations came with the territory—always had. He did have a few advantages that most of the other unit leaders didn't. He glanced at Sophie and smiled.

"What? You looking at my boobs?"

"Tempting as that is, not this time. I was just thinking how lucky this BAU is to have who we have. Not every specialty unit at the Bureau can say that. In fact, none of them can."

"Manny?"

"Yeah. I know I keep saying this, but I've not seen a profiler like him, even with all of the distractions over the last two years. Not to mention, he knows how to get to the heart of a problem. His talk with me was vintage."

"Oh, tell me about those talks."

"But he's not the only one. This team is a true team, and that's hard to find."

"That whole 'work together' thing is still a little weird to me. Never been part of a real team until I joined up with Manny. All of that loyalty and patience crap, he's strange that way. I tolerate it just to humor the boy."

This time he laughed out loud. "That's so good of you."

Sophie turned onto the exit leading to the Federal Building as he squeezed the list Flores had given them. He felt the answer was here, or part of it, then he shook his head. That "feeling" world belonged to Manny, but every now and then...

"Good job with the questioning in there. What made you ask the last one?"

"When Manny and I would talk about profiles, it seemed like all of the real psychos flew under the radar. There are some exceptions, like Gacy. Manny, and my Mom, always said to look out for the quiet ones. They're both right, so it seemed a question that needed a little love."

"What do you think about him? Samuel Crouse, I mean," he asked, watching her face.

"I think it's damn weird that he's Crouse's ex for one thing. We need to get the lowdown from her. Being married to her might mean he's got some knowledge about how cops do what they do."

"True."

"He also fits, at least in part, some of the profile Manny put together, so he's a good place to start. He might not be any more of a suspect than any of the other assholes on that list, but the 'keep to yourself' bit and arguing about the price of a sword, puts him at the top, in my book."

"You're right."

"I am? I mean, I am," she said, grinning.

Gliding the SUV to the security gate, Sophie drove to the front of the building. Josh got out and handed the stack of papers to the agent he'd called to meet him.

"I want background checks on everyone on this list, starting with Samuel Crouse and the owner of the fencing clubs, Flores. I want to know everything you can find out about them. And I want a list of sword dealers from every damned corner of the globe, including what any of those people sold and to whom over the last three years."

"Yes, sir."

He started to walk away, but turned back to the agent. "I need one more thing."

Josh told him what he needed.

The agent looked puzzled and shrugged. "Okay. That's weird, but okay."

"It is, but something tells me Special Agent Williams will want that information."

"What would Manny want?" asked Sophie.

"If any of them owned an animal research lab."

"Good one. He would want to know."

A moment later, Chloe and Dean emerged from the building.

"How'd it go at the fencing clubs?" asked Chloe.

"Not bad. We'll fill you in on the way to El Yunque."

"Yeah, can't wait to see that mess," she shivered.

Dean and Chloe climbed into the backseat and Josh noticed, with some amusement, that Dean had gotten into the passenger side. It lent a better look in Sophie's direction. The man was gone, for sure.

As the vehicle left the circle driveway, Sophie pointed to a man sprinting across the median from Carlos Chardon Avenue. He jumped the yellow curb and was running directly at them.

"What the hell's going on with him?"

Josh watched the picture unfold in front of them as three more men came into view, running after the first man, two of them had weapons pulled and were yelling.

"Hey, isn't that first guy Detective—?"

Dean didn't finish his sentence because the first bullet that hit the windshield caused him to duck.

In an instant, Sophie yanked the vehicle to the left, away from Detective Ruiz and the weapon he had in his hand.

CHAPTER-52

"Sweet mother of Jesus," whispered Alex. "This just went to the top of the list."

Not able to speak at that moment, Manny only nodded. The climate in the rainforest had accelerated the decaying process, and all four bodies were bloated to the size of Thanksgiving Day Parade balloons. Add in the repulsive, metallic stench, the buzz of blow flies, and a few other insects he didn't recognize, and you could chalk this crime scene up to one of the worst he'd ever witnessed. More sleepless nights and a visit or two to the FBI's shrink staff were on the horizon. And he'd be lucky if that was all.

He scanned each body slowly and was suddenly struck with his own mortality. It had entered his mind a time or two over the years, especially in Galway, Ireland, but to see what this maniac was capable of drove the point home. God had watched out for him—he had no doubt regarding that—but we all have an appointment with destiny. Louise was proof, and he suspected every-one, deep down, knew it. Knowing and accepting were about as compatible as fire and ice, and he thought most people knew that, too.

"You're trancing, and I think I need to learn," said Alex.

"No. Just thinking."

"If it's about death and dying, forget it. It'll make you crazy, and that's not why we're here."

"You're right on both counts."

Standing, he ran his hand through his hair and tried to get a feel for what had gone down in this little area of paradise. You can't do this to four people unless you surprise them like a trained jungle guerilla. Or maybe they were taken off guard because the killer seemed harmless. Maybe they knew him. His vote this time was for knowing the killer. No one would seem harmless approaching a campsite early on Saturday morning. If he was right, what exactly did that mean? Relative? Jealous coworker? Professional associate?

He squatted next to Alex, both of them feeling the heat and perspiring to prove it.

"Tell me something good," said Manny.

"You first."

"All right. I think these people knew him. It's hard to surprise more than one or two folks without one of them getting the opportunity to escape or at least scream for help."

"Yeah, but even if you knew him, after the first swing of the blade, maybe the second, the others would be on their way to anywhere but here, right?"

"Right, but I don't think they were all together. If you look close enough, you can see subtle breaks in the vegetation and the dirt over there has drag marks. Let me show you something else."

Still on his haunches, Manny pointed to the cracked cement slab. "There are small streaks of blood on that slab, and you'll let me know for sure, but it looks like there's a crossing pattern, indicating that more than one body was dragged over it and from different directions."

Inhaling from his mouth so as not to take in too much of the smell, he pointed to the ground behind the faded bench supporting the heads. "There are different angles of blood splatter on the leaves and the stones. Also, the amounts vary. To me, that says he killed them one at a time and at slightly different times. And not to put a damper on your 'run screaming into the woods and hope for the best' theory, but where in hell are you going to run if he's coming in from the same direction we did?"

Alex surveyed the area, then nodded slowly. "You're correct. It's almost a natural boxed-in location, but he couldn't have known that, right?"

"That's probably true, unless he knew the area and had that in mind when he planned this one. Even if he didn't really realize it, he may have counted on the fact that the rainforest is a tough place to navigate."

"Sounds true."

"Your turn, what do you have?"

"Right. First, I gotta say that I thought some of the shit Argyle pulled was something from the dark ages, but this is something to make Count Vlad the Impaler proud."

"No argument from me."

Standing up, Manny stood with him. Alex was still sweating, but he wore a paler shade than when they first arrived. He probably did, too.

"They've been dead for about three hours, but these conditions make it appear longer. You talked about the blood patterns outside the body area, and that makes sense. We'll have to go over the perimeter to see exactly where they were all killed, but I won't lie, the moisture and the rain will make that tougher. We have our ways, luminol, for one, but these conditions are going to be a factor. Also, look here at the cuts on the abdomens of both women. It's like he was thinking of playing a little more, then decided not to."

"Maybe he was running short of time."

"That's probably it, but once we get them cleaned up we'll get a better idea. Also, if you look at the area where the heads left the bodies of three of them, the angle of cuts, at least to the naked eye, looks the same. The head on the far left belongs to the body on the right, and the cut looks like it angles slightly up, but for the most part, the man could be a damned surgeon with that kind of precision."

Manny frowned. "Would you say that this victim was a little taller than the others?"

"I would. But—oh. If the angle's a little on the up slant then—"

"We might be able to get a height for him, and that's a great start."

"One of the blues is about the right height. I'll get him over here and see what I can figure out."

"Good."

Alex raised his hands in the air. "There are more obvious things to do. There must be about a million places to collect samples of dirt and bugs, and I have to start taking pictures now."

"Have at it. I can handle going to the other scenes. It might even be better to be alone."

"That works. Because I need to be here when the CSU, hopefully two units, arrives. I'm going to have to stay and make sure they do it right."

"It'll take me a few hours, but I'll call you if anything jumps out at me," said Manny.

"I'll do the same."

Manny left, careful to avoid any area that could hold a clue, and headed for the SUV. He drove through the roadblock, looked at the map of the five murder sites, and decided to start with the first victims, then he would go where Amanda Griggs and her husband died, then the Britton Tower, then where Josh's brother was killed.

Moving up 191, he was halfway to his starting point and stopped the vehicle. He ran the set of pictures from the first crime scenes in El Yunque over in his mind, then progressed to the last one where Caleb was killed.

The altar-like site was a better place to start. He didn't know why, but it was right. Protocol had always called for beginning at the beginning and going forward. But what if backtracking from the last to the first could reveal more? Who knew . . . maybe the killer's boldness caused him to make a mistake, or at the very least, his arrogance might lead to something.

Driving back down 191, he moved through the roadblock and, ten minutes later, reached the Palo Colorado parking area.

He stuffed the map in his pocket, grabbed a bottle of water, moved across the road, and started down the Bano De Oro trail.

Manny never noticed the large, dark man exiting the pickup parked a few spots away from his SUV, following him.

CHAPTER-53

The black Traverse rose over the curb in front of the Federal Building and skidded in a semi-circle on the grass as Sophie cranked the vehicle to the left. Her reaction caused the SUV to roll up on two wheels, hesitate, thump the lush grass, and settle facing Ruiz's direction, but at an angle forty-five degrees from where it began. She quickly scanned for Ruiz and didn't see him, but noticed that the three men chasing him were running in the other direction and disappeared around the corner a block away.

"Where in the hell is Ruiz?" shouted Sophie.

"I don't see him," said Chloe.

"Me either. Shit. Maybe's he's down. Those three weren't throwing water balloons," said Josh.

The calm in his voice surprised her, but at the same time gave her a shot of confidence.

That's why he makes the big bucks.

"C'mon. Anyone see the Detective? Dean?" asked Sophie.

"I don't. But then again, I'm just pulling my head out from between my legs. I thought we were going over."

"Not on my watch."

"Still don't see—oh damn. He's lying on that section of grass over by the flag. See him?" said Chloe.

Gripping the wheel, Sophie ran the movie they'd just witnessed backward in her mind and realized that maybe what they thought they saw wasn't the truth.

Caution was the word of the moment.

She popped open the door, pulled the slide back on her Glock, and stepped out.

"Where are you going? He could be just waiting for this very thing," barked Josh.

"I don't think so, but get your ass out of the truck and cover mine."

Looking at her with more than a little doubt, he finally opened the door. A moment later, Chloe and Dean did as well, and Sophie led them toward the crumpled figure on the ground.

"You think he wasn't shooting at us?" asked Dean.

"Not sure, but maybe he was just protecting himself and was trying to get our attention. We'll find out in a minute."

By then, she heard an alarm bugling from the Federal Building and the accompanying shouts. The infantry was on the way.

Moving with less caution, Sophie approached Ruiz, who was on his side facing away from them. After another step, his arm fell toward his back and he flipped over, causing each of the agents to stop with weapons poised, but there was no need. The blood on his shoulder and chest said so. Detective Ruiz opened his eyes, focused on Sophie, and pleaded with her in the way an injured animal pleads for help without uttering a word.

Holstering her weapon, she rushed to him and kneeled. She could see the twin holes in his right shoulder and rib cage, both oozing blood at an alarming rate.

"Easy, Ruiz. We're getting help."

She turned to Josh, but he was already on the phone, requesting an ambulance.

"I—I need . . . to talk . . . to you."

His voice trailed off, and unexpected compassion ransacked her thoughts. This man had lived enough hell over the years, now he may not see another day. It didn't seem fair, but who said life was fair?

Shit.

"Don't talk. Save your strength. You can tell me later."

Ruiz's eyes cleared, and he moved his head back and forth, wincing as he did. "I'm not sure I'll have the chance." His voice was steady but weak.

"That's crazy talk."

"Just listen."

He swallowed hard, pursed his lips, and continued. "Fogerty's men. I was on his payroll. I hooked up with him through a friend. So sorry. I had all of those bills from . . . Anna's counseling."

The detective coughed, and it was so harsh that a chill ran up her spine.

Somewhere a siren was bellowing.

Ruiz closed his eyes and began to breathe shallower. At that moment, she hated everything about being a cop, but she also knew doing what you had to do was part of the job, so she did it.

"Ruiz! Don't you do this," she yelled, and then shook him.

His eyes fluttered open and that awful wince was far worse than the first.

"Yeah, getting tired, agent. There's a record of the money. In a book at the house. Desk drawer by the computer. Blue. Anna's favorite color . . . I think. Pictures of some of the drops from his man, Bra—Braxton. Sorry. I've been giving him . . . info on you, all of you. He knows a lot. Sorry. Thousand a month is good money. You can nail him, though. Also names of other cops on . . . his pay . . . roll. I did it for her."

Trying to laugh, the blood bubbled from the hole in his ribs, and scarlet foam ran at the corner of his mouth.

"Guess I—that's what all dads say when . . . they screw up. Had to try. Is she. . . ?"

Sophie put her hand on his, glanced up at Josh, and fought off the emotion. Later. She'd think about it later.

Like I have a choice.

"Still alive. We just can't find her, but we've got leads. We'll do it."

The siren was ever so closer. Sophie thought it was no more than a block away. It might as well be in Lansing.

His eyes drooped shut, then sprang open, even though his breathing was even more labored, and the color of his skin was on the wild side of pale.

"I—something. Professor she liked. Might. Able to help . . . criminal justice. Tall . . ."

"Okay. You did good, Ruiz."

The ambulance pulled around the corner, and she heard the doors slam as the EMTs got their act in motion.

Glancing at Ruiz, she squeezed his hand. "Help is here."

The detective's eyes told her it didn't matter. They were staring at a world no one gets to see until you go through the door yourself.

Chloe inhaled in an effort to control her emotion. She failed.

Josh swore as he motioned to the crew from the ambulance.

Sophie wiped at the tear in the corner of her eye, vowed this was her last case. Then she got out of the way as the EMTs went to work, even though they were too late—again.

When do I get a good déjà vu?

Dean took her arm and escorted her away from the detective, with Chloe and Josh close behind, and she let him. His hands were strong, comforting, and almost furry. Odd. She hadn't noticed that before.

They reached the SUV, and she leaned against it.

"That sucked," said Josh.

"It did. Good God, I hate this shit," she answered.

"But we've got more work to do. Like Manny says, we can cry tomorrow," Josh responded.

"Yeah. I don't know how in hell he does that. That off-to-on cop-mode thing, but I need to get better at that or find another damned job," she answered.

"You? The rest of us ain't exactly gonna sleep tight tonight, ya know?" said Chloe.

"No truer words," whispered Dean.

Josh stood a little straighter, and the look on his face got her attention. Was that worry?

"We've still got to get to the rainforest. I don't like it that Fogerty knows more about us than we apparently know about him. I'm sending a team over to Ruiz's to get that book and pictures. If he was telling the truth, we can nail Fogerty for bribery, maybe extortion, and start the ball rolling to put this guy away for a long time."

"Wait. Go back to what you just said. He knows more about us? Does he know that Manny and Alex are at the rainforest?" asked Chloe.

He rolled his eyes in disgust. "Shit. I got a text from Manny that Alex was staying at the new crime scene —alone—and Manny was headed for the other sites—alone."

Pulling the phone from his shirt pocket, Josh stepped away. "I've got to make a call, hang tight."

Panic for Manny had never really been on Sophie's radar. Maybe a little after Louise had died, but he'd always been the man; big, strong, and smart. He'd always been able to take care of himself. So, why the freaking red flag now? Was it because of the concern in Chloe's voice or—

"Get into the damn truck. We're heading out," Josh ordered.

Josh turned to Dean. "Listen. Chloe, Sophie, and I are going to El Yunque. You're going with the team to Ruiz's house and make sure they don't screw anything up. We can't have that evidence tainted. I just talked to Detective Crouse. I don't have the info yet on the background checks for the SJPD, but I think we can trust her. She's going to meet you there."

"Like hell. I'm going with you. You're my team and —"

"Dean. Some of our agents could be on that payroll list. You have to make sure that's covered. We've got Fogerty nailed. Got it?"

The CSI turned his palm to the sky and started to speak just as Sophie came around the front of the truck. Another thing that had to be done, but this one would be far more pleasant.

She stood on her toes and kissed Dean on the cheek. "Thanks for being willing, but Josh is right. Lots of shit flowing, and we need you to shovel on the other end. Okay?"

The CSI was still touching his face and wearing an incredulous look to boot as she guided the SUV off the lawn and onto the road, racing to the rainforest.

"Well done, Lee," said Josh.

"Yeah. I had to do something. I've kissed worse."

The voice in the back seat was less comforting.

"Manny? Call me, and I mean now, man."

Sophie glanced at Chloe in the rearview mirror as she slammed her phone down on the seat and swore. She picked it up again, left three more messages, and clutched it to her chest, anxiety draping her face.

Pressing the accelerator, Sophie's heart began to race.

CHAPTER-54

The knock on the door surprised him. He'd only been back from the rainforest for a few minutes and hadn't had time to clean up. He wasn't in any hurry to answer the door wearing the results of his morning pilgrimage.

Lucy. You got some 'splainin to do.

Ducking into the bathroom, he washed his face, stripped, threw on a tank top and another pair of shorts, and made his way to the door, weapon in hand. Samuel Crouse had always been a cautious man—his mom and his tart of a wife had taught him the importance of that. He snorted as he bent to the peephole. It was hard to believe his bitch of a wife had been able to teach him anything, other than women are not to be trusted on any level, unless it was your mother, or maybe a grandmother.

Peeking into the hole, he felt relief, then his anger rose. Relief that the authorities weren't there because of his nocturnal and early morning activities in the rainforest. Illegal activity was always hard to explain, even in the name of science. His anger spiked at the balls of the man standing outside his door. The son of a bitch was just as responsible as his leg-spreading ex for the year of misery that had accompanied their divorce.

He leaned away from the door and let out a slow

breath.

Once, he and the man on his veranda had been fast, tight friends. The kind of friend you could call at two thirty in the morning when you had a flat tire, and he'd get out of bed to help. The kind you'd consider dying for, because to lose a friend like that would rip a hole in your soul that might never be woven back together, at least completely. Hell, he had even been the best man at his unfortunate wedding. But that time was over. His love for this man had been replaced with a hate that seemed impossible to placate.

Time to find out what this piece of shit wanted, and then he could get back to the single thing that kept him from going absolutely mad. Although if he took a poll, most would label him that already.

Gripping the brass knob, he pulled the door open.

His visitor stood with his hands behind his back, and his gray eyes regarding Samuel up and down. It had been a long time since they'd met alone. At the fencing club, once in a while on campus, even in El Yunque, but in this setting, it'd been years. He imagined what it would be like to run him through. It would not be the first time his mind had gone there, especially in light of recent developments.

"Hello Samuel. You're looking good. Did you lose some weight?"

"Why are you here? I tolerate you in public, but this, well, this is crazy on your part."

"Perhaps. However, the trip to your door was necessary."

One lunge and this rotten prick would be just another unfortunate statistic of random violence.

"Necessary? Like giving me a hard row to hoe with

that last Katana we were bidding on? No wait, maybe it was the porking of my wife and letting me find out about it by 'accident' that brings you here today. Or giving me static about my research. Am I getting warm?"

His eyes were seeing red, and he was scarcely maintaining a semblance of civility. The gray eyes of his visitor never wavered, never turned away.

"Ah. I get it. You're here to give me your condolences on the loss of my mother a few months back."

"We never did talk about that, but no, that's not exactly it either. Although you're in the ballpark with that one, as they say. It seems I didn't see your name on the guest list for my own mother's funeral. At any rate, I came here to warn you, then I realized that wouldn't do. Because once the FBI got here, you and they just might put two and two into some formula and figure it out."

"FBI? Why would they come here? And figure what out?"

"Let's just say I have sources, and I can't allow anyone to get lucky when I'm so close."

Samuel never saw, let alone anticipated, the incredibly quick move by his uniformed visitor. But he felt it. The Katana disappeared between the fifth and six ribs, gashing his heart. His visitor pulled out the blade as Samuel Crouse went to the floor, finding it strange that he couldn't breathe.

Looking up, he saw the flash in the late morning sun and barely felt the smooth metal as it entered the right side of his neck.

***

He pushed Samuel's headless body back inside the

front door, careful to avoid the blood that seemed to paint the doorjamb and the floor in a garish red. Using the Katana, he wedged Crouse's severed head next to his right hand, then lifted the hand so that it was resting on the top. He laughed. It looked like a man stroking his faithful pet. Wiping off his sword, he double-checked for blood splatter, and then he closed the front door. He walked back to his car, whistling an old Puerto Rican love song.

CHAPTER-55

Fifteen minutes later, Manny was standing in front of the Baño de Oro pool. The green circle had a calming effect on his psyche, and thank God something had. He noticed the old fishery tanks on the right side of the trail and thought they resembled the pictures he'd seen of old Mayan ruins as they were discovered. He'd read somewhere that the tanks represented an ill-fated attempt at introducing trout to the La Mina River. It didn't make sense to him, but he was no biologist.

Crossing the short, wooden bridge hanging over the stone embankment glistening with the trickling waters of the La Mina, perspiration ran freely down his back. He hesitated before he finished going completely across. Manny leaned on the railing, taking in the exotic vision surrounding him again. No wonder people enjoyed camping in El Yunque. No predators large enough to harm a human, warm nights and days, lush trees, and an array of flowers ranging from striking reds to subtle pale yellows made it a true paradise.

Predators.

Except there had been a predator, hadn't there?

The worst kind—human.

And this one knew his way around the rainforest and had tainted paradise with his personal concept of . . . of what? Pleasure? Recreation? Justice? Whatever it was, and for that matter, whoever he was, needed to be dealt with. But how? They'd better figure that out quickly.

Maybe people were right. The reason this planet was going to go to hell in a handbasket was because of the pervasive attitude that people were entitled to everything their hearts and minds could dream up. He didn't know what was worse—the want or the people who satisfied it.

Finishing the walk over the bridge, he proceeded to the camping area where Caleb Corner had breathed his last. Five minutes later, he stood outside the still-present, yellow police tape and scanned the killer's 'altar,' if that's how the killer thought of it. The dark burgundy stains had been mitigated by the rain and conditions of the rainforest, but they were still plainly visible. At least four people had died here, and the killer had gone to great lengths to accomplish that. It's one thing to bring them all in one spot, he even understood that, but to take the four victims back to their campsites and set up the morbid displays was more than compulsive. All except Caleb. Manny had thought it was personal, that maybe Caleb knew this man, but now he wasn't so sure. Maybe the killing had more to do with the act than anything personal. Hell, it could even be both.

The phone vibrated in his pocket, and he ignored it. Whatever it was could wait for a few minutes. He was getting close.

He ducked under the tape. Beneath the tree, the area was raised, about two feet by the growth of the root system. To the left, the clearing was disturbed, like it had been scraped, but nothing struck him as odd. He turned back to the right, and saw that some of the brush had been uprooted underneath one of the plush plants, displaying a patch of bare soil. *That* looked unnatural.

What the hell? Why hadn't someone gotten pictures of this?

Frowning, he pushed back two of the wide leaves to get a better look. The markings resembled a rectangle. The kind you'd find ... where? He couldn't place it just yet.

Walking back to the middle of the clearing, he stopped and looked intently at the altar, then back to the right, then back to the altar.

Where four people had died.

My God! That was it. The unsub had taken the campers back to their campsites because he didn't want anyone to know about this spot until he was ready. If that were true, the killer wanted, or needed, more time. But for what? And what did that have to do with anything?

There's more. What am I missing?

Then, as if his mind were guided by divine inspiration, it all made sense. The killer had evolved to this point, no question. So that meant he was deep in the game. And that always indicated a message, a communication to confound the cops and elevate the ego of the killer.

Glancing back at the moist, bare soil and its relationship to the tree, he eyed the dirt, then he did it again.

He walked around the two areas from every angle. He wasn't getting it. Then Manny remembered something he'd read once: when in doubt, go up.

Grabbing a thick vine covered with green moss, he put his foot on the strong roots of the Palo Colorado tree, boosted himself up to the next vine, and found another foothold. He pulled several more times and found himself about twelve feet above the ground—where the message the killer had left became as plain as the sun in the sky. A rough semblance of a block number "2" extended from the base of the tree to the cleared soil. He reached for his phone, took two pictures, and put it back in his pocket. He smiled. Sophie'd be proud that he figured out how to use the camera.

Climbing down, he took out the phone again to call Alex and tell him to get pictures of the new crime scene from above, and that he was going to the other three sites to do the same. Unless he'd missed his guess, the order of the killings would have corresponding numbers. He had no idea what the numbers would represent, but when they got together, it just might come to them, and that's all they could hope for.

Alex's number rang once then went directly to voicemail.

Damn it. The reception was still spotty up here.

"Alex. Listen, I need you to get pictures of the murder area from the top, maybe ten or twelve feet up. I know it's weird, and I'll explain later. Just do it. Thanks."

Stuffing the phone back in his pocket, he turned to the trail leading back to 191, so he could get to the other two campsites and the tower.

They were close to discovering what was next, and if Josh and the others had any luck, maybe even who. Nothing like good police work, and a trance or two.

He turned the bend and stopped in his tracks. One of the biggest men in the Caribbean stood with his legs spread apart and wearing a wide, white grin that reminded him of Eli Jenkins.

Fogerty.

"Agent Williams. Good ta meet ya, mon. I'm Braxton, and I'm here ta send Mr. Fogerty's regards."

CHAPTER-56

Watching the episode unfold in front of him, Fogerty rolled the window up in the Mercedes and began to tap the Beretta on his leg. His anger expanded to a near inferno. He'd sent three of his best to get rid of Ruiz and whoever had been standing guard at the detective's house, and this was what he got for his trouble.

Ruiz gets out of the back, steals a cruiser, and almost makes it to the Federal Building before one of the morons working for him blows out a tire on Ruiz's ride.

Ruiz didn't die right away, giving him time, in all likelihood, to implicate Fogerty for numerous felonies. Not a pleasant situation for him or anyone else Ruiz might have mentioned.

He tapped the gun faster. He'd deal with the incompetent hit team later but, for now, he had to think about what was best for him. Having contingency plans was a way of life in this business. He had several, and he was going to execute one.

It'd be just a matter of time before his house in Barbados was crawling with cops from every drug agency in the world, in spite of his monthly "contributions" to the local government. Especially when they find the body—and they were going to find him—of the undercover FBI agent he'd killed in the limo. He wasn't sure how Ruiz had found that out, but he had. Funny how life works. He'd eliminated the chink in his security armor, but now it would lead to more trouble than he'd dreamed possible. It might even shut him down. The gun moved even faster.

Marriage, once again, was responsible for causing him great difficulty.

Losing Amanda had brought him here, and just as he'd always expected, she'd be a major problem to him and the business one day. That day was here. At least Williams and the FBI had been right about her murder not being a message or retaliation from his competitors.

Give the man a cigar.

Even though the money end was where his first thoughts had migrated, she *was* his daughter and, in his own way, he'd miss her. Hell, maybe even find some time to grieve. But wasn't there a time for everything? He'd find time for that later. He had more pressing matters.

Fogerty cracked the window again, just as the Traverse carrying the Feds streaked to the east—no doubt, to the rainforest. They'd probably figured out that he knew where Williams would be; maybe Ruiz told them that too. But they'd be too late. Braxton didn't make mistakes.

He was going to miss Braxton. He'd been his best number one. But he did hire that piece of shit Domingo. Besides, money could always buy another best number one. Always.

He'd drive south, then pick up Highway 1, and eventually drive west to a place that only he knew about. Well, he and the sexy realtor who had brokered the deal, but he was pretty sure she wouldn't be speaking to anyone, ever.

After a couple of days, he'd take the yacht over to St. Thomas and then skip to Antigua, where they ask even fewer questions than Barbados, and have a meeting with his "suppliers" to get the train back on the track.

But first things first, he had to make sure Braxton had accomplished his mission before an anonymous call to the proper authorities would end the big man's life of crime forever.

Pulling off on a side street, he cruised into the parking area of a large drugstore chain, went in, and came back out with two pay-as-you-go phones. Just as he was getting into the car, he heard the quick blat of a siren. A very close siren. He spun around just in time to see two white SUVs leading three SJPD cruisers into the parking lot.

Four plainclothes cops sprang from the first SUV.

"Randall Fogerty. You're wanted for murder, extortion, and bribery. Put your hands on your head and face the car," ordered the agent on the right.

Usually prepared for the worst, he hadn't seen this coming and was frozen in place.

How did they find me? I changed cars twice and I was the only one to know it.

For a brief moment, the thought of blowing his brains all over the parking lot wore an intoxicating appeal. If he went to prison, he might last two days. He might not last that long if he were housed in one of the local jails. But then again, that's why he paid those leaching attorneys all of that damned money—to keep him out of jail. Besides, he wasn't one of those noble types who'd rather die than bend to the system. He was a survivor.

"Last request, asshole," yelled the agent.

By this time, there were fifteen cops surrounding him with raised weapons. He swore he heard each cock of the hammers.

Fogerty put the phones on the roof and raised his hands over his head.

"Certainly. No need to get nasty. I'm cooperating."

Just then, one of the phones began to cascade from the roof of his vehicle. He instinctively grabbed for it.

"He's reaching for a weapon," screamed a voice.

The last thing he heard was the roar of gunfire as he slammed against the Mercedes. Then he slowly sank down the door.

CHAPTER-57

"Any reason Fogerty can't do that himself? I'm a pretty social guy, and if he wants to say something to me, I'm all ears," said Manny.

"Oh. No doubt wid dat, Agent, no doubt. But it be da damnedest ting. He don't like people so much, so I got de job."

Doing a quick inventory, he felt the Glock in the small of his back instead of hugging the left side of his chest. He'd changed holsters when they got to Puerto Rico because of the weather.

Can I move that fast?

The huge man leveled his arm, revealing one of the largest handguns Manny had ever seen. It looked like a .50 caliber Desert Eagle, but he was as close to it as he cared to be.

"Before you tink 'bout gettin' stupid, mon, I tink dis big ol' boy would send ya hafway to Sint Martin, yes?"

"I suppose that's true."

The big man stared at him, shifting his gun to the left hand. Braxton rolled his head to one side, then the other. Manny felt like he was being sized up for a meal.

The rainforest had grown quiet, and the smells that he'd thoroughly enjoyed during his trek on the trail had turned sour. Amazing what a little stress and anxiety can do to the human senses.

The day was getting longer, and the sweat ran more freely down his back and arms as he continued to match gazes with Fogerty's lackey. In his mind, whoever twitched, blinked, or even belched, lost . . . except . . .

"I don't suppose you were sent here to give me an ass-whooping. You know, to teach me a lesson, then report to that piece of shit how I moaned and begged. Hell, you could even do a video. If that's it, let's get to it. I've got a bigger piece of shit to deal with, the one that killed Fogerty's daughter, and I'd like to get to it."

"You be right on a ting or two, Agent. I was sent to make tings hurt for you, no doubt, den, put dis cannon to dat head, and see how many pieces dat slick brain of yours make in da process."

There it was again. Manny had read much about the expressions a face can make stimulated by the subconscious. Micro Expressions was a fairly new technology based on the slow-motion analysis of videos recorded when people were relating facts about a particular incident. But some people had a natural ability for it. The theory said that if you instinctively knew someone's motivation, could always tell when someone was lying, or even had a natural dislike for another without a concrete reason, that maybe you had the gift.

Braxton's face was giving him away. There was almost a smile at the corner of his mouth each time he spoke, like he knew something Manny didn't. Not unusual for cold-blooded killers who enjoyed their work, but this expression was different. And his eyes. They sparkled more than they should. He sensed no real dread in them. Most people who had been in shoes like Braxton's would have no compunction for regret, but the corner of his mouth and the lines running across his forehead said differently. And his dialect had slipped, ever so slightly, but it had. Maybe he had some formal education.

Taking a step forward, Manny prayed he was right. He had no choice. The killer wasn't going to wait, and they still hadn't gotten to second base in the investigation.

"When do we get this dance started?"

Braxton didn't react, just held his ground like a curious bull.

The perspiration flowed faster as he felt his foot take the next step and crunch the small twig. The sound echoed loudly through the clearing.

"You tink you know what you're doing, Williams? I don't tink you do." The wide grin gave Manny a little more confidence.

I'm a foolish moron. He's going to blow my brains out after he breaks every bone in my body.

Except Braxton hadn't started that assignment. Why? Was he that confident in his size and his arms disguised as tree trunks?

Taking the next step, literally, was Manny's only option. He did and now was just a few feet from the man. He could hear his breathing, and the weapon took on the profile of an artillery gun.

Then, as if cued, Braxton dropped the gun to his side, and grinned even wider, if that were possible. A second later, he had Manny's arm in one hand and drew him within an inch of his face. Manny's toes were almost off the ground. Braxton's grip was more like a vice than any vice Manny had used. This guy could cause serious damage to his arm, if he had a mind to. But there was almost a gentleness . . . and there was that damn twitch around his mouth.

Fifteen seconds later, still staring at each other, Manny smiled.

"Are we going to kiss or are you going to tell me how long you've been under?"

Releasing him, Braxton stepped back, scowled, then broke into a full belly laugh. "I read dat profile dat Ruiz sent to Fogerty, the one dat said you were the FBI's new BAU Wonder Boy, but who can believe all of dat shit. But I do now." There was only a hint of island dialect in his booming voice now. "How did you know?"

"Let's just say that your face gave you away."

He nodded. "Micro Expressions. Been working on not letting dat show. What if you'd been wrong, mon?"

"Fogerty would have gotten that video of me bleeding all over the rainforest, I suppose. So how long?"

Reaching out a hand that engulfed Manny's, they shook, and Braxton laughed again. "I'm Braxton Smythe, and I've been working for the DEA for almost nine years, but we can talk about dat later. Can I use your phone? If tings went well, Fogerty's in cuffs and that would sure as hell make my day."

Manny plucked it out of his shirt, and then noticed he had nine messages from Chloe. He'd turned the sound off when he got here, and this was the first time he'd looked at the screen. She was either worried about something or had butt-dialed him several times. His vote was on worry.

"Hurry, up, mon." mocked Manny. "I need to make one too."

"I will. Dis must be a good spot for the phone. Don't get dat everywhere up here."

A few moments later, Braxton handed back the phone. His smile had disappeared.

"What?"

"Good news, bad news, mon. The good news is dat Fogerty's dead. A few days ago, I was able to put a new chip in his phone while he was in da throes wid some hooker in Barbados. He thought I was taking the GPS out, but really I put a very sophisticated one in. We thought we were getting close to nailing his ass, but he always seemed to have dat sixth sense, and we wanted to make sure he couldn't run and hide. Not sure why he didn't toss it away, but it was a pretty phone with 4G so I guess dat's why he kept it. Anyway, after he killed one of your undercovers this morning, we had enough."

"Wait, we had an undercover, too?"

"Yeah. Domingo. Someone dropped da dime on him, and Fogerty killed him. It was all I could do to control myself and not tear his head off his shoulders, but God knows I had to. Fogerty had information on the South American operations that would have saved him from the gas chamber, and he would have squealed like a pig, because, as he used to say, he knows information is life. Hell, he probably would have gotten a retirement farm out of it. The San Juan DEA agents followed him to a parking lot, where something went wrong, and they killed him."

"I wish I could say I was sorry, but I'm not," said Manny.

"Me either. It would have been nice to get dat other information, but we're working on dat in other ways, so maybe it's all good, ya know?"

Manny ran his fingers through his hair. "You said there was bad news."

"You better stop that or you're going to go bald . . . like me," said Braxton, running his hand over his clean-shaven brow.

"I'll remember that. So?" he asked, as he began to dial Chloe.

"My face is all over the Caribbean as Fogerty's number one and I know a ting or two, myself. So—"

A second later, Manny felt the shot whiz past before he heard it. Instinct sent him to the ground as he yelled for Braxton to get down. Too late. There was a second shot. Braxton listed to the left and then crumpled to the ground, blood gushing from his head.

CHAPTER-58

Dean stepped out of the truck as the agent driving followed. He was scoping the exterior of the neat, stucco bungalow located on New San Juan's north end, where Ruiz had lived. A moment later, Detective Crouse pulled in behind them. She and another suit got out of the car. The other suit stayed as she worked her way in his direction, the white stone crunching under her steps. She'd been crying, and why not? Ruiz had been her partner. From what Dean could tell, Ruiz had been a good man, mostly. Then again, didn't that apply to all of us? He shook off the thoughts sending him down Philosophical Lane. He had work to do and the sooner it was done, the quicker he could get back to his team, and Sophie.

"Sorry for your loss, Detective."

She waved him off. "He made his own bed. I'm just pissed I didn't see—"

"And that he didn't ask for help?" he suggested, adjusting his green paisley shorts.

"Yes. That too. But I'll deal with it. What choice do I have?" she said quietly.

"None, I guess. So, are you ready for this?"

Nodding, she stepped up the cement-gray steps and moved to the door just as another white SUV pulled up wearing the FBI logo. Three more agents got out and stood beside the vehicle. All wore dark sunglasses and moved to the side of the truck closest to the house, with arms folded.

"Nothing like a little overkill on the backup," said Dean.

"I guess I don't blame them. This could be bad for the department and the FBI. Hell, *it will* be bad for both departments," she responded.

Dean found himself liking her a little more. She was at least honest.

Reaching under the potted Azalea near the front window, she grabbed the key, unlocked the door, drew her weapon, and walked in, Dean following behind her. A few moments later, three other sunglass-clad agents were on their heels.

"Where do we go?" asked Crouse.

"Computer room file cabinet, blue notebook," said Dean.

Julia led them through the small, neat family room and entered a tiny bedroom set up as an office. Near the glass computer desk stood the file cabinet Ruiz had told them about.

Detective Crouse began to reach for the drawer, and he stopped her. "I'll do that. Sorry, but please go stand by the door. Boss's orders."

He expected a full-blown pissy fit, but for a change, she simply nodded, moved to just inside the door, crossed her arms, and leaned against the red wall. For that, Dean was grateful. There was enough shit going on, here and in the rainforest, where he'd much rather be.

Reaching into his pocket, he pulled out a pair of gloves, snapped them on, then tested the handle of the drawer. He was surprised that it wasn't locked, and even more surprised that the blue notebook was still there. Visions of conspiracy plots had been dancing in his head, and he was sure the book would be gone.

Damn. Too many crime novels.

Pulling it out of its bed, he leafed through a couple pages, then a couple more, and whistled.

"This looks like something out of a 'hooker tells all' book. Let's go."

He quickly dropped it into an evidence bag and turned for the door.

"I'll take that now."

The young agent who had driven Dean to the house was standing in the doorway, gun drawn, with a look on his face somewhere between fear and evil.

"Are you sure you want to do this? You're going to have to shoot all of us to—" said Dean.

He racked the slide on his Glock. "Don't worry about that; just give me the damned book."

A second later, the young agent was out cold. He never saw the long leg that Julia Crouse flashed, hitting him square on the jaw, sending him and the gun flying.

Letting out a breath, Dean headed for the door as the other three agents pounced on their fallen comrade like zombies in a Zane Bradey novel.

"Thanks, Detective. I didn't have time to die today."

She grinned. "Funny boy. I guess we know one of the names in that notebook."

"We do."

Glancing at her, he suddenly felt the need to ask. "So, does that mean we won't see your name in there?"

She didn't speak and moved outside to the small stoop. She played with the key in her hand, and then stuffed it in the pocket of her black jeans.

"You know, I guess I thought there was something wrong when Carlos told me about all of those therapy bills for Anna," said Crouse. "I figured he'd found a way. I should have been nosier. Maybe things would have been different."

"Maybe. But you can't put Humpty back together again."

"You're right. We don't get many do-overs, do we?" Folding her arms, she sighed. "No, Agent. I won't be in there. My ex and I both came from money. But who's to say, given the right circumstances...?"

The three agents carried the man Julia had cold-cocked past them just as the officer who had accompanied her walked up. He spoke to her in Spanish for few moments, and Dean watched her lips form a long, thin line.

"Shit, does it ever stop?"

"What?"

"There's been another package delivered."

"This is worse than LA. Where?"

"On the hood of a squad car parked at a restaurant. The officers had stopped for breakfast and never saw a thing."

"Did anyone open it?"

"They called for backup, checked it out for explosives, but they were pretty sure it was the same MO and box type as the other two. So yeah, they opened it."

"And?" Dean asked, knowing her answer wasn't going to make his day.

"Heart," she said, absently. "It was a human heart."

CHAPTER-59

"I suppose it's true. Nothing lasts forever, and that's probably an enlightening way to digest the path we choose in this life. Wouldn't you agree?"

The bed whispered a soft complaint as he crossed his legs and smiled at Anna. Her eyes were closed, and she lay so very still. That seemed appropriate, giving all she'd been through. After all, hadn't she been a major help to him? And she had the heart of a lion. He grinned.

But the conversation was not going to be as interesting as it could be. One-way discussions seldom were, but they did have their advantages. He'd taught his students, uncountable times, to speak concerns, facts, and passages from textbooks out loud. Hearing helped. The audible could also assist one in advancing to the next level of thought. Like his next step, and his last in the crusade that had evolved into more. Much more. El Yunque was the love of his life, but the line between that love and his newfound pleasure had grown fuzzy after the first "lessons."

Over the last few days, he'd come to realize just what the words "enjoy your work" really signified. And how the rules didn't pertain to men like him.

"Parting is such sweet sorrow, my twisted Anna. But I suppose you know that by now. For people like us, it's no longer a matter of the heart."

He laughed, then louder. "That was funny, don't you think?"

Standing, he reached for the camera on the dresser. He gazed at her and, noticing the thin line of sunshine diagonally across her nude body, marveled at the effect. After taking several more pictures of the bloodied woman on his bed, he bent low, kissed her on the forehead, and moved to the door.

"As I said, this is goodbye. If everything goes according to plan—and it will—I will be avenged, El Yunque will be a better place, and I'll have the euphoria that the screaming masses will provide. You have been instrumental in all of it. That should make you feel good, if you could."

He closed the door and strolled to the front room where a bundle of ancient rapier swords and Katanas rested on top of a long, black duffel bag. Just to the right stood a small metal briefcase, and to the right of that, a larger, blue, nondescript suitcase. Resting on the wide top of the luggage was an airline ticket envelope.

Taking his time, he carefully loaded the blades in the bag and ushered them to his SUV. He came back for the blue suitcase, loaded it, and returned to the living room. As he carefully rescued the metal satchel from the floor, he stood in place, and then did a slow, deliberate three-sixty, trying to decide what his mother would think of his journey. She'd always been proud of him, no matter what he did, but what about now? Would she encourage him and say that he was her reason? He was abruptly struck with the notion that maybe what he was doing wasn't exactly . . .

Don't be ridiculous.

He jumped. The deep voice ringing in his head had

startled him.

"I know you're right, but . . ." he said.

There are no damned buts. Don't forget what your mother looked like at the bottom of those steps.

That image was eternal. He still saw her on every turn and in every dream. He grasped the handle of the valise and squeezed.

Not to mention the, well, let's call it what it is, the bloodlust. Have you ever felt anything so right? So perfect?

He hadn't.

Then the voice was gone. But that was of no consequence. He'd accomplished his goal; the game was on and in full glory. Tonight would be a night that Puerto Rico and the rest of world would never forget. Life was full of tradeoffs, and tonight he'd switch one icon for another, his way.

Moving through the front door, he gingerly placed the case on the front seat, strapped in with the seatbelt, and smiled as he backed out of the driveway.

CHAPTER-60

Another shot smashed into the dirt beside Manny's leg, and the spray from the dark soil peppered his arm, stinging like so many angry insects. He rolled on his back and slid down the small embankment that sandwiched a tiny tributary running to the La Mina River, hopefully out of sight of the shooter. Then he pulled his Glock, glancing at Braxton. The big man was motionless, and the blood had begun to form a small pool around his shaved head.

The next shot caused Braxton's body to lurch from his resting place as the bullet hit him in the back.

Shit. He strained to see if Braxton was still breathing, but couldn't tell.

Manny had always told Jen that life had defining lessons and not all of them would be the kind that made us feel good. Some would separate us from the comfort we enjoyed and force us to either embrace or reject our convictions, completely or in part. How could he expect her to accept that as truth if he didn't live it himself, so right now he was about to do just that. He couldn't leave the Braxton out there. He was probably already dead, but maybe . . .

A fourth bullet splintered the root of the Tabonuco tree to his right, a foot from his head, immediately releasing the pungent smell of its sap.

Now was the time. There had been at least a few seconds between shots. He scrambled out of the ditch. A moment later, he had Braxton's shirt in both hands and was pulling with all he had. The man was an easy three hundred pounds, but adrenaline was magic.

The next shot went high; maybe three feet, and he and Braxton tumbled into the alcove, Braxton on top. Blood still was coming from the first wound, but not as heavy. Manny pushed, managing to roll him over on his back, while another shot echoed through the clearing. Except . . . this one sounded different. That's when he heard the shouting. A few more shots erupted, accompanied immediately by a scream of pain that caused a visit from the Goose Bump Fairy. Straining, he thought heard a woman yell. The source was much closer than the first shouts, and then he saw her. Chloe was swearing in Gaelic, a trick she said she'd teach him. She called someone a name, then began shouting Manny's name. He couldn't help thinking about the reputations redheads have for losing their temper. He reminded himself, again, not to walk on that wild side.

"I'm here, and we need an ambulance," he yelled. "Now."

Chloe burst around the bend leading to the bridge, Josh and Sophie right behind, followed by an unexpected fourth. Alex was panting, but running just the same.

"Are ya hurt man? 'Cause if you die on me, I'll kill ya."

"Not me. Braxton here has been shot twice. We ne—"

Leaping into his arms, Chloe held him tight, trying to stifle a sob he guessed was born of pure relief. He understood. He almost lost it.

Is there anything better than the love of a good woman?

"I'm okay. A little shook up, but okay," he whispered.

She nodded without taking her face out of the crook of his neck. "Don't smell all rosy, though, do ya?" she said, her voice gaining strength.

"What the hell happened?" asked Sophie as she bent to Braxton. "And why is Fogerty's Goliath your new best friend?"

Chloe stepped back, running her finger under her eye. Good God, she was more beautiful each time he saw her.

"He's undercover with the DEA."

"That explains what the shooter was doing," said Josh.

"Damn, he looks dead," said Sophie.

As if to answer Sophie's statement, Braxton moaned. It was like music to Manny's ears. Then his hand reached for his head. Sophie grabbed it. "Don't touch that, big man, your meat hooks are dirty. We've already sent for help."

His eyes were glassy, but he tried to sit up, cringed, grabbing his back, and seemed to think better of it. "Damn, dat wasn't funny."

Moving Sophie out of the way, Alex looked at the wound on his head, pulled out a pair of latex gloves, and began to gently touch the area where Braxton had been hit.

"Gloves? Still?" chided Sophie.

"Bite me. They come in handy, right? Anyway, I think it's just a graze. It looks much worse than it is.

He'll make it, I think."

"Whoa. What about the shot in the back? That made me sick when it hit you." said Manny.

"Dat Kevlar is good stuff," Braxton responded. "I'll be sore, but living."

He began to sit up again, seemed to think better of it, and laid back down. "I'll just wait for dat ambulance."

"It'll be here in a few. There's one up by the hut with the four bodies," said Alex.

"Good," said Manny. He motioned toward Josh.

"You said something about explaining the shooter. I suspect I wasn't the main target, but two for the price of one? And why are you all here? Not that I'm complaining, mind you."

"We had some inside info that Fogerty probably knew where we all were this morning and took it from there."

"Inside info?"

"Ruiz. Seems he was talking to Fogerty and his people real often," said Josh.

Raising his eyebrow, Manny stared at Josh. "Ruiz? I didn't have him pegged for that. He was a little nervous, then the whole thing about his daughter seemed to have him more than distracted. What else did he say?"

"Ah, not much. He's gone. Fogerty again. Ruiz was able to give us that much before he died, plus we sent Dean to pick up some evidence Ruiz said he had at his house that would give us names and places," said Josh.

Manny bowed his head. It was hard not to think that Ruiz's torture regarding his daughter, and maybe life in general, was over. He hoped that the detective really was residing in that "better place."

"Sorry to hear it, truly. His life hadn't seen too

many bright spots the last few years."

"No, it hadn't. Maybe a little peace now, huh?" said Chloe.

"I hate to seem cold, and I always say we can cry tomorrow, but it's true. So, what about the shooter that kept Braxton and me company?"

"Must be Fogerty figured something out about Braxton and sent the man up here to make sure Braxton took care of you, then he would be next. We called Alex to see what direction you'd headed and were on our way to the first scene when we just happened to hear a shot," said Josh.

"Yeah. What a dumbass," said Sophie. "You could almost see him from the curve where we parked. It didn't take long to find him, and we were up his butt. And then he got dumber."

"What do you mean?"

Sophie smiled at Chloe. "She figured out in a heartbeat what was going on, that maybe you started from the last to the first, and she was right. She beat us to the shooter and told him to stop, he took another shot, then she took one of her own and hit him in the left cheek, the one below his waist."

"Didn't want to kill him, but the next one would have ended his miserable life. I would've tracked Fogerty down if this one had done his job," said Chloe.

"I bet you would have," said Manny.

Fogerty.

"Oh shit. I just remembered."

"What?" asked Alex.

"Braxton got a call from one of his agents. Fogerty's dead."

"Dead? How?" asked Josh, surprised.

"Dey got him trying to escape. Dat's all I know," said Braxton, eyes still closed.

"I guess that's good enough for now," said Josh.

The ambulance crew came around the bend hauling a stretcher and two medical kits and quickly went to work on the big man. Manny smiled. He didn't know how they were going to get him on that stretcher and back to the vehicle, but it was going to be a show. He was as large as the two EMTs put together.

He bent down to Braxton. "We'll talk more later, but we've got to go. We've got a bead on a few things with this crazy bastard, and we have to compare notes."

"You can bring me flowers, but you're right: you need to find dis one. He don't feel straight."

Sophie volunteered to go get the other SUV. Ten minutes later, Manny was standing by his vehicle with Dean and Chloe, who wouldn't let him move two feet from her. Sometimes smothered is good.

Josh was on the phone, trying to reach his office and then Dean. Alex had followed Josh's lead and wanted to see if the lab had anything for him, plus a status on the latest murder site processing from the local CSU.

Out of nowhere, Sophie tore into the parking lot steering the FBI's SUV, skidded to a stop, revved the engine and then hopped out.

"That thing moves, I got to tell ya."

"You're going kill yourself one of these days," said Manny.

"Maybe, but not today."

"Good ta know," grinned Chloe.

Sophie turned to Manny. "Alex said you found something at that last murder scene, what was it?"

By then, Josh and Alex had joined the rest of them.

"It looks like he left the number '2' on the ground at the murder site, but you really couldn't see it until you got up ten or twelve feet."

"How'd you think of that?"

"It sort of popped into my head. I just remembered something from a class a long time ago."

"But the question is: did he do it at the other murder scenes or am I'm smoking dope?"

"Let me answer that," said Alex. "I took the liberty of sending two CSIs to the tower after I got your message and I'm waiting for those images. Meanwhile, I got one of the blues to climb the big tree near the south end of the hut. Look at these."

Alex opened up his tablet and flashed to the pictures.

On the right side of the hut, closest to the sun, was a distinct "1" carved into the embankment.

CHAPTER-61

"We've got a boatload of information to share, and we've not exactly been in a place to do that until now," Josh announced, standing at the head of the table inside the conference room at the Federal Building.

Josh turned to Crouse. "How's your relationship with your ex?"

"What? What the hell does that have to do with anything?"

"Just tell me."

Crouse folded her arms in that familiar position of rebellion. "Not a relationship at all. I haven't seen him for at least a year. We were married for five months and nothing worked for us. The sex was good, but I loved being a cop more than I loved him. He loved his work and that stuck-up fencing club more than me. Tell me why that's important."

Sophie shared the information about the fencing clubs and their conversation with Donald Flores.

Crouse snorted at the part about putting Samuel Crouse on the top of the list. "He never liked Sam much. He was better at the game than Flores and had more money. Plus, they didn't like each other from some political shit at the University that cost Flores a class or two. He didn't need the money, but his ego is bigger than a cruise ship."

"What about the part about your ex losing his mom? I'd bet you a million this unsub had an event that triggered this spree," said Manny.

She shook her head. "His mom passed over a year ago. I went to the funeral in Miami and that's the last time I saw Sam. Not a few months ago, if that's what he said."

"We'll have Flores picked up to talk some more, but we finished checking out his story, and were able to verify that he was out of town when the murders started," said Josh.

"Anything else?" asked Manny.

"That's it. Except how he loved those old swords he spent a fortune on. It all added up to a perfect storm for divorce and not being in each other's world. Oh, wait. He's a suspect, isn't he?"

"Yes. A viable one."

Manny leaned closer. Chloe had filled him in, she hadn't mentioned names.

The phone in Josh's shirt pocket rang, and he answered. It didn't take long for the expression on his face to reflect a new development. "What do you mean he's dead? Son of a bitch." Josh spun away from the table, then spoke into the phone. "Okay, get a team out there. Alex and Dean will be busy for a while."

Punching the stop button, he tossed the phone on the table. It rattled and then stopped in front of Manny.

"Who's dead?" Manny asked.

Rubbing his face, Josh scoped the table and stopped at Julia. At that moment, his boss appeared older than Noah after the flood.

"Sam was a suspect, along with a few others, but not anymore. I sent two agents over to talk to him, and they found him inside the front door. It wasn't pretty."

"Sam's . . . dead?" Crouse stammered.

"I'm afraid so. I'm sorry to have to tell you this way."

The rest of the room grew silent. Their faces displayed the same mixture of surprise, anger, and sadness that Josh was feeling, and none of them had ever met the man. Cops would always feel deeply for another cop's loss, because they knew they were only a call away from the same fate. Manny recalled the day his old partner Kyle Chavez had died, and then Louise's face flashed across his mind. There really wasn't any escaping those ghosts. Julia would have to learn what he already knew: you live with them and hope they don't visit too often.

Exhaling, the San Juan detective stared at the table, then got up and paced back and forth, struggling to find poise that was doing its best to elude her. Manny hated that feeling.

"You should leave . . ." said Josh.

She stepped around the room, then sat down, jutted out her chin and swore in Spanish, smacking the table with the flat of her hand, tears smearing her makeup.

"I could, but . . ."

Josh's voice grew soft as he spoke. "There are a few rules about working the case of someone close. I—"

Chloe took Julia's hand. The detective lifted herself from the chair, brushing at her cheeks. "For once, there's a freaking rule that makes sense. I need to think." Then she left, pushing away Chloe's attempt to console her.

Josh motioned for Manny to return his phone, then dialed a number and waited. "I'll call the department's counselor and let them know she just left. They're probably expecting her anyway."

He finished the call and looked around the room. "Manny's right. It's going to be tough, but we can't do anything about what's already happened. We need to find this guy before anymore funerals are scheduled. Let's get to this. Sophie? Flores's list?"

"Yeah, you're right. It just seems like it gets harder," she answered.

"Let's hope it never gets easier," said Manny.

"I'm done if it does. All right. There were six names that fit what we were looking for, at least from the roster Flores gave us and the killer's approximate height based on what Manny and Alex put together at the latest murders. Josh sent teams out to each address, but it's Saturday and who in the hell knows if we'll find any or all of them at home. Besides, these guys are just leads, like Sam. Maybe the killer never even belonged to one of these fencing outfits."

"That's true, but it's a good start. What about the auction houses that specialize in those swords?" asked Manny.

"We're checking out that angle and, with any luck, we won't need subpoenas to get records," said Josh. "Meanwhile, we'll keep pounding the other leads."

"What about this number thing?" asked Sophie.

"I don't know what it means—"

"Wait," interrupted Alex. He was looking at his laptop screen, scowling as he did.

"I got an e-mail back from my friend in Michigan. He worked late, and I owe him tickets to the Redwings and the Tigers, but he's got something on the metal we sent. He says it's unique to the sixteenth century, a rapier with a slightly wider blade and a grip that was probably quite ornate. He said the steel was pure, but littered with small idiosyncrasies that went with the steel folding criteria of that time. German, he thinks. He says this type of sword was kind of a hybrid between a thrusting blade and a cutting blade. That makes it a six-teenth-century weapon, probably designed by someone named Peter Munich Solingen. Then he says 'Go Blue'—he hates the MSU Spartans."

"Excellent. Let's get that information over to the auction houses, too. That'll narrow the search," said Josh, becoming a little more enthused. Manny was glad someone was enthused because he was having a hard time gleaning information into something that made sense. It was making him crazy.

"Manny?" said Sophie. "You here?"

"Yeah. Just thinking."

"While you're thinking, let Dean and I give you some more information to stoke over," said Alex, squirming in his seat. He stood, shifting to one leg, then the other.

"What the hell's wrong with you, Dough Boy? Underwear issues?" teased Sophie.

"Sort of, but that's none of your business."

"Rash, isn't it? What have you been doing?"

"Maybe, but like I said; it ain't your business, wench."

"Wench? That hurt, and don't say I didn't warn you about those gloves."

"Later, you two," warned Josh, though his eyes were smiling.

Alex grimaced and shifted again. "Anyway, we've got all of the pictures from the other two murder sites and we found more numbers. Site one had a '2', site two had a '0', site three had a '6' the altar site had the '2' Manny found, and the last site had the '1,' which gives us, in order, 2-0-6-2-1."

"You could reverse it," said Dean. "But either way it makes no sense to me. I took a few classes on numerology and cryptology, and there's about a million things those numbers could mean."

"The Zodiac killer did this in the late sixties, but his code was more complex, and he made mistakes in it, supposedly. But if this is all we got, it's a start," said Manny.

"Could the numbers be translated to letters?" asked Chloe.

"They could, but the trick is to find out which numbers correspond with which letter. It'd be too easy to start with A as zero," said Dean.

"We have to think simple and go from there. I mean start from the most obvious and work our way up. Maybe Occam's Razor will apply here. God knows we need a simple, obvious explanation," said Manny.

"Damn. This could be anything. In the movies, the numbers are always a longitude, latitude clue," said Sophie.

"Good guess, but not enough numbers," said Dean. Manny noticed the CSI's look of worship toward Sophie was back and wondered briefly if he did the same thing himself when he looked at Chloe.

"Could it be a significant—wait!" Manny jumped up. "Alex. I need to see the pictures from the morgue. I thought there was something weird there. I couldn't figure out why he'd dragged the body. I thought he was simply screwing with us."

Still trying to get comfortable, Alex punched a

couple of keys and turned the computer in Manny's direction. "Have at it. Just push this arrow to go to the next one. This will take you back to previous one."

The others had gathered over Manny's shoulder as he clicked pictures of the dark red smears running in different directions on the floor. They watched in silence as he worked the slideshow.

"You might get this tech junk yet," said Sophie.

"God forbid. How do I isolate four pictures in an up-and-down row?"

"Which four?" asked Alex.

After Alex had them lined up, Manny could only stare.

"Well, kiss my ass and give me a Valentine," whispered Alex.

The large "P" was rough, but unmistakable.

CHAPTER-62

The sounds of the casino echoed through the lobby as he sat patiently in one of the padded chairs in the lounge, pretending to play on his tablet. He'd already been for two walks, and then decided he couldn't risk taking any more. He didn't know when Special Agent Manny Williams would return to the hotel, but he needed to be here when the object of his hatred showed himself. The arrogant prick would probably be surrounded with "his" people, but that didn't matter. Williams would go to his room, eventually, and when he did, it would be his time to shine. And shine he would, wouldn't he? He hadn't prepared all of these months to fail. That wasn't in the cards: his or Williams's.

"Do you mind if I use that outlet to plug in my phone?"

The heavyset man with the Southern accent smiled at him, and he smiled back.

"No problem. I'm not using it."

"Thank you. I'm waiting for my wife and that could be a while. Being married to her sure has taught me patience, but she's been worth it."

He stood, stretching his legs to his full height. "I know exactly what you mean. Rewards come to those who wait, do they not?"

"Oh, are y'all waiting for the love of your life?"

"Something like that."

CHAPTER-63

"Great. Now we have a 'P'. What good does that do?" asked Sophie.

Manny ran his hand through his hair, studying the pictures. "I don't know, Sophie, but I think the puzzle's still not complete. We've found what he left in El Yunque and the morgue, but what about the body parts? Especially the last one. Dean?"

"The heart?" answered Dean. "What about it? Same MO for delivery, same box type, same amount of puking when the cops opened it. Even the label print had the same sub-pattern inside the letters, but—"

"But what?" asked Alex, tapping him on the shoulder. "You didn't have any 'buts' when you and Julia left the office, and the techs took the heart for more work."

"I don't know, I think Mucus's butt is kind of cute," said Sophie.

"It's Mikus. And . . . really?" asked Dean.

"Focus, Mikus, focus," said Manny.

Dean searched Manny's face, glanced at Alex, then raised his hands in surrender. "I wasn't sure, okay? Besides, the CSU was in a hurry to get the thing processed, and that's just my first impression. I'm a science guy so I don't like to guess, but I kind of have a thing for spatial relations. You know, how something should be in comparison to other traits. I thought there was something wrong with the size of the heart. Like—"

"Like it was male, not female?" asked Manny.

"Yeah? How'd you know?"

"I didn't, but given his profile, a change-up like that is no surprise. He's telling us to think differently because he is, so I'm betting you're right."

"Anna could have had an enlarged heart," said Alex.

"True, but it didn't seem like that. Most men have a twenty-five percent larger heart than women. That's what it seemed like to me," said Dean.

"Okay. Say you're right; where did he get it and what does 'change-up' mean?" asked Josh.

"I can answer that," said Chloe quietly, "at least the 'where he got it' part. It's probably Sam's."

Sophie nodded. "If it's the same killer, and Josh said it wasn't pretty, then that only makes sense."

"Say Dean and you are right. The question is why? He takes a hand and a foot from a female, from Anna, then Sam's heart, then makes sure the police get it, guaranteeing that we see it too," said Manny.

"Yeah, but maybe he doesn't care if we see it. Maybe he's in his own world and just doing what comes next in his mind," said Sophie.

"Or maybe what the voices are telling him. This kind of psychosis probably includes some delusional activity," said Chloe.

"Both good observations. If he's hearing voices, then the game gets more complex, but those killers tend to be more reckless because the voice is almost always God, or at least an authority figure the killer wants to impress. That usually leads to some kind of public appearance to strut their invincibility. But say that's not the case. Say he's sending these displays to get a message to a particular group, maybe even to a special individual," said Manny, leaning on the edge of the table.

"Taking that further, I can see trying to play with the FBI because we get that all of the time. But if you're correct; who is he trying to connect with?" asked Josh.

"I don't know. I may not be right, but this has a different feel. He's not following the profile completely, and that worries me. This escalation is unique even for serial killer."

"He's not like Argyle?" asked Alex.

Manny shook his head. "No. His thought development was incredibly exclusive. None of these people do things the same, but the reasons for doing them don't fall far from the tree."

One of the local agents brought in more coffee and a tray of sandwiches that made Manny's stomach rumble. It was almost two p.m., and they hadn't had lunch. The five of them dove in, eating quietly. Manny was sure they all had thoughts of what to do next haunting them. Then Sophie broke the silence.

"This feels like a freaking last meal or something."

"Naw. More like it'll be a while before we do this again," said Manny.

His confidence in that statement wasn't exactly brimming. He couldn't shake the feeling that Sophie was right. Add the fact that he was sure they were running out of time, quickly, and that made a recipe for disaster unless they got it together soon.

Writing on his legal pad, Manny wrote out 2-0-6-P-1-2, then drew a hand, a foot, and a heart. After that, he mapped out, to the best of his ability, the murder sites in the rainforest in relation to how highway 191 wound through. Next, he wrote down his first impressions of the crime scenes individually, then what he believed they had in common, and finally what differences they had.

Alex and he had always debated the concept of instinct versus a subconscious analysis of the facts that led to conclusions that led to clues that led to solving a case. Right now, he didn't give a rat's ass how it all worked; he just needed to find some answers.

Chloe leaned over to see what he'd written, touching his arm with her breast. It was like a static electricity shock, but fifty times stronger. By the way she jerked back, and then smiled, she'd felt it too.

Not now, Williams, not now.

"What were you writing like a crazy man? And you two stop touching. It makes me nervous," said Sophie.

"We weren't touching, sort of. Anyhow, let's do this the old-fashioned way, it might shake something loose. Josh, go to the dry board. We're gonna brainstorm."

The collective moan was substantial.

"Just do it. You never know."

"What could the numbers mean?" asked Manny.

"License plate?" said Dean.

"Post office box or bank vault box?" asked Alex.

"This is killing me, but how about an address or birthday?" groaned Sophie.

Twenty minutes later, they had five categories of questions posted on the board: the numbers, the reasons for intentional placements of body parts, the murder site pattern in the rainforest, the reasons for the altar, and what the sites had in common versus what was different about them.

"This is all good thinking, but I'm not getting it,"

said Josh.

Manny turned his scribbled-up notebook over. "This is damn frustrating. He's left some clues consciously, but it's not ringing my bell either."

He ran his hand through his hair. "Wait. If he's giving us this junk on purpose, maybe we have to sit on the other side of the table and see if he's giving us anything subconsciously."

"Great. How in the hell do we do that? Group hypnosis?" asked Sophie.

"Better than that. Close your eyes. Open them, look at each scene, close your eyes again, I'll call your name, then just start writing your first impressions."

"Aw Manny, I tried this in school doing a book report and got sent to the principal's office. He said people didn't want to know any of my first impressions, ever."

"Knowing you, the book was something about whips and chains," said Alex.

"Did I tell you that one before?" she grinned.

"Come on, just do it," Manny snapped.

"Okay, okay. Grouchy jerk."

The room grew quiet. A few minutes later, Manny stopped them.

"Okay. One word from each of you. I'll go first. Puzzle."

"Art," said Josh.

"Precision," said Dean.

"Horny," said Sophie.

"Horny?" asked Manny.

"Hey, I warned you."

"Picasso," chimed in Chloe.

Jumping up, Manny clutched Chloe's arm. "What did you say?"

"Are ya deaf? Picasso."

"That's it . . . I never . . . Alex, can you pull up pictures of Picasso's paintings?"

"You think this guy is a frustrated Picasso wannabe?"

"No, but if I'm right—just pull them up."

Alex shrugged and did what he was told. The excitement coursing through the room could have been bottled, it was so thick. He hoped his memory was right. More than that, he hoped he'd hit on the key to where this murderer was going.

"Here you are. Do you know which one you want to see? Wait. Never mind, I think I found it," said Alex.

On the screen, Picasso's black and white masterpiece, *Guernica*, told a story that would appeal to the killer. To the left, a person was in utter anguish, holding a dead loved one, then came the ensuing chaos of war, a broken sword, and body parts, including a severed head, and one could make a case for another severed limb among the animals. It ended with a person with hands held in the air. Frustrated, angry, and maybe isolated. Even though the painting was commissioned by the Spanish Government to display at the 1937 World's Fair and turned into one of the most dramatic antiwar paintings of all time, the killer had used it to model just the opposite. Manny was sure the irony wasn't lost on the killer. It certainly wasn't lost on him.

"So, the killer used that work to . . . what? Get his ideas for his MO?" asked Sophie.

"Maybe, but I think it might go deeper. The figure holding the dead person on the left represents his trigger event, I think. The rest is just a model for him. But he may identify with the idea of ending a personal war, and this helped. At least that's my best guess," said Manny.

"Your guesses usually work. But what war?" asked Josh.

"I'm not sure, but maybe it has something to do with the rainforest. I read at the visitor's center that there is going to be about eleven hundred acres set aside for public development. Maybe he thinks the forest is being destroyed and decided to protect it."

"That might explain the random killings to start with, but you're saying he fell in love with that part of it and isn't really concerned about protecting the rainforest?" asked Chloe.

"No. I think he probably tells himself that protecting El Yunque is his primary goal, but his psyche has developed into much more than that. Like I said before, he's looking for a bigger thrill."

"Now comes the so what?" sighed Dean. "What does that all mean?"

"I don't know," said Manny.

Pacing in the silent conference room, Manny felt much of what they had discussed was true, but did anyone on the list from the fencing club fit this profile? For that matter, had they guessed right? And maybe more important than the *who* was the *where*. This guy was primed to do something public, but what? And what about those damned numbers and the letter "P"?

"Any more thoughts?" he asked, trying to keep the angst out of his voice.

"Hey, I can smell the smoke, but I don't know where the fire is," said Sophie.

"That sums it up for me, too. But I know we're overlooking something," said Josh.

Manny sat back down. His mind was racing, but just maybe . . .

"If this guy had an altar mentality and acted on it where Caleb and the others were killed, say in this case the rainforest, then if he stays true to that, who would he sacrifice to next? Who would he—"

Chloe grabbed Manny's arm, hard. "Would he sacrifice to Picasso's painting?"

"Maybe. But that work is still in Spain. Wait—is there one on the island?"

"I can answer that," came a voice from the doorway where Julia Crouse stood. Her tears were gone and she had grit in her voice. "I'm not going to be on the sidelines for this. I can't."

"I thought you left?" he asked.

She walked over to Josh. "I couldn't. I went into the ladies room and, well, it may need a little repair. Listen. I'm good. Please let me help. You know damn well how hard it is to go through this and to be told you're not needed. I don't care about the regs."

Josh smiled. "That sounds like this group. Talk to us."

She sat down. "A bunch of us cops helped with a fundraiser to bring a couple of paintings to San Juan. It took some wrangling, but they're here. The elite, bluenose private showing is tonight," she answered, as she stood straight up.

"Where?" asked Manny, standing with her. The others followed suit.

"In Old Town. A place called Galeria San Juan. The address is on San Francisco."

The next instant, Alex had the Galeria up on the screen. As Manny looked at the announcement, it all fell into place. The address was 206 San Francisco, the date January 18, and the main attraction was Picasso. 206 P 18.

They had found the where.

CHAPTER-64

Parking the rental in an abandoned lot two blocks from the Galeria of San Juan, he carried the metal case and the duffel up the street toward the old Fort, El Christóbal, and turned left. Another block later, he nodded to the security guard, flashed the stolen ID, and entered the huge oak door fortifying the back of the art gallery.

The Galeria of San Juan had been an ancient mansion that was gutted and redesigned for the purpose of restoring native culture, which he appreciated. The old building still carried an aroma of the past that simply couldn't be remodeled away. But then the "money" got involved, and now it was used for private gatherings, like the one tonight, and for the first time since that had happened, he was glad. One hundred guests would show up tonight for the viewing of two of Picasso's works, wearing their tuxes and glittering gowns, each trying to out-impress the other like flamingos in heat. How he hated them. It was odd how people like himself, who knew the Master better than most, would never get an invite to such a glorious event. Those impossible invitations were always contingent on the size of the check written to the gallery. But that was all right. He'd found another way to attend and show his respect. A new beard and set of coveralls he'd borrowed from the maintenance crew's locker room did the trick. It was all he needed, and no one could imagine the level of homage that he was going to show in less than three hours. Picasso had been right.

People thought the painting *Guernica* was a protest against war, but he knew better. All one had to do was to look closer. The painting was about justice—and at any cost. The loss of a loved one led to a transformation that was far more than an attempt at revenge, but a right of wrongs. The Master understood that and passed it on to those who had eyes to see, and the willingness to finish what Picasso had started. He'd gotten it. And when this lesson was taught, he'd go to the next place where justice needed to be delivered. Where the rich and the politicians dictated what came next. The "few running the many" was getting old, and he would certainly have no problem finding that situation on this globe. He closed his eyes as he thought of how he and the blades would work in unison. He felt himself becoming aroused and welcomed it, eagerly.

But first, this strike for freedom, and then of course, his inner satisfaction would be carried out. Hot blood raced through his veins, and he wondered how he could ever wait the time required, but he would. Besides, he had a few things to set up. Walking through the next set of doors, he stopped. He wondered where the security guards might be, then realized it was customary to have them inside the exhibit and at the entrances. The folks putting on these events didn't want to alarm the attendees, so security was camouflaged as much as possible. Another blue-blooded, and deadly, way of thinking.

Double checking to make sure he was alone, he shoved the duffel under one of the long reception tables covered with white, ornate, floor-length cloth near the locked doors of the exhibit's entrance. A perfect place for when heaven and earth collided. Perfect for him at least. He smiled.

The smile grew wider when he thought about the game he'd played with the cops and the FBI. Even if they figured things out, it was already too late. His plan was in place. He'd be lying if he said he hadn't expected more from them, after all of those years of being fed propaganda on how good they were.

"I guess not," he whispered.

A few moments later, he was in the lower level putting the finishing touches on his "surprise, I got you" package, and then he sat down, counting the moments when this world would be his . . . alone.

CHAPTER-65

Manny exited the SUV, adjusting the tie of the tux and feeling the beads of sweat already forming on his lip and forehead. He turned to the west and noticed the sun had drawn closer to the horizon. In spite of the situation, it was almost impossible to ignore. He didn't.

The streaming reds and purples and the tux worked together to bring back a sense of nostalgia that he hadn't expected. Louise and he had kissed, then made love, on their first night in San Juan two and a half years ago in a world eerily similar.

His heart dove a little deeper, and he fought to bring it back. These momentary reminders of his life with the amazing woman who was his first love shouldn't surprise him. Sophie had been right. They'd spent too much time together, gone through too many ups and downs, and raised Jen, to ever think the memories would disappear. He wasn't sure he wanted them to.

It was something he and Chloe had talked about, several times, when he'd spent that month in Ireland. The purpose was to get to know each other better and, of course, to address any demons that clawed at either of their psyches. Her demons were far less considerable than his, except for one. Is there a worst condemnation for a person than loneliness? He thought not. She'd bared her very soul that night, expressing guilt that to get what she needed only happened as the result of Louise's death. It broke his heart, but he understood. He reminded Chloe that fate had its own agenda and it wasn't her fault. It just was what it is.

He remembered holding her tight and kissing away tears, not sure if they were all hers, and thanking God for working that awful situation in his life into the love that he and Chloe had. Then that dream . . .

Blinking at the sunset again, he smiled. Louise still had it.

"What the hell you smiling at?" asked Sophie.

"Something special, and no, it's none of your business."

"Whatever. You'll tell me; men just can't help it. It's about how hot I look in this dress, isn't it?"

"No, it's not. But you do look hot in that red dress. Ask Dean."

"I just might, but I think he's had enough of wiping the drool from his shirt, and look, even Dough Boy looks good in that monkey suit. Who would have thought?"

The other three doors closed almost in sync and the five FBI agents stood in a "U" around the front of the truck.

"You all ready for this?" Josh asked, wearing a white tux that matched Manny's.

He looked better than he had at any point in the last two days. The shock of his brother's death and the plane crash had finished working their voodoo. It was good to see.

"We've no choice now, do we?" said Chloe, that hint of Gaelic lilt dancing in her voice. She looked every bit an Irish queen of old. He didn't know how she got those curves in that blue satin dress, but he'd like to help her out of it.

Easy, boy.

Josh grinned. "I suppose that's true. And I'm sure no one else noticed, but you two women are as gorgeous as any on the island."

Sophie reached up and kissed him on the cheek. "You still have a way, Boss," she grinned. "And I've got my throwing stars in a place most men only dream about seeing."

Chloe laughed out loud. "The same for my gun."

Dean swallowed hard; so did Manny.

"Okay, enough stirring up the help," said Josh.

Turning serious, he looked Manny's way. "So, this is the best way?"

"Yeah. Pretty sure it is. We couldn't put those people at risk knowing that the killer could be planning something big, so the next best thing was to fill the place with cops and hope he still shows."

"That's not a bad thing," said Alex, tugging at his cummerbund. "Aren't we supposed to be protecting the public?"

"Yes, we are. Canceling this exhibit would give us zero chance to catch him and stop this crazy prick from killing even more people, so we have to hope we guessed right, and get that chance. It wasn't much of a problem to get a hundred cops to show up here, impersonating high society, I just pray we didn't tell the wrong guy to stay home."

"Do you think we did?" asked Chloe.

"Only three people on the guest list were members of the fencing clubs, one of them a woman, so our chances are good that we didn't lose him there. I'm more worried about, and I hate to say this, the unsub being in law enforcement. But we checked each of them out, so we should be good," said Josh. "Not to mention, he may not even be here. He may have led us here and has something else planned altogether. That's not likely, but . . . listen. We all feel nervous about this one, but I don't see another way. We couldn't risk any more civilians dying," said Manny.

"Do you think he's already in the building? If the chances are good that he is, then maybe we should storm the place and see who's not a cop," suggested Dean.

"Grasshopper. Have you forgotten the little head-explosion trick he pulled at the morgue and what Josh just said?" said Alex, putting his hand on Dean's shoulder.

"Good point. So maybe he doesn't show at all?" asked Dean.

"Like we talked about at the office, that's possible, but I don't think so. This is his *coup de gras*, his reason. And I think he's driven to get personal. Real personal. He'll be here, if we've guessed the clues properly. The questions are when and how," answered Manny.

"We don't want any cops to get hurt either, and Crouse's CO can stop the event at any time he feels there could be a serious problem, but I doubt he will. He wants this over with too. He said if this iffy plan doesn't work, the people that couldn't attend will be pissed and call on their political contacts to have his ass. He said the governor would be his new proctologist."

"Even though we'll all be cops, it still sounds dangerous," said Dean. His face caused Manny a slight tinge of nervousness, but he dismissed it. They just had to do their job, that's all.

"Okay. The gallery is a block in that direction. We need to get into position. The four of us will go through the back. You all know where you're supposed to be, and don't forget to keep in contact with each other. These wireless intercoms aren't cheap. Dean will hang around across the street from the front door and keep us posted."

The CSI nodded. "That works for me. I'll watch your backs. I hate tuxes anyway."

"And for God's sake, and your own, don't get stupid. We're a team, act like you know what that means. If something is wrong or goes down, call first, act second. Got it?"

The collective nod said they did.

When they reached the backdoor, they walked in, spoke to the cops disguised as guards, then they were in their assigned positions. Manny looked at his watch. Thirty minutes until the doors were supposed to open to display one of the planet's best. He felt more anxiety, or maybe it was excitement. At any rate, a few deep breaths were required. This man, this complex psychopath, was more than unpredictable. Had he changed his MO? Was this going to be some kind of bomb attack? Gas? No. It didn't fit. He was fairly sure of that. Besides, the gallery had been scanned and searched for all of those things. At the front door, "guests" were arriving in elegant style, the long limousines and the sparkling necklaces making the ruse look authentic. He saw Chloe on one side of the room and Alex on the other. Josh and Sophie had taken the assignment inside the room where the Picassos were encased in bulletproof, fireproof glass as clear as a Caribbean morning. Just in case the killer was also a thief.

Out of nowhere came a loud, crashing sound and Manny reached for his weapon. Turning quickly to face the wine and hors d'oeuvre table, he saw a tray of black caviar staining the expensive Oriental rug.

"I'm so sorry," apologized the large woman officer. "I just bumped it."

"No problem. I'll get maintenance up here to take care of this. Accidents happen," said her date.

Letting his Glock drop back into the holster, Manny released a breath he'd borrowed from hell. His heart told him he couldn't take too many more of those, and from the look on Alex's and Chloe's faces, their hearts were speaking the same language.

The clock seemed to move slower as everyone in the room anticipated something that might not even happen. In spite of that, he felt, somehow, that show-time was quickly approaching. How? Where? And Good God, who?

Still scanning the crowd, he only partially noticed the cop maintenance man as he began cleaning up the spilled caviar. The man looked in Manny's direction and went back to work.

What the hell?

He knew that face, even with the dark beard, didn't he? Then it hit him. His head swam because it was impossible. He'd seen the pictures; this man was dead, butchered into so many pieces.

But if he were here, then what had really happened in El Yunque? Manny's mind was swiftly flooded with the rest of the truth. He pulled his Glock, stepped around two cops, and stood ten feet behind the imposter.

"Caleb Corner! Stand up and put your hands in the air."

CHAPTER-66

Caleb froze in mid-motion as his head bowed. Manny watched the flexing of his right hand and knew that he was looking for a way out. Even in that second, his mind still rumbled with the fantastic reality of Caleb's state.

This will kill Josh.

By then, out of the corner of his eye, he saw that Alex and Chloe had noticed his posture, and his gun, as had some of the fake guests who were standing near him. Chloe hiked up her dress and pulled out her Smith and Wesson from her thigh holster and started to run in Manny's direction. Alex was right behind her.

Standing to his full height, left leg stiff, Caleb dropped his hands to his side, never turning in Manny's direction.

"Agent Williams. I guess you figured it out. But it's too late."

"Raise your hands! Don't even think about pulling that blade. Do it now."

What the hell did that mean, too late?

Josh's half-brother hesitated and kept his right hand still, hovering like a cobra ready to strike, but then he moved quickly. He drew the blade from his coveralls, then grabbed the female cop who had knocked over the plate of caviar, and slit her throat. Then he hacked at her date. The accompanying scream told Manny that he'd struck well.

Cops weren't supposed to panic, but that was now a reality. Guns, blade, yelling, and two more agents hurrying to confront the killer was a sure fire-incantation for disaster. The yelling coursed through the room, and people scrambled to get away from Caleb and started pulling weapons, but in the confusion, it was simply too close of quarters to get a clear shot—for anyone. Four cops ended up directly between him and Josh's brother. Caleb seemed to sense his chance to make a break and headed for the door. His movements were fast and graceful. Manny raised his gun and yelled for him to stop, wondering if that ever worked, and tried to get a bead on him, but he had no shot, at least one he wanted to take. Damn it. He hadn't thought about the close quarters. This was turning south in a hurry.

Caleb pushed two people out of his way, slashed at one of the security guards, and the woman went down screaming as the gash running across her face flowed a scarlet river before she hit the marble floor.

"Stop! Now!" yelled Chloe.

But Caleb didn't stop. Instead, he pushed an older cop in her direction and rushed her. Manny still had no shot, and he worried that someone else wouldn't exercise such control. But so far so good.

The older cop crashed into Chloe, causing her weapon to fly from her hand. It discharged, and the shot hit some five feet above the ornate bay window on the wall to Manny's left. Two more shots rang out while someone yelled to cease fire. What happened next could only occur in real life—no one in Hollywood could have dreamt it.

355

Catching the cop Caleb had tossed her way, Chloe steadied him as Caleb wound up to swing the shining Katana in a full arc. Reacting like a woman of her substance would, she swung the cop to the side as Caleb's blade began to move forward.

There is no horror like the repeat of one a man has already endured. In a blink, Manny knew that Chloe was going to die.

Enter Alex Downs. With a push of his left hand, he sent Chloe sprawling, getting a shot off, but he missed and Caleb didn't. Alex's left hand spun to the floor landing gracefully, palm up, before Alex ever realized it was his own. Then Manny had a shot and took it, just as another gun exploded from behind him. Caleb took one slug in his shoulder and another in his leg. The killer, the brother of a friend and more, crumbled, the sword skidding across to where Alex sat on his knees staring at his wayward limb. Glancing behind him, he saw Josh Corner's gun still smoking. He hadn't hesitated to shoot his half-brother, even though the shock at seeing his brother alive had to be akin to seeing him dead.

Caleb had now joined the ranks of the screaming, as chaos began to settle, and fifty cops pulled their weapons. But it was the wrong kind of scream. It was not from pain, but from the frustration and the madness that he so willingly embraced. He pulled a smartphone from his pocket and the screams turned to laughter, the kind that haunts any respectable insane asylum.

"I'll kill all of you!"

Before Manny could react, there was a third shot and a whir as something sped past his ear. The bullet from the third shot caught Caleb's left ear, tearing it off as the throwing star hit the hand holding the phone. The next set of screams Caleb indulged in was from unadulterated pain. Maybe the experts were right: nothing like a little agony to clear one's mind. He knew where the star had come from, and he could hear Sophie breathing hard two feet behind him. He looked to the front door, where the shot had originated, and saw Dean lower the gun and sprint toward Alex.

Manny rushed to Chloe, helped her up, and held on like there would never be another morning.

"I'm okay, I'm okay. But Alex—" her voice caught as she whispered.

Alex.

Releasing Chloe, he dropped next to his long-time friend, The man, maybe his best friend and the hero of Manny's life, was on the floor, but not alone. Dean had barged through the crowd, grabbed Alex's left arm and looped a nylon wrist restraint around the lower part of his arm and pulled it tight. Immediately, the flow of blood was reduced, but the floor was covered.

"Someone call for an ambulance," yelled Manny.

"Done," answered a voice who sounded like Detective Crouse.

The siren blaring somewhere near confirmed it.

Looking back at Alex, Manny's self-control left the building as panic called his name.

Sophie had slid behind Alex and was holding him in her lap, rocking back and forth and talking to him softly, sobbing at the same time—the way people do when they're ready to say goodbye.

CHAPTER-67

Josh looked at the injured and bleeding Caleb Corner, hesitated, then took three steps from his family and squatted by Alex, his eyes glistening.

Our worlds are shaded by our choices.

Manny sat down and raised Alex's arm to help stop the bleeding. He could see that Alex's eyes were glazed over, but he was there.

"Did we get him?" Alex asked, steady as a rock.

"Thanks to you," said Manny, his voice not really his own.

"Chloe?"

"You saved her life."

The CSI smiled. "Hey, Sophie, that's nice."

Alex smiled wider and then closed his eyes. Manny's spirit fell into a black, bottomless pit, and his tears flowed, unashamedly.

Sophie kept talking to Alex until the EMS team steamed into the room. The look on the first one's face only added to the awfulness of the situation.

The second one felt for a pulse, raised her eyebrows, and began barking orders to two others. "Let's get him into the unit. I can't get a pulse. I want 3ccs of epinephrine and crank up the defibrillator. Move it."

The woman who was barking out orders touched Sophie's hand.

"You've got to give him to us, okay?"

Sophie nodded. "I'm going to ride with him."

"One of you can, but that's it."

"We'll be right behind you, you go," said Manny.

Then, not sure why he did it, Manny reached down and picked up Alex's hand and gave it to the third EMT. "This is part of him."

One minute later, Alex was out the door, into the ambulance, and on his way to the hospital, Sophie at his side.

"What about *this* Corner?" asked Julia. "He's in tough shape, but it doesn't look like he's going to die anytime soon."

"Too bad," said Dean.

Just then, the second ambulance pulled up outside the double doors.

"I guess that answers that," said Chloe.

"You three go after Sophie and Alex, you're going to need each other. I'm—I'm going to ride with Caleb," said Josh.

"You're sure?" asked Manny.

"He's my brother. Maybe he'll talk to me. Maybe."

Manny knew he wouldn't. The Caleb Corner that Josh had known was gone, way gone.

***

Seven hours later, Chloe brought Manny and Dean another cup of coffee and Sophie a cup of tea. The waiting room had grown quiet, and Manny was grateful. There was a time and place for confusion, but this wasn't it.

The EMTs had managed to get Alex's heart beating, but it had taken five minutes, then they'd lost him again, but got him back much faster. By the time they'd reached the hospital, Alex had left and returned three times—not ideal, but he was fighting. Sophie had said they rolled him right into the ER surgery room, and that's where he'd been for the last six hours and fifty minutes. No updates from any doctor, or any nurse, just the ticking of the wall clock, the stack of old magazines, and the smell of dread.

Josh had come in twice and then gone back to Caleb's room after he was out of surgery. He said that Caleb would survive, maybe have a limp, but healthy enough to go through the justice system when the time came. However, Manny had guessed right. Caleb had not said a word to anyone. But that could change in a heartbeat with men like him, especially if he thought it could work to his advantage.

Moving back to the worn leather chair directly between Sophie and Chloe, he sat down, put his coffee on the floor, and folded his hands together. For the one-hundredth time, he asked God to fix this. He had to because no one else could.

The vision of Alex's blood flowing from his arm and spilling on the marble showed itself. It whispered that not even your God can fix this. He tried, but the truth the vision spoke was far too difficult to ignore.

"Is he going to make it?" asked Sophie, her dark eyes scanning his face.

"I don't know, Sophie. He lost a lot of blood, but he's fighting like a madman."

She offered a slow nod. "I've been praying, ya know. I've been talking to your God."

"That's good, real good. Me too."

"So, seriously, does He listen, really?"

Before Manny could answer, Chloe did. "He does, and He will. I don't think I could live with myself if—well, I mean, he was so brave and that kind of bravery doesn't die early. I know it."

"That whole thing about faith being the substance of things not seen kind of works here. I don't see how, but we don't have to. We just have to ask," said Manny softly.

Dean came back in from the restroom and sat on the other side of Sophie. Manny noticed his knees were red. Apparently he was on the same page as the rest of them.

"Okay," said Sophie, "but I feel so helpless."

Then she reached for Manny's hand.

At that very moment, the door from the waiting room swung open and two blue-clad doctors strode directly at them, neither smiling.

For the second time in one night, Manny's heart disappeared.

No!

The four of them stood in a group just as Josh came through the other entrance to the waiting room. He took one look at the doctors and ran toward them.

"I'm sorry we couldn't do more. We're not sure if the hand's going to make it," said the tall, slim doctor on the left.

"What?" said Sophie. "His hand? What?"

"Someone had the good sense to make sure it got here with Mr. Downs."

"His hand. What about *him*?" asked Sophie.

The second doctor grinned. "Oh, he's going to live. In fact, he's awake. We reattached the hand, but it's touch and go. I apologize, we don't like doing things this way, but he made us promise—how did he say that?—to scare the hell out of all of you first."

"That Dough Boy's gonna wish he would have croaked," growled Sophie.

She pushed past the doctors and headed for the recovery room, Manny close behind.

CHAPTER-68

"Hi guys. SO GLAD to see you. They got this great pain stuff, and I've never felt better in my life. Did you know I can control it? Look at this." Alex punched the tiny button near his right hand and leaned back, smiling.

Forgetting her promise to kill him, Sophie was laughing out loud. She stepped closer, careful to avoid the left side of his body. The arm and hand were in a cast up to his shoulder with about a million tiny pins sticking through the creamy cast. She cradled his face in her hands. "Think that was funny Dough—ah, Laughing Boy? Your joke *did* scare the hell out us."

"Yeah, but I noticed you were laughing when you came in. Why are you holding my face like that, Princess? Are you going to kiss me? I know, you know. You always say bad things to me to cover up your true feelings, but I know. I'm so sorry, but I'm going to have to break your heart. I love my wife. But you do have a great rack. Are those natural?"

Quiet laughter filtered through the room. Manny wasn't sure if it was relief or the fact that Alex on meds was akin to a standup comedian, probably a little of both. Chloe moved beside him and palmed his hand, her tears were light, but her gratefulness was clear. . . Manny's wasn't far behind.

Sophie stepped back laughing harder. "Well, I guess I'll just have to get over it, and of course my boobs are real, but that's not something you should ask a princess."

Alex leaned over to her and spoke in an exaggerated whisper. "Okay. Don't worry; your secret's safe with me."

Looking around, his eyes lit up again. "Did I say it is SO good to see you all? My friends. My life, sort of. Hey, look at this. I can control this wonderful pain filling, er, killing stuff. Just watch."

He hit the button again, smiling wider than the last time. The laughter in the room grew louder.

Sitting up suddenly, like he'd just remembered something, his face as serious as an IRS agent, he said, "You know, I had my hand whacked off, my left one, and it doesn't even hurt. You should see what they did to put it back on. Great surgeons, you know. I should be able to use it in a day or two."

"That fast?" grinned Manny.

"Yep. That's what they said."

"You know, Laughing Boy, it was a good thing it was your left hand," said Sophie.

His eyes grew wide. "Why?"

"Because if it had been your right hand, you'd have no sex life," she laughed.

Putting his hand over his mouth, he giggled. "That was funny. But Barb handles all of that. Get it? Handles?" Then he burst into another infectious laugh that would have made a dead man smile.

"Oh. Hey, Dean. Come here."

"Will do." Dean did as he was told. "Yes Sir. What can I do for you?"

"I just wanted you to know that you're the best damn CSI I ever saw, well, except for me, but you're a better shot. Anyway, thanks for the tunakit, or whatever the hell they call those things you put on an arm to stop the bleeding."

"You remember that?"

"Hell yeah," he said, tapping his head. "I never miss a thing."

The doctors came in and gave them a few more minutes, but not many. Alex needed to rest, and tomorrow the pain medicine wouldn't be as effective, after the local anesthetics wore off.

"Okay. We have to go, but we'll be back, tomorrow, and with a surprise," said Manny.

"Damn. I love surprises. Can't wait. But I need to talk to Chloe first. Come see old Alex, Irish Queen."

"Ah. Now I'm a queen?" she smiled as she sat on the edge of the bed.

"Always were." Alex's eyes focused, and he put his hand on her arm. "Listen. Don't feel bad. I'd do it for you and Manny, a thousand times over. A million. Second chances are rare, and you both have that. I just couldn't stand by, got it?" he laughed. "And that's just how we roll."

Kissing him on the forehead, she let the tears run. "Thank you, Alex Downs. You bet your ass that's how we roll."

"It is. Say, did I tell you guys I can control this pain medicine?"

His eyes grew heavy. "Manny? I love you, man. Josh. Your shorts are too tight, but you're the best."

Then he was out.

CHAPTER-69

The next morning, they met for breakfast in the hotel's restaurant, but Manny was a little late. He'd checked with the concierge, and Tina had everything arranged, including calling the hospital to make sure Alex was okay to participate in what Manny had planned. They weren't happy, but finally agreed. He made one more call and knew where he had to be at three o'clock that afternoon. It was awesome when a plan fell into place.

He sat down at the table and took in the brilliant aromas that accompanied every breakfast buffet in the Caribbean, and this one was a good one.

Sitting beside Chloe and looking across at Dean and Sophie, he realized he wasn't the only one who was late.

"Where's the fearless leader?"

"He got a call, left the table, came back, got another call, and hasn't come—oh wait, there he is," answered Chloe.

Josh slid into his chair. "Like I started to say; good morning. Let's eat, then we can talk."

Manny thought he was doing well, but there was no question it hurt to see his brother this way, even worse to contemplate what Caleb had done. Manny knew a little about those life lessons.

After they all had made a second trip to the buffet, Josh ordered a pot of expensive coffee and sighed. "I want you all to know that I'm doing all right. I guess it helps to realize that Caleb isn't the same man I've known over the years. But I'd be a liar if I said I saw this coming. Anyway, early this morning, he decided to talk, but he only wanted to speak with Detective Crouse. He said we, the FBI, only wanted to analyze him. Apparently, he and Julia had some torrid affair, one she didn't tell us about, and it added to the fire that fueled her divorce with Sam. She said they hadn't talked in a long time and that she hadn't really kept track of him. She was a little freaked by his request, especially since he'd killed her ex, but she's a tough one, so she agreed."

"That had to be interesting," said Manny.

Sipping coffee, Josh nodded. "It was. You'll all get copies of the interview, audio, video, and transcripts, but basically, Manny was right. It seems he was bent on finding his mother after he'd been taken away from her in Chicago. But he couldn't do it until he got out of college and she got out of prison. I never knew that part. His mom had stabbed a guy in a bar fight and went away for twenty years.

"Before that, she'd left the guy she moved to California with after her daughter had been killed in a car wreck, and her husband offed himself. Caleb and she had settled on the south side of Chicago. A couple years after she went away, dad got a call, and I had a new brother. He was always kind of to himself, but smarter than a whip."

"Funny how people want to take up with their real parents," said Dean. "I know I wanted to, but never could find my biological mom."

"That explains some things, Mucus," grinned Sophie.

"It's Mikus. And I suppose it might," Dean sighed.

"Anyway, she was killed in a freak accident in El Yunque, and that was the event that led to his evolution. He admitted that it started out as a war against the defilement of his first real love, the rainforest, but after the first murders, it became something more. That's when he decided to stage his death, figuring it would make him harder to catch. He found a single camper about his build and age, and well, we know the rest, more or less."

"That poor camper must have been one of the missing persons reported," said Sophie.

"He was," said Josh.

"Voices, delusions, and a bloodlust. Obviously, not a good combination," said Chloe.

"At any rate, he detailed all of it, including how the whole thing had taken on the game flavor and how he thought he'd won. He almost did have the last laugh. That phone Sophie starred out of his hand was a trigger device for a bomb he'd set up underneath the reception room. It would have been devastating if he'd gotten it to blow. But apparently, that was only a backup plan for him. He'd found a way to disconnect the main light breaker, then he was going to have a sword party," said Josh.

"He would have killed dozens," said Manny.

"Yeah, given the bag of swords we found, that's right." Josh's eyes flickered brighter. "Oh, as a sidelight, I forgot to tell you that they found Anna Ruiz alive, barely. She's hanging in there. After we left the gallery, Julia took over and decided to go to Caleb's house. It was still taped off tight because we thought he was a victim and they didn't want anyone to go inside until I got there. She had a brainstorm, checked public records for home ownership, and found that he had a beach cottage on the other side of town. They stormed that one and found Anna."

"That's good, but Anna's under guard too, right? Although I don't know how dangerous she is with a foot and a hand missing," said Manny, remembering the conversation he and Sophie had had with her father.

"She is, and it never hurts to be too cautious."

Josh refilled his cup and continued. "I want to thank you all for a great job. We'll debrief some more when we get home, but that won't be for a couple of days. You all deserve a little rest, so take some time. I'll send a jet for you on Tuesday. I'm going back tomorrow."

"Interviews?" asked Sophie.

"No sense in trying to fool you. Yes. The race has started, and solving this case makes my BAU unit look like the best thing since margaritas."

"Well, I for one, hope you screw up the whole thing, Sir," said Sophie. "Just saying."

"Thanks, I think," smiled Josh.

They talked a while longer, then Manny made a request. "I know we're all heading up to see Alex this morning, and his wife Barb should be there by now, but I need you all to show up at three thirty."

"Why?" said Josh, his eyes narrowing.

"You'll find out when you get there, but don't be late, or I'll send Sophie out looking for you, got it?"

Josh shrugged. "Okay, sure, if that's what you want. I guess we can spare some time from shopping and the beach."

"Oh man. Shopping." Sophie got up, pulled Chloe from the chair, and ushered her toward the door. "We're going up to see Laughing Boy, then we're going shopping, then we'll be back. I forgot about the shops on the Condado Strip. Even on Sunday, that place is special."

Then they were gone.

Five hours later, after Manny had made the run he needed to make, he ushered his gift for Alex into his new double room. It was still cramped, but would do. He scanned the room and saw that almost everyone was there, including Barb Downs, and the guest Manny had requested through the concierge.

Alex looked up at Manny, then to his right, and broke into a grin. "Jen Williams! It is so good to see you, girl."

Jen rushed to Alex and gave him a hug. "Glad you're doing good, Uncle Alex. Dad told me what you did. Pretty brave for a science guy."

"Not really, but thanks." He said, grinning. "Did you come down here just to see me?"

"Well, that's part of it. Dad needed me for something, and I'm, like, ready to do it. Now is as good a time as any."

Jen left Alex and walked over to Chloe, taking her by the hand. "I'm forever going to miss my mom, but it's time for me to do what she would have wanted, and give my dad to you. But, you'll have to take care of him, okay?" Then she hugged her.

"What are you talking about? I—"

Looping her arm through Chloe's, Jen pulled her over to Manny and motioned to someone outside the door. The guest wearing the white collar joined them.

The room grew silent as Manny went to a knee. "Chloe, I want you to marry me today, right now, in front of the people that matter to me. We made a commitment in Ireland, and now it's time to make good."

Chloe twisted the Claddagh ring on her hand, tried to speak, but nothing came out.

"Ya better answer the man, girl, ya got him where you want him," came a response from the door. Chloe's mom, Haley Rose stood there. "I didn't fly this far ta hear any excuses."

"Mum?" she looked back at Manny, more shock on her face. "You know how ta get things done, I'll give ya credit for that."

"We'll do the big wedding later, Maybe even in Galway, but this will have to do for now," said Manny.

"I'm holding you to it, man," Chloe said.

After the hugs and greetings, and a thousand more tears were unleashed, the priest began.

"Do you have another ring?"

Reaching into his pocket, Manny pulled out an exact copy of the one Chloe was already wearing. He handed it to her. She reached up and kissed him, then again.

Ten minutes later, with Jen at his side, and all of the people that meant anything to him at his back, Manny said I do to his Irish Queen.

***

After a meal of fast-food burgers, fries, and shakes, the nurses finally booted the wedding party out of Alex's room. They drove back to the hotel and headed for the casino. Manny was grateful when the guard smiled after he sized up Jen, then waved her in.

Sophie took Jen by the hand. "I got her for the rest of the night. It's been awhile since the girl and I have had some time together."

"Yeah. Like a week," said Manny.

He handed Jen a room key. "Not too late and no drinking. Got it?"

"Dad! I'm only seventeen. Besides, Sophie might need help to her room."

"You mean *will* need some help to her room. I'm ready for a couple Long Island iced teas," laughed Sophie.

Looking at Chloe standing next to Manny, her hand in his, Jen tilted her head. "I don't know if I said this, but welcome to the family. I'm still working through some stuff, but it'll be cool." Then she disappeared into the casino.

"She's a good girl. I hope I don't disappoint her, ya know."

He kissed Chloe. "How could you ever disappoint anyone?"

There was a bump from behind and then loud laughing. He turned to see Haley Rose flanked by Dean and Josh, all with drinks in their hands.

"Excuse me," grinned Haley Rose. "These fine gentlemen have agreed to teach me the art of counting cards at the blackjack tables, and I expect to be rich before the night's done."

Without warning, she pulled Manny to her, kissed him on the cheek, then stepped back. "You're a good man, Manny Williams. A little old-fashioned, but then again, maybe we need more of that."

She hugged her daughter again. "What the hell are you two still doing down here? It's your bloody wedding night. Move your asses. I just might be needin' a grand babe or two."

"Holy smokes, she's right," said Josh.

"TMI," smiled Dean, "TMI."

Then Chloe and Manny left, hurrying through the lobby.

"I'm thinking there'll be a hangover or two tomorrow," smiled Chloe, almost shyly.

"There will, but not my problem," he grinned.

Their eyes met, and she drew him in tight. "I'll not be waiting another minute," she whispered.

When they reached the door of her room, Manny picked her up, found a way to work the slide key, and carried her in.

The room had been decorated with shaving cream, colorful balloons, and condoms all over the bed, but neither of them really cared.

They stood, kissing, as Manny slowly worked his way down both sides of her neck. Her small moans said he was getting it right. His hands were surprisingly steady, he thought he'd be more nervous, but was instead on the other side of excited.

She pulled his shirt over his head and kissed his shoulders. The feeling was next to unbelievable. Returning the gesture, he helped Chloe slip off her blouse. She shook her red mane, and her eyes grew wide.

He slid his hand around to her smooth back and popped her bra loose with one flick.

"Nice touch," she said, thickly.

"A little out of practice, but it worked," he breathed.

He teased her breasts with his fingers, then kissed them gently as he ran his other hand down her hip and cupped her backside. She reached for his belt and loosened his khakis, and they slithered to the floor. Her hand found what she was searching for and squeezed. He gasped.

He lifted Chloe to the bed and finished undressing her with steady hands and a steady purpose, relishing each movement and wondering how his life could contain such joy. Three hours later—and another robust session of getting to know each other— they leaned back on the bed, sipping champagne and talking. Every move of her mouth, every motion she made, only added to his appreciation for his new wife. She was completely intoxicating, and completely his.

Getting up to pour more champagne, he heard the knock at the door.

"Great. They were supposed to leave us alone," he lamented.

"Get rid of them, Special Agent Williams, and I'll make it worth your while, I will," she said.

"I'm looking forward to collecting on that one."

Manny threw on a robe and peered out the peephole. Crazy. Word must have spread fast. The copilot that had flown them to San Juan stood outside the door, gift in hand.

Rolling his eyes, he wasn't going to open the door, then decided that would be rude. After all, the man was bearing a gift. He opened the door.

"Sorry to bother you, Agent, but I've a gift for ya."

It was impossible to ignore the Irish tint in his voice. Manny cocked his head. He didn't remember that accent from the jet.

"Thank you, but it's not necessary."

"Oh, but it is. Some gifts are just better than others."

Dropping the package on the carpet, he thrust the long knife deep into Manny's chest.

"One never knows, Agent. One never knows," he said, then sprinted down the hall.

As Manny dropped to the floor, his hands gripping the hilt of the blade, blood gurgling from the wound, he heard Chloe scream his name.

Then Manny Williams greeted the darkness.

ACKNOWLEDG-MENTS

I want to thank my wife for her hard work and dedication to what we're trying to accomplish. It can't be that easy working with your husband who doubles as a writer. I love you.

Inexpressible thanks to my editor, Janet Green (www.wordverve.com), for running her hand through her hair and doing an amazing job.

Cover Art by Katy A. Whipple, Nice work, Katy.

Formatting by Robert Houston Formatting Services. Great job, Bob.

Special thanks to Retired Ingham County Detective Mark Bowser for answering my endless stream of questions.

I want to thank Amazon, Barnes and Noble, and the other outlets that drive the e-book revolution. I'm extremely grateful that this media has helped me live this dream.

Thank you Sarah Murgittroyd, Sue Teachout, and Marie and David Gold for being the best beta reading team ever assembled. I'm more than grateful, as I run my hand through my hair!

I want to thank all of you readers, I'm just not sure how. You are the true reason authors get to share the stories in their heads, and you have made this journey seem more like a fairytale than a vocation. I tip my hat to you and say . . . much appreciated.

Lastly, and most importantly, I want to thank God for His great gift: Jesus. Nothing I write could express what that means to all of us. He's lifted me up and taken me from Hell to Heaven, and I'm eternally grateful.

****

Thank you so much for reading Caribbean Rain!! Please go to rickmurcer@gmail to tell me what you think.

FUTURE WORKS.

I have several projects in mind for the next two years, God willing, including the next Manny Williams thriller. I have an anthology schedule with six very talented writers, due out in June, 2012. Then my first Non-Manny thriller to be releases by the middle of August.

Carolina Rain: Murders in Hilton Head, South Carolina, and Ashville, North Carolina, send Manny on his toughest case, contemplating the hardest decision of his life. Great weather, grisly murders, and a few surprises that will have you wondering what's next! Due by December 15, 2012.

****

ABOUT THE AUTHOR

Rick lives in Holt, MI with his wife. They have two great kids, three amazing grandchildren, an equally amazing daughter-in-law, and the best blind writing dog ever, big Max.

****